MW00533331

THINGS YOU NEED

KEVIN LUCIA

Let the world know:
#IGotMyCLPBook!

Crystal Lake Publishing
www.CrystalLakePub.com

Copyright 2018 Crystal Lake Publishing

All Rights Reserved

ISBN: 978-1-64440-605-2

Cover Design:
Ben Baldwin—http://www.benbaldwin.co.uk/

Interior Layout:
Lori Michelle—www.theauthorsalley.com

Edited by:
Monique Snyman

Proofread by:
Amanda Shore
Tere Fredericks

This is a work of fiction. Names, characters, businesses, places, events and incidents are either the products of the author's imagination or used in a fictitious manner. Any resemblance to actual persons, living or dead, or actual events is purely coincidental.

No part of this publication may be reproduced, stored in a retrieval system, or transmitted in any form or by any means, without the prior permission in writing of the publisher, nor be otherwise circulated in any form of binding or cover than that in which it is published and without a similar condition including this condition being imposed on the subsequent purchaser.

WELCOME TO ANOTHER CRYSTAL LAKE PUBLISHING CREATION.

Thank you for supporting independent publishing and small presses. You rock, and hopefully you'll quickly realize why we've become one of the world's leading publishers of Dark and Speculative Fiction. We have some of the world's best fans for a reason, and hopefully we'll be able to add you to that list really soon. Be sure to sign up for our newsletter to receive two free eBooks, as well as info on new releases, special offers, and so much more. To follow us behind the scenes while supporting independent publishing and our authors, be sure to follow us on Patreon.

Welcome to Crystal Lake Publishing—Tales from the Darkest Depths.

OTHER CLIFTON HEIGHTS TITLES BY KEVIN LUCIA

OTHER COLLECTIONS BY CRYSTAL LAKE PUBLISHING

Or check out other Crystal Lake Publishing books for more Tales from the Darkest Depths.

As always, thank you Abby for your love and support. I couldn't do any of this without you. Thanks also to Skip Novak, who continues to offer the perfect antidote to my terminal case of Conjunctivitis. And my eternal gratitude to those readers who long for the odd streets of Clifton Heights. May you someday find what you need there.

Most importantly, thank you to the One who wrote— and is still writing—the Greatest Story of All. My mere scribblings are but a pale imitation of Your Great Tale.

PUBLISHING ACKNOWLEDGEMENTS

The Office—*Beauty of Death*,Independent Legions Publishing, 2016

Out of Field Theory—*Shock Totem 9.5,* Halloween Special, 2014

Scavenging—*Chiral Mad 2*, Written Backwards Publishing, 2015

The Way of Ah-Tzenul—Createspace, 2015

A Place for Broken and Discarded Things, Previously Unpublished

The Black Pyramid—*Shadows Over Main Street*, Farolight Publishing, 2016

When We All Meet at the Ofrenda—*Gutted: Beautiful Horror Stories*, 2016

Almost Home—*Horror Library 4*, Cutting Block Press, 2013

Out
Of a great need
We are all holding hands
And climbing.

"A Great Need" by Hafez

The things
we need most
dwell darkly
in our innermost
cracks
we dare not look
too long,
for fear
of madness
over which
we cannot reach.

"Need" by Jeremiah Bassler
The Nameless Hunger

I.

HOW'D I END up here?
It's a long story. That's the thing about life, though. Never can tell how it's going to go. As Woody Allen once said: "Want to make God laugh?

"Tell him your plans."

Anyway, I certainly didn't figure on *this* being my life's work. But it is what it is. If you're interested, I can share how I got here. To start the story right, though, so you can understand my perspective better, I need to ask: You ever get fed up?

Y'know, your job sucks. The spouse is a pain. The kids are sucking your life away. Finally, one day, you blow your fuses and think: *Hell with this. I'm out of here.*

Ever feel that way?

Sure you have. Everyone gets fed up eventually. Unless you're a robot. Or a Vulcan, or a Zen Buddha Hare Krishna Weirdo, and those guys *have* to get fed up sometime. You show me a Zen-bot who never gets fed up and I'll show you someone with a few interesting ways of blowing off steam.

Me, I was lucky—or at least I told myself so. In my old life, I never got fed up because I was always on the move. Living out of my suitcase. Spending most my time in rental cars and motel rooms.

Which suited me fine. I lost my parents when I was young. Until recently, I couldn't even remember their faces. Anyway, before I graduated high school I moved from one foster home to another. I got used to always moving, so you could say my career—what I used to do, anyway—was a perfect fit.

See, in my former career I visited high schools along the East Coast, conducting magazine drives for fundraisers. Public schools booked me to raise funds for proms, class trips, and post-prom parties. Private schools usually ran drives to raise funds for their tuition assistance programs, which aided their less-affluent students.

It wasn't bad. At least, not in my prime. I was one of the best East Coast Representatives for Mass Media Sales Incorporated. I visited high schools and performed a song and dance about school spirit, community, and working together. A kind of motivational speaker, I guess. Instead of motivating them to accomplish big things, however, I was motivating them to sell magazine subscriptions.

After my opening spiel came the presentation of the "prizes" they could win, based on their sales. Smaller prizes for "Sellers of the Week." Cheap trinkets, honestly. Likewise cheap trinkets for "Highest Sellers of a Brand." For example, say one kid sold the most Ladies Home Journal subscriptions? A cheap prize for their troubles.

The Sellers of the Month got slightly better prizes, not as cheap as Sellers of the Week, but still lame. Sellers of the Year usually got a cash prize, but I always noticed the kids who won that were from rich families where Mommy and Daddy probably sold magazines for them.

Of course, that wasn't any of my business. I was the Vanna White of magazine drives. Showing the goodies which could be theirs, if only they put a little muscle into their hustle. I had no say in *how* they earned those prizes. Long as I reached my subscription quota per school, I smiled, danced, handed out their prizes, and moved on.

How'd I get myself into it?

It was only supposed to be temporary. I'd graduated college with a Bachelor's Degree in Advertising. I was aiming to be a big shot at an advertising firm in New York. And believe it or not, after two months of unemployment, writing freelance ad copy for a handful of AM radio stations to keep a roof over my head, I still entertained those dreams. Wouldn't be much longer, I told myself, and one of those big firms I'd sent resumes to would call me for an interview. I'd run through their hoops with a winning smile, and then I'd be in the game with the big boys.

Five months later with no calls and my freelance jobs drying up, I was less optimistic about my prospects. So when I saw an ad in the paper about an opening for "creative individuals willing to go an extra mile," I jumped. I was a creative individual, right? And the way things were going, I was willing to go more than the extra mile. Hell, I'd go several hundred.

You can imagine my dismay when I discovered Mass Media was basically offering the position of traveling salesman. They said lots of things, however, which made it sound great. *Imagine*, they told me, *what a couple years in sales will do for your resume. Not only will you have field experience, you'll know— firsthand—what sells and what doesn't.*

They said lots of other things, too. Buttered me up real good. Told me how beneficial my education in Advertising would be. I could be an integral part of the process. Develop advertising strategies for each magazine campaign. Give feedback that would shape future campaigns.

Integral part of the process my ass. They sent me already finished brochures, flyers and ad copy, with little sticky-notes reading, "What do you think of the border color? Does it clash with the text?" or "This is our slogan. Any thoughts?" and "Is this font too distracting?"

Yeah. I was *real* integral.

Why'd I stick around?

Well, wanting to eat and keeping a roof over my head proved powerful motivation. But why'd I stay with Mass Media all those years? Why didn't I jump ship, aim for those stars, as I'd planned when I'd graduated college?

Honestly?

You get accustomed to living within a certain budget. A year or two into the job I started thinking it was nice having steady cash coming in, plus bonuses when I exceeded my quota. It was also nice not getting harassed by my landlord for rent (even if I was spending more time in my car and motels than I was my apartment), and hey: Mass Media paid for the rental cars, hotels, and meals when I traveled. I still wanted to make something bigger of myself, but I'd be lying if I didn't admit I enjoyed knowing when my next meal was coming.

Five years down the road I was still sending out resumes, sure. But I was on the road so often, even if I'd landed an interview, I wouldn't have had time to keep it. By then my savings was fattening a little, so I bought some Mass Media stock options, thinking, "What the hell?" I'd open a 401k, too.

Don't ask me how the next ten years passed. They simply did. One year after another. On the road, all the time. New state, new city, town or village. New school, new fundraiser. And then one night, drinking alone in some little bar in a small town, I realized something. My edge had been sanded away. It wasn't coming back. I couldn't make it in New York Advertising if the best job was offered on a silver platter.

Doesn't sound fulfilling, does it? But it wasn't awful. The travel and the same pitches got a bit monotonous, but I had it down to a science. It wasn't hard, and truthfully, the kids did all the selling, not me.

Sure, I had to get them energized. I had to be organized and give a slick presentation, but mostly it was out of my hands. Either the students were into the sale or they weren't. Either folks in their town were buying, or they weren't. It was a big crapshoot. I'd visit a school to kick off their magazine drive and then a few months later returned to close it. They either did their thing or didn't. I got paid, either way.

I never fell under my quota, you understand? Never. Every magazine drive of mine always sold the minimum amount of subscriptions because I was one of the *best*. I couldn't account for schools where the kids didn't give a rat's ass (and believe me, those schools abound), but when I hit a school where the kids were even halfway into it, I cleaned up. Had them eating out of my hands. I knew how to talk. Still do, I guess.

I never believed half of what I said, of course. I was selling magazine subscriptions, for Pete's sake. To raise money for the prom. Or the senior class trip, or to save the whales. Whatever the cause, I could sell it. I put on a good show. I came out with the microphone, smiling and yelling, "Good Morning Townsend High!" or "How's it going, Ridgeview Academy! You ready to make some MONEY?!" The kids would be screaming—most of them, anyway—the teachers appeared only half-bored, and the administrators were smiling with that hungry expression they all get when they sense money rolling in.

I cleaned up.

Usually.

As I said, it was a dice roll. Maybe the school was full of stoners. Maybe it was a little podunk high school out in the middle of the sticks. A country school full of kids taking shop and Home Ec classes, or kids who couldn't care less about raising money for this school event, or for that cause. Maybe they had no school spirit.

Other schools?

They *loved* it. They got the job done. I made my quota, got my bonuses, kids raised the money they needed, and everybody went away happy.

So when you total things up, it wasn't bad. And, as I said, I was always on the move, so I didn't have to worry about getting fed up because, hell—I was always leaving. Half the time, I only got back to my apartment three or four days a month.

THINGS YOU NEED

Say I had to hit a high school in Montrose, Pennsylvania on Monday, Tuesday, and Wednesday. Then I worked a gig up in Syracuse at the end of the week. Maybe I made it home to my apartment for the weekend, maybe not. Most likely, I had to head down to Elmira the following Monday, Tuesday, and Wednesday, so Mass Media would put me up in a crappy motel in nearby Horseheads for the weekend. Maybe afterward I was scheduled to swing down to a Catholic school in Pittsburgh, or to a little hick school in York, Pennsylvania. I was always on the move, from school to motel to school.

It was okay, I guess. The scenery changed, at least. A little.

I mean, the motel rooms didn't change much. Once you've seen one motel room you've seen them all. Also, the bars were the same. A dimly lit joint with a counter, rows of liquor bottles behind it against a mirror no one wants to look into, a gruff bartender and a few hardcore drunks. Maybe a 30-year-old lush gal (who may or may not be older), with peroxide hair and tight clothes that didn't quite fit anymore.

I'd be lying if I didn't admit to having occasionally enjoyed the overnight company of Ms. Maybe-I'm-30-But-Probably-35. Of course, when I was younger, she was Maybe-I'm-27-But-Probably-30, so I suppose *she* changed some, but mostly she remained the same, too. Tired, with slightly glazed-over eyes, desperate for something better, too much make-up caked on her slack face, tight clothes holding in the rolls, over-teased hair, and a vapid, loose grin.

Thing is, she aged to Maybe-I'm-40-But-Probably-45-or-Maybe-Even-50 almost overnight. Sometimes

7

after a few shots, if the place was dark enough and I was lonely enough, that was okay. But toward the end, it wasn't. Near the end of my run I wasn't exactly in my prime anymore, but I sure wasn't wearing Depends. When the bar hounds started looking more like toothless alley cats than cougars, I got choosier. There's lonely and willing to be flexible, and then there's desperate. I didn't want to be the latter.

There were strip clubs, of course, and most of those motels had free WiFi, so I suppose there was porn, too. But I avoided strip clubs, especially out in the sticks. In those backwoods clubs, two kinds of girls worked the pole: Ms. Maybe-I'm-45-But-Probably-50, and Ms. Underage-Jail-Bait. The first category was barely acceptable under dark lights and through beer goggles. Seeing them remove their clothes (with their same glazed-over eyes and vapid grin) crossed *way* over the line in *desperate*.

The second category? The underage girls swinging their thing around a rattling pole? Given my profession, spending all my days in high schools and how my livelihood depended on my reputation, you can see my concern. That's why I always hit bars several towns away from the school I was working. You don't piss in your own pool, right?

As for internet porn . . . well, seeing naked women having sex (and doing other things) on a computer is interesting the first few times. After a while, however? It makes you want the real thing. All porn did was make me thirsty for drinks I couldn't afford anymore.

See the thing about sex . . . not to make you uncomfortable, because this probably ain't the story you wanted to hear . . . you know the old saying, "If you don't use it, you lose it?" Believe it or not, that's how it was for me. As options got less desirable, my urge kinda disappeared. Not completely, of course. Sometimes, I decided nighttime company was worth lowering my standards, or occasionally I got lucky and nabbed a Maybe-I'm-35 (they were never much in the looks department though).

For the most part, toward the end, after working a gig I went to a local bar outside town, had a beer or two, enjoyed some wings, watched the game on the big screen, then headed back to my motel room alone.

Don't get me wrong. I didn't think of myself as lonely. Actually, sitting at a bar alone was a relief. I spent my days pretending to be enthusiastic, positive and friendly, so sitting in a dark bar, ignored by everyone, was sorta nice.

Especially toward the end. When I started wondering if there was anything more to life. Wondering if I was going to someday quit in the middle of a gig. Tell a gym full of students where to shove their damn magazines. Walk out, get into my car, and head for parts unknown. Or if one night I'd go back to my motel room, sit on the bed, drink a bottle of JD, and then calmly pull out the .38 I bought a few years before (for protection, I'd told myself), stick the muzzle into my mouth and pull the trigger.

I know.

Funny how things work out. I finally got fed up. But there wasn't anything for me to drive away from because that's all I ever did: drive away.

So there it is. My life before this. To be honest, I'm still not sure which option I would've chosen. I'd prefer to think the first one: I'd drive to my bank, withdraw all my cash and disappear. Maybe get a part-time job in some city working at a bookstore or something. It's a nice thought and I think a probable option. On my worst days, though, I wonder.

I wonder.

Because that's why I'm here. No matter what I want to think, the muzzle of my .38 was a lot closer to my mouth than I care to admit. In fact, the day I stepped into Handy's Pawn & Thrift, I'd say I was two steps away from giving my .38 that long, last kiss goodbye.

2.

IT WAS MY first visit to Clifton Heights Junior/Senior High School. Right from the start, I thought Clifton Heights was a strange town. Nothing obviously wrong with it. Not on the surface, anyway. Place was the same as any of the hundreds of towns I'd visited over the last twenty years. Homey little department and hardware stores, restaurants, and knick-knack shops. A town hall, three churches, the requisite small town diner and two high schools. A library, a lumber mill, and a little creek running past the town, with a bridge over it called Black Creek Bridge.

There was a modest lake—Clifton Lake—to the east, and folks referred to the hills as "the Heights." The clean streets were patrolled often by Sheriff Baker and his deputies. He seemed a decent guy. Certainly not the stereotypical small-town crook, who ran his little kingdom with an iron fist. Trust me; I ran into plenty of that sort back in the day.

The students of Clifton Heights High were a bunch of hard-working go-getters, the kind which usually brought in droves of subscriptions. Right from the start I knew they would deliver.

The teachers and administrators were friendly and accommodating. The kick-off went well, the student body enthused, and everything was running five-by-five. Normally, I would've headed out to a bar (in the next town over, of course, always in the next town over), and settled for Ms. 40-Maybe-50. If she looked okay, of course, and if I'd had enough Jose Cuervo.

For some reason when I returned to my cabin at The Motor Lodge, I started to feel restless. I'm not sure why. Like I said, there was something *off* in Clifton Heights. It didn't make sense at the time. It was quaint, homey, rustic but not a tourist trap. The people were friendly. The kids at the high school had been outgoing. The English teacher there—a Gavin Patchett—had taken me out to dinner at The Skylark. The meal had been everything you'd expect from a small town diner; heaping portions of great food. When I'd left The Skylark, I was full-bellied and content, maybe interested in a little company later.

On my way back to The Motor Lodge, I started feeling twitchy. Uneasy. As if I was being *watched* or something. Sounds crazy, I suppose. Anyway, even after showering and prepping for my night out, I still couldn't settle down. My good mood had vanished. I no longer wanted to chat up an aging bar whore with a loose grin and glazed-over eyes. At the same time, I was far too restless for sleep.

So I found myself driving aimlessly around town.

Which was strange.

I'd never before had any desire to explore the town I was visiting. I usually checked into my motel the night before, maybe hit a bar one or two towns over, called it an early night so I could wake up fresh the next morning. The next day I'd wake up early, get myself organized, head to the school, and do my thing. After, I'd return to the motel, eat somewhere then head out to another bar a few towns over and maybe score some female company. The next morning, I'd be on my way to another gig.

I'd never bothered to see more of the towns I visited, so I didn't understand why I was doing so that night. Maybe I was curious. You never know if something interesting might be lurking in a humble little town, right?

As I turned onto Asher Street, I pulled my rental up to the store at the end. It appeared to be the only one open. Handy's Pawn and Thrift. That was interesting: a thrift store in a small town open at 8:30 at night, when everything else appeared closed.

At the time, I didn't know why I'd stopped there. The joint caught my eye for some reason. Maybe there was something valuable inside, hiding in all the junk. Treasure among trash, y'know?

But something else was at work. I felt pulled there. By what, I had no idea at the time. Now I know, of course.

It was Fate.

I was meant to stop at Handy's.

And nothing would ever be the same after.

3.

FROM THE OUTSIDE, Handy's Pawn and Thrift was like any other second-hand junk store. Random items filled both storefront windows. Old radios, ranging from transistors to stereos with combination eight-track players and tape decks. Rusted old milk cans. An old tricycle next to a plastic Big Wheel. A jumbled assortment of sports equipment—deflated basketballs, footballs, scuffed baseballs and dinged bats. Helmets, a pair of hockey sticks, and a few pairs of old basketball sneakers. Old mason jars filled with marbles, a pile of hammers, saws, another mason jar filled with assorted screwdrivers. A few stacks of old books, and leaning next to them, old records in faded sleeves.

Standing on the curb, I saw nothing particularly enticing or remotely interesting. In retrospect, I think it was the sign hanging in the window that sealed it. Maroon with gold trim and gold lettering, it read:

HANDY'S PAWN AND THRIFT
WE HAVE
THINGS YOU NEED

I snorted because from where I stood, Handy's didn't sell anything but junk. Nothing sitting in the window looked valuable. I couldn't for the life of me imagine I needed anything Handy's was selling. In fact, I was about to turn and leave when I glanced down with some surprise to see my hand turning the doorknob.

Even more surprising, I pushed the door open and stepped inside.

I stood there for a few seconds, my eyes adjusting to the dim murk. After my vision focused and I could see better, I glanced around and saw the inside of Handy's didn't appear any different than what I'd seen through its storefront window. A collection of junk no one would be interested in. Of course, that was my initial reaction. As I've since discovered—like other things in Clifton Heights—Handy's Pawn and Thrift needed much closer examination to gain a true appreciation of its offerings.

An aisle led from the door to a sales counter, and on either side stood rows of double-sided shelves. More old tools hung on the wall to the far left. The wall to the right looked interesting: Several framed paintings (nothing valuable, mostly pastoral scenes) and a few framed movie posters from the fifties and sixties.

I almost left right then.

This was what my life had come to?

Haunting a junk store because I didn't want to sit in a dingy bar chatting up fifty-year-old lushes?

A surprising tide of self-loathing rose up inside. For a second, I imagined spinning on one heel, marching out of Handy's, and heading back to my cabin at The Motor Lodge to finally use my .38 . . . until a voice stopped me.

"Anything you're looking for?"

I glanced up, startled. No one had been standing behind the counter when I'd entered the store, but someone stood there now. I'd heard nothing. Not the creaking of a door or the clinking of a latch, or a shoe squeaking on the floorboards. One minute, the area behind the counter was empty, the next, a tall, shadowed form stood there. The way the shadows fell, I couldn't see a face. Disconcerting as hell, let me tell you.

But I knew how to sing the song and dance the jig. Smiling, I stuffed my hands into my pockets and wandered casually down the aisle toward the sales counter, pretending the man's shadowed face didn't bother me.

"You're open late," I noted, sidestepping the man's question, "especially considering all the other stores on this street are closed."

As I neared the counter, the shadows pulled back to reveal (much to my relief) an ordinary, if slightly weathered face. With a neatly trimmed white beard matching his hair, the guy could've been anywhere from his late forties to early sixties. He was smiling amicably, revealing white, even teeth.

"As Mr. Handy always says, you never know when someone's going to get an itch for what they need. So we try to stay open for folks of all hours."

I stopped at the counter, arrested slightly by the guy's vivid green eyes. "So you're not the Handy of Handy's Pawn and Thrift."

The man smiled wider, eyes twinkling, as if he

thought the idea funny. "No, sir. A humble shopkeeper is all."

I grunted, casting a glance back over my shoulder at the assorted odds and ends of old toys, soda bottles, yellowed china and tarnished silverware, aimlessly cluttering row upon row of shelves. "An itch for 'what they need' huh?" I faced the man, offering him a smile I hoped wasn't too sarcastic. "Nice hook on your sign. 'We Have Things You Need.' Catchy."

The guy's smile never wavered, and he appeared about as genuine as they came. "Catchy and true. We do have things people need. And a surprising number of them seek what they need after regular hours, so we stay open late."

I smirked a little. Couldn't help it. I mean, the guy *looked* sincere, but he was laying it on a bit thick. For some strange, mean reason I felt compelled to probe his bubble. I'd be lying if I didn't admit it was because he'd gotten to me a little. "C'mon. A small town thrift store has what people need? When folks these days can get whatever they want online and have it delivered by air drones to their doorstep in hours?"

The man tipped his head as if conceding the point, though still disagreeing with me in principal. "But isn't this the age-old conflict wrestled with by philosophers, theologians, and psychiatrists all through the ages? What we *want* is so rarely what we need. What we *need*, we hardly *ever* want."

Outwardly I scoffed, shrugging as I glanced around the store, but on the inside, I gotta be honest: What he said struck a chord. Again, against my will, I thought of the .38 in a box under my bed back at The Motor Lodge.

A thought occurred to me; a way to steer our increasingly disquieting conversation back onto more comfortable ground. I glanced at the guy, giving him my 'just-between-us' grin. "You guys do good business here, I bet."

A smile and a nod. "I must admit we do. Only Mr. Handy knows the exact details, of course. However, I've certainly rung up enough sales to know we're in no danger of closing any time soon."

"I bet. Take that old milk can." I gestured at the black, rustic Crowley's milk can standing in the corner. "Folks come to the Adirondacks from out of state, see it with the date embossed on the side—1950, is it?—and because they found it *here* in an Adirondack thrift store, they'll be far more willing to pay top dollar for it than if they'd come across it in a yard sale, where Mr. Handy probably bought it for ten bucks. And that's if he didn't get it lumped in with a bunch of junk in an estate sale, or came across it for free in someone's abandoned barn."

I gotta admit feeling proud over my little spiel, which makes sense, I suppose. All those years on the road selling magazines—hell, selling the *idea* of selling magazines—and I'd never gotten the chance to flex my marketing muscles. Granted, what I'd offered wasn't exactly the most insightful market analysis, but it felt good regardless.

It must not have been far from the truth, because the shopkeeper (yeah, I never did get his name; weird, huh?) gave me a knowing smile and winked, as if we were two old friends sharing a secret. "You know your thrift stores."

I shrugged. "Nah. I know marketing. Well," I

added, giving him a whimsical smile I hoped didn't show my hidden despair, "I used to."

Something flickered in his eyes again. "Are you sure there's nothing you're looking for in particular?"

I had to hand it to him: he showed some salesman moxie himself. I wasn't about to be handled so easily, however. I tipped my head—in what I hoped was a bored gesture—and said, "You mean, am I looking for what I *need*? I dunno. Guess I'll have to browse a while." I grinned. "As you said, most folks only know what they want. Not what they need."

Making good on my words I meandered to my right, approaching the farthest aisle. It was crammed with plastic and ceramic figurines, plates, mugs, and more of those old soda bottles.

"This is true," the shopkeeper agreed, "people know exactly what they want, but it takes time to search for what they need. No rush. Take your time."

I spied a Magic Eight Ball nestled on a shelf between some slumped over Barbie dolls. Y'know what I'm talking about. That corny fortune-telling game we all played as kids, which delivered vague answers like Future Unclear or Answer is Hazy. On a whim (I admit, a slightly cruel one), I snatched the eight ball, turned on my heel, held it up with a grin and said, "Here it is. This is what I need, right here."

The shopkeeper folded his arms, pursed his lips, narrowed his eyes and *examined* me silently for about a minute or two. I swear, he literally examined me, taking me at my word, as if by some mystical clairvoyance he could determine if, indeed, I did *need* the Magic Eight Ball.

After another minute, he shook his head and said, sounding regretful, "No, I'm afraid it's not."

I felt a little bad about stringing him along—for the most part, he seemed genuine—but I couldn't stop. The showman in me was on a roll.

I spread my hands in mock appeal. "C'mon. I'm on the road all the time, working a dead end job with no upward mobility but which pays me too comfortably to quit. I've got no family or friends, no one at home. If there's anyone who needs to know the future, it's me. See? Look."

I addressed the Magic Eight Ball, earnest as could be, bringing all my showmanship to bear. "Magic Eight Ball. Will I ever get off the road and find some sort of life . . . "

will I go back to my cabin and shoot myself between the eyes

" . . . besides pitching magazine sales to bored teenagers all over the East Coast?"

I shook the Magic Eight Ball, suddenly and inexplicably angry. I didn't know why, but standing there, holding the damn thing, I'd spoken truer words about my own life than I'd ever allowed myself to think. I swear, the bit about shooting myself had been on the tip of my tongue. In fact, to this day I'm still unsure whether I thought it or actually spoke it.

The little hexagon suspended in milky liquid inside the Magic Eight Ball finally floated to the surface. Predictably enough, it read "Future is Hazy" in faded letters. I had to restrain a sudden, violent urge to heave it the length of the store.

Instead, I smiled at the shopkeeper. "'Future is Hazy.' Figures. Maybe I don't need this thing after all."

He nodded in sincere agreement. "You certainly want to know the future. We all do. But that's not what *you* need, I don't think."

For some reason, my grin felt forced. "Is that so? What do I need, then?"

It was his turn to shrug. "I can't say, for sure. You'll know when you find it. As I said, take your time. No rush. Once, a man—also from out of town—visited us around this time, and he didn't find what he needed until nearly 10:30. I was happy to wait. Turned out he needed an old turntable."

His straightforward answer popped my bubble. I couldn't keep up the show. All my snark faded, leaving me empty, used up . . .

And thinking about my .38.

"Listen. I'm sure you mean well. You seem sincere and all." I tossed the eight ball hand to hand—fidgeting, for God's sake.

His expression sobered. "*Sure* you're not looking for something?"

I shook my head and approached the sales counter. "Thanks for chatting. Got a long drive tomorrow. Gonna go and . . . "

get my gun
shoot my brains out

" . . . hit the sack." I placed the eight ball on the counter. The shopkeeper gazed at me silently, as if he could see inside my head. As if he knew all about the .38.

"Have a good night." Not waiting for an answer, I turned on one heel and walked down the middle aisle without looking back.

He didn't answer.

The only sounds were my shoes squeaking the floorboards, and the door as I opened and closed it behind me.

You know what I did then? I stood outside Handy's, staring into space. I didn't see anything. Not the street, the dark stores on the other side, or my rental. All I saw as I stood outside the store?

My .38.

It crept up on me, y'know? The idea of *actually* using it. I certainly hadn't been thinking of it when I'd woken up in the morning . . .

but I knew it was under the bed
felt it there
like a sliver in my brain

. . . and I certainly hadn't been thinking about it while I was performing for the cheering student body of Clifton Heights High, or during dinner with Mr. Patchett. All right, so maybe I thought about it a *little* when I returned to my cabin . . .

pulled the box out from under the bed
opened it, and held it

. . . but nothing more. I put it out of my mind as always and ended up at Handy's Pawn and Thrift, for no reason at all. After a little conversation with an eccentric but well-meaning shopkeeper, there I was, halfway convinced if I returned to The Motor Lodge I'd finally put my .38 to use.

are you looking for something
we all know what we want
not what we need

Standing on the sidewalk, staring at nothing, the

weight of my life loomed. I had no idea what I wanted. If I was honest with myself, I had no clue what I needed, either. For the first time in a long time, I had no idea what to do next.

I felt it tugging at me, a mental fish-hook in my mind: *Handy's Pawn and Thrift. We Have Things You Need.* I slowly turned, and before I quite knew what I was doing, I grabbed the door knob and tried to turn it.

At first it wouldn't open. I don't mean the door was locked. The knob turned fine, but when I pushed, the door wouldn't budge. I rattled it a few times, and was about to shrug and walk away.

But I couldn't.

I know. It sounds crazy. I'd started the night thinking about hitting a bar for a few drinks. Maybe finding some company for the night. But there I was, rattling the door to a hokey used pawn shop with a ridiculous sign promising "We Have Things You Need." Convinced I might actually need something in there, when what I needed was back in my cabin at The Motor Lodge . . .

in a box under the bed

"Please," I whispered, twisting the door knob, rattling the door against its frame, "please let me in, I . . . I need to be in there, I'll do anything. *Let me in.*"

I know.

I'm not proud of how I acted. I can't explain why I needed to get inside so badly. All I can say is a short conversation with a weird shopkeeper had stripped away the shell I'd created over the years, leaving me exposed and raw—an open nerve.

I thumped the door, laying my shoulder against it. "Let. Me. *In.*"

And with a click the door swung open. Without hesitation, I stepped inside. The door closed behind me, and I gotta tell you, it shut soft as a whisper. No cliché slam. A soft click, nothing more.

Right away I sensed something different. I can't explain it, not even after all this time. All I can say is the air inside felt heavier. Everything was blanketed by an oppressive silence. Y'know how it sounds inside a building when it's empty? Or maybe how it *feels* is a better way of putting it. The store didn't sound empty so much as it *felt* empty.

Which didn't make sense. Even assuming there was a rear exit for the shopkeeper, I hadn't stood on the sidewalk for long. No way he could've closed the store and left.

Glancing toward the counter confirmed my suspicions. All the lights were still on. And, sitting where I'd left it, was that hokey Magic Eight Ball.

I'm still not sure what pushed me forward. Why I didn't turn around and leave. Crazy as it was, the guy had obviously closed and gone home. It seemed weird for him to have left the front door open and the lights on, but maybe those were security lights, right? Maybe the door's lock stuck as old ones do. Maybe he'd thought he'd locked it, but hadn't.

I meandered forward, glancing around the cluttered shelves. My gaze didn't settle on anything in particular, gliding over used tools, old board games, discarded dolls and other cast-offs. By the time I reached the counter, most of my unease (okay, fear) had passed. The human brain is interesting, if you think about it. It doesn't want to be afraid or think about things hiding in the shadows. It hates ideas that don't make sense, or things that trouble us deeply inside . . .

like the .38 under the bed

. . . so our minds slide around these things, winking at them, nudging them softly aside. That's what my brain was doing, I guess. I'd gotten over my nerves and figured I was right. The shopkeeper had thought he'd locked up, but the front door's lock was broken or didn't work right. Or, maybe he was out back and hadn't heard me come in. Either way, so long as I didn't think too much about the weird heaviness of the air in the store . . .

or my .38

. . . I felt fine. It was a weird night in a weird little town. That's all.

I stopped at the counter, placed my hands flat down and leaned over. I tried to peer around the corner. All I saw was a dimly lit corridor reaching into darkness. I supposed it was possible someone was back there, but I heard nothing. All I could see was a vague suggestion of shelves, and boxes piled on the floor.

"Hey," I called, "anyone back there? Mr. We-Have-What-You-Need? Hello?"

Silence.

And the weird thing was, my voice didn't echo at all. I wasn't expecting an echo, of course. Place wasn't a cave or anything. But I expected to hear something, I guess.

I got nothing.

I grunted, dismissing it. So my voice sounded weird. So what?

My gaze fell on something I hadn't seen before, to

my far left on the counter. An old tape recorder. One of those big reel-to-reel jobs. And the odd thing was: the power light glowed an eerie green.

It was on.

I stared at it, frowning. I didn't remember seeing it only ten or fifteen minutes before, when I was talking to the shopkeeper. Of course, I hadn't looked around much, either. Was mostly focused on the guy and his weird ramblings. But I would've bet my bottom dollar it hadn't been there when I'd first approached the counter.

And it was *on*.

Which bugged me most of all.

Why would it be on?

I found myself reaching for the "play" switch before I even understood what I was doing. I stopped short, clenching my hand, gripped by strange, conflicting emotions. I couldn't understand why I felt compelled to press "play" and at the same time, I didn't understand the feeling of . . . *foreboding?* . . . which checked my hand.

It was an old tape player. What could possibly be on it? Disgusted, I pushed aside my strange reluctance, reached forward and pressed play. I heard nothing but clicking, hissing static as the reels turned, then, a deep voice cleared its throat and . . .

THE WAY OF AH-TZENUL

EVERYTHING GOT STRANGE when the new moon cycle started last April. Course, things always get strange when the moon changes. My goats and chickens act up, coon dogs howl more than usual, cows won't milk. It figures, I suppose. We're all tied to the moon more than we think. *Farmer's Almanac* says so, same as John George Holmnan's *Long Lost Friend*. Hell, moon pulls in the tides and such. Makes sense it messes with other things too.

I'm rambling like an old fool. Happens when you get my age. Take a seat there on the sofa, son. Didn't catch your name.

Ah. You're the new fella, ain't you? Fresh in town from medical school. Pleased to meetcha.

Anyhow Doc, I'm much obliged, you coming to see my Betty. Dr. Jeffers, he's on vacation. He recommended you. Said you was a fine sawbones, which is fortunate. My Betty, she's in a bad way. Has been since last April. As I said; moon pulls on all of us, but this business with my Betty? Well, that's something else altogether. Something unnatural.

What's that?

Oh, she's resting now. We'll go see her by'n by.

27

Lemme catch you up with everything, first. Things got strange around the new moon last April. Right when *The Way of Ah-Tzenul* said to start planting, but like I said, the moon always brings out strange things. If I think back, it all started with *The Way* itself. Everything started changing after I found it. Wish to God I'd left the damn thing where it was. Maybe none of this would've ever happened.

Too late now, though. Here's how the whole damn thing started.

I wasn't looking for nothing in particular the day I found *The Way of Ah-Tzenul* in the recycling dumpster at the Webb County Landfill. Now, don't get the wrong idea. I ain't no garbage picker. No, sir. I ain't one of those fellas who drives round town the night before garbage day, going through junk on the curb. I'm as curious as the next fella, though. When I was dumping our paper into the recycling dumpster at the landfill, something caught my eye. Two cardboard boxes. One of 'em spilling a mess of pamphlets, papers, and letters stuffed into opened envelopes. The other was stuffed full of old books.

The one full of books drew my attention. I talk a little rough, but I ain't dumb. Did fine in school, wanted to attend Webb County Community but couldn't cause of Daddy dying and me having to take over the farm. By the time Momma passed I was married with a little one on the way, so my chance for college had passed, too.

But I never stopped reading. Got me a nice little library out back, filled with all sorts of books crammed on bookshelves made by my own two hands. Books like Tom Sawyer, Edgar Allen Poe stories, Huck Finn and *The King in Yellow*, (that last one I don't read much cause it always gives me strange dreams), some old mysteries, a clutch of Lovecraft's books (they hurt my head, too, so I don't read them much neither), my Hardy Boys books from growing up, and a whole bunch of newer ones by Stephen King and Dean Koontz.

Got some heavy thinking books, too. The family King James, *The Book of Mormon*, *Long Lost Friend*, also got *The Traveler's Gate* and *The Witch Book of Throop*.

Anyhow I love books, so when I saw that box in the recycling dumpster at the landfill I couldn't resist. I dumped my load to the side, leaned in, snagged the box's flap, and dragged it out. Didn't take time to look through em right then, just pretended I wasn't doing anything out of the ordinary. I needn't have worried cause there wasn't no one around so early anyway. I got into my truck and headed to The Skylark for my usual Saturday morning pancakes.

In the parking lot I rooted through the box for something to take into the diner and read. Didn't find much of interest at first. Only a few books with plays by Shakespeare and a book by Melville called *Benito Cerano*. Past those, I came across something promising. An old journal. Name on the inside cover read JEREMIAH BASSLER, which of course caught my interest, Bassler being an important name round these parts, what with Bassler Road, old Bassler House and Bassler Memorial Library. Flipping through it, I saw it was written in other languages and such, maybe

Latin, which I can't read. But I knew some hill folk—especially a hoodoo man named Clive Hartley—who could read Latin, so I put it aside for later.

I looked back into the box and of course, that's when I found it. The book that's caused all this trouble. *The Way of Ah-Tzenul*. Course, that's not what's printed on the cover. There's a picture of some sorta tribal man squatting down with both hands raised to the sky etched into the cover and traced in silver. Otherwise, it's a plain-looking book, all bound in pebbly black leather.

The title was printed on the first page. See, this book was also handwritten, but a whole lot neater than the diary. All in English, too. Under the title, whoever had written the whole thing wrote an explanation of who Ah-Tzenul was. Apparently he was the Aztec nature and harvest god. Another name they had for him was "He Who Brings Life from the Earth."

You got it right, Doc. From what I was reading, *The Way* was a planting book for ancient folks, like the Aztecs. I didn't read all of it while sitting there at The Skylark, just flipped through. From what I could see, the book was an older version of the Farmer's Almanac, which was mighty interesting, seeing as how planting season was coming on. Every year, I raise one of the best pumpkin patches round. I usually get one monster in the top three of Clifton Height's annual Halloween Pumpkin Contest. Our other produce Betty cans and freezes for the winter months.

Unfortunately, last year's crop of pumpkins was one of the worst I'd had in years. Only a third turned out, and they was just little blobs which rotted on the vine. First time in ten years I didn't have an entry in the contest.

Anyhow, I finished up them pancakes, closed *The Way,* and headed back to the farm. Soon as I was pulling in the driveway, my old lady—Betty—she come out and lit into me as she always did about wasting my Saturday morning at The Skylark chewing the fat with the other old codgers, instead of plowing and getting things ready for planting.

One thing you gotta understand about Betty and me, Doc. We have our tussles now and then. She's a good country woman, my Betty is. Raised the kids right and proper. The boy is attending Cornell University studying Agricultural Science and my girl is down at Broome Community College in Binghamton, working on her degree in Social Services. They turned out right cause of their momma.

Betty also runs a tight ship. Leastways she did before her troubles. Time was, she had dinner on the table around five, clothes were always washed, mended and folded in my drawer, the house neat as a pin. She had several flower beds around the property she tended with about as much sweat and blood as I poured over my fields.

Thing is, Betty has a temper (still does, in a way). Came with her red Irish hair, I suppose. She got something on her mind, she said it, and she didn't spare no one's feeling about anything. She'd light into you or Sheriff Baker or anyone else, she get her dander up.

Ain't always a bad thing. My girl and boy learned their manners and did their schoolwork. They minded their mother because if they didn't, she'd bring down hellfire on their heads. Even I can admit to a strain of shiftlessness. Suppose if I was left to my own devices I'd putter around town all morning, chewing the fat with the boys at The Skylark. Sometimes, it's good for the soul to know you're gonna catch hell at home if you don't get work done.

Problem is, there's a few things about Betty that really chaps my ass (used to, anyway). One: Much as her fire was good for the soul, she didn't rightly know when to quit. Especially when she found her groove. Whole week coming up to the Saturday when I found *The Way*, she was riding my ass. Couldn't let last year's bad harvest rest. Every minute I spent doing something other than plowing the field or turning the mulch she was hammering away about how I needed to get my ass moving, or we'd have another poor harvest. That Saturday morning she was pushing me to my limit because I'd heard the same riff all week long.

Another thing is, she hates books. Hates me reading them so much, too. Now, she don't hate school learning, else she wouldn't have been so hard on the kids, driving them so hard they got the highest marks in their classes and got scholarships for college. No, what she can't stand is the idea of reading for pleasure. She never took to school herself. Quit at age sixteen. And though she made our children attend school and college so they could someday have better lives than us, she didn't cotton to the idea of a grown man sitting around for even ten minutes reading something for enjoyment.

According to her, I was a farmer and nothing more. I was to spend all my days with my hand on the plow, not on a book. Fact, she went so far as to never clean my study. Kept the rest of the house spotless, but she never cleaned my study. Said she hated being near some of the strange books I kept, claiming they gave her the heebie-jeebies cause they was Satan's own words, bound in evil and lies.

Mostly, I think she couldn't stand the thought of me sitting in there reading them heavy thinking books or a Stephen King yarn for fun. She wasn't ever much of a reader. Meaning my old lady no disrespect, Doc, but I'm not sure how much she could read herself. I think a lot of her ire came from being jealous of all the simple pleasure I took from it.

Lastly, Betty always did poke fun at my pumpkins. Said I spent too much time fretting over them, claiming last year's harvest was so bad cause I wasted too much time trying to save the pumpkins. For true, might be something to what she said. Got a bit taken with the pumpkins last year and probably did spend too much time trying to save them.

But Betty, she never though my winning one of the top three spots at the Festival was much to-do. Never mocked me outright, but was always sarcastic about it, see? This past year, after all my pumpkins died on the vine? Well, she was in hog heaven, for sure.

Don't get me wrong, Doc.

I love my Betty. But she nags, sometimes. Leastways she used to, before all this. Hell, I'd trade it all back to catch some of her nagging.

So anyway, you can imagine her consternation. There she was, standing in the front door, wiping her hands on her apron, scowling, and she says, "What the hell kinda trash you dragging in now, Seamus?"

I open my mouth to speak, but she holds up her hand and says, "No, lemme guess. Some fool dumped a box full of those useless books yer always reading and you fished em out and brought em home so you can waste more time reading instead of plowing the field. Ain't gonna have nothing to eat, winter comes."

Now truth be told, there was something for her to be frustrated about. I had dawdled a bit all week. Hadn't plowed the field as I should've, especially my pumpkin patch. I'll admit I spent a patch of time in my study, reading the *Farmer's Almanac* and *The Long Lost Friend* to see if I'd missed anything that could help with the crops.

Still, much as I love my Betty as only a man could love his God-given wife, sometimes she can't get it through her head how much gets in the way of plowing and planting, come spring. For example, that whole past week, besides reading the Almanac for planting ideas, I had to re-shingle the roof on the backside of the house. I also spent a whole Tuesday repairing the fence around the goat pen. Wednesday, Betty had me fetching mulch from the landfill for her flower gardens. The tractor's engine broke down Thursday. I spent the better part of the day fiddling with it until I finally threw up my hands and called Jeb Hawkins (mechanic who runs a little shop up in the Heights) to come fix it for me. Of course with the tractor out of commission all day I couldn't plow, but I didn't tell Betty that cause she'd just get her dander up and accuse me of lying to get the day off.

So anyway I *was* behind in my plowing, but not because of loafing around, as Betty said. When she lit into me about those books I'd scavenged from the dumpster, I scowled and says, "Don't start. If I don't figure what went wrong with last year's crops it ain't gonna matter how soon I get the fields plowed, same thing as last time's gonna happen."

Betty folded her arms, scowled and says, "Hell, ain't no mystery why the crops failed last year. Went in with Cletus Smith on them cheap seeds he found in Booneville. Got taken for a ride, Seamus. Which I told you last year, if you remember."

Thing is, Doc, Betty wasn't *exactly* wrong about that, neither. I *did* throw in on a deal with Cletus Smith to buy some wholesale seed from this place he'd heard of in Booneville. Folks around those parts swore on the place. Well, they may have sworn so, but the seed Cletus bought grew some of the weakest plants I ever seen, no lie there.

Even so, the subject was still sore despite her being right. You show me a man who don't mind being proved wrong, I'll show you a man who ain't got much in the way of balls. I snorted and says, "Ain't nothing wrong with the seed we got from Booneville. Something else went foul. Soil, mulch, weather. Something. And if I don't figure out what, same thing is gonna happen this year. Then we'll be up the creek. Plus, I ain't missing out on the Halloween Festival two years in a row. No way in hell."

She shakes her head, wiping her hands on her apron the whole time. "You gonna spend the whole day reading them damn fool books you dug outta the dumpster, trying to figure out how to save yer precious pumpkin patch? Or are you gonna get on yer tractor and do some plowing today?"

Now, plowing wasn't what I wanted to do right

then. Truth be told, I wanted to hole up in my study and start flipping through *The Way*. Of course, I couldn't say so to Betty without riling her up even worse, but an idea came to me, quick as flash. "Depends. We got any venison left in the freezer for dinner?"

She thought for a minute, then shook her head. "Used it up in a casserole night before last.

"We got any meat at all?"

Her face scrunched up. "Nope. Was planning on spaghetti tonight."

"Well then," I says with a smile, "best head out to Clifton Lake, hook me some bass for dinner. Can always plow Monday."

I'd offered her a perfectly logical explanation. We was out of meat, and she didn't like spaghetti any more than I did. She knew I had good luck with the rod and reel. More than likely, I'd bring home at least ten or twelve bass and pan fish.

But she knew me, Doc. Knew I could plant two rods in the ground, sit back, kick my feet up and browse through a book to my heart's content. She also knew what I knew, deep down in my heart: I was putting off plowing the field.

She smirked, wiped her hands on her apron once more and says, "Fine, Seamus. Do whatever you want. I'm only yer wife. Hell, when we're begging for food at the Methodist Church food pantry in the Fall cause the plants didn't grow right cause you spent all yer time trying to conjure how to grow prize-winning pumpkins, don't complain. Hell, you'll have plenty a time to read then, sitting on your ass in an old church pew every month waiting for a handout."

With that, Betty turned and walked back into the house, muttering under her breath something I couldn't hear but figured wasn't complementary. I thought *Hell with her anyway.* Doc, I love my wife as much as the next man, but she couldn't ever consider anything from a different perspective. Besides, what did she know about planting? I'm the one been doing it all these years.

Plus, something in my head was whispering *The Way of Ah-Tzenul* had all the answers I'd need. If I could find some time to sit and read the damn thing, all our planting problems would be solved. I would finally take first place in the Halloween Pumpkin Festival.

Turns out I was right, Doc. *The Way* did have all the answers I needed. But honest and true? I'd take it all back, sure as God rules in Heaven and the devil dwells below.

⤜∞⤏

Luckily I keep all my tackle and poles in my truck, and there's bait coolers at the Quickmark on the way, so I didn't have to weather Betty's disapproving glare while gathering my fishing gear. In no time at all I was rambling down Main Street, turning the corner at the end and heading to Clifton Lake. I parked at the trail-head, gathered my gear—*The Way of Ah-Tzenul* in my jacket pocket—and tromped down to my usual fishing spot, under an old elm on the deep end, whose branches reached over the water. Bass congregated there.

I cleared a space on a big rock, set and baited my poles, cast one, then jammed the end in the crook between rocks. I cast the other, fixed it up, then settled back against the elm and opened *The Way*, hoping to find something for better crops.

Honest truth, Doc? Part of me was thinking Betty was probably right. The whole thing was a waste of time. Some other part of me, though—deep inside— knew what I needed was in *The Way*.

Course, I read maybe a page or two before bass started hitting both my lines. Don't know how much fishing you do, Doc, but fishing with two poles, you gotta be on your toes. Especially when they're biting, like they were that morning. I hadn't gotten much past the second page before I landed five bass and two pan fish, all of them big enough to plop right in a bucket I'd brought with me. Anyway, I felt a mite better. If I brought home a mess of fish for dinner, Betty would be pacified for least a day or so.

Anyhow, the first couple pages didn't tell nothing more than basic advice about planting. When to start plowing and when to seed. What types of soil grew plants the best. What plants to start indoors, what made good fodder for mulching. Ironically it mentioned using fish guts for starting corn seed, which I'd heard tell of some old timers doing, but hadn't ever tried myself. I'd need a whole lot of fish guts to cover my field.

About an hour later, after landing ten bass and four pan fish, things started slowing down. It was getting on eleven in the morning, after all. Fishing always slows down around then. So I settled back and dug into *The Way*. For the most part, it still didn't say much more than what you'd find in the Farmer's Almanac. I was getting mighty disappointed until I

38

turned to a new section titled in slightly shaky handwriting, *Invoking Al Tzenul's Harvest.*

That sounded interesting, seeing as how the whole journal had been named after this Aztec planting god, but it hadn't yet mentioned him. So I perked up. From then on it all sounded different. Even the writing sounded older, using the kinds of words Clive Hartely and other pow-wow fellas conjured with. Anyway, the first paragraph said invoking the spirit of Ah-Tzenul in a "treasured vessel" wasn't to be taken lightly, cause once Ah-Tzenul has "come among the harvest and blessed it he's forever hungry because his belly's empty after bestowing his blessing on the land."

Or something as such, anyway. I don't remember it word for word. Anyhow, the first thing needed to invoke the spirit of Ah-Tzenul was nothing special. Plowing, tilling and mulching the land. Which let me down. I started thinking the rest of the journal was as Betty would say. A waste of time, and I was just desperate because I was afraid I'd lost my touch.

Let's be honest between men, Doc. That's the real reason for putting off plowing my fields. I was afraid I'd never grow plants again, or—stupid as it sounds— grow prize winning pumpkins again. Men don't take blows to the ego well. I heard tell of one fella, over in Eagle Bay, who had a nice business guiding tourists to good fishing spots. Been doing it for years, and he always found folks the best spots without fail.

Well, one summer he lost his touch. Couldn't find any fish at all. Lost all his customers, one right after the other. Wasn't long, folks hadn't seen him around town for a few days, and when they finally broke into his place, they found him in the tub, wrists cut and bled out. I'm not saying I'd thought about doing something similar, but I ain't saying I *hadn't* thought about it, either.

Anyway, I was ready to quit until I read this line: *Invoking Ah-Tzenul's Harvest requires a nightly propitiation to Ah-Tzenul by the offering of the planter's seed.*

Offering of the *planter's* seed.

You understand what that means, Doc? Guess by the way yer staring at me, you DO. So, according to this book I'd found in a dumpster, for a good harvest I hadda go onto my field at midnight, chant a bunch of mish-mash, grab myself and, well . . . get it up . . .

And offer my *seed*.

On my damn field, under the moon.

You'd think I would've caught on, right then. Maybe this whole Ah-Tzenul's Harvest wasn't something to be messing with, right?

Yeah.

You'd think so.

I read more of *The Way* while fishing. Thing is, can't remember much of what I read. My head's fuzzy after the part about "offering the planter's seed." Guess it threw some gears. Anyhow, best I can remember, what I read afterward said something again about a "treasured vessel" meant to bring forth Ah-Tzenul to bless the harvest, and how Ah-Tzenul is always hungry after.

Wanna know the real strange thing? I sorta remember tending to my rods every now and then, hooking the odd bass or pan fish while I was reading, but it didn't seem more than two or three. When I finally blinked and looked at my watch, saw it was near two o'clock in the afternoon, you know how many fish I'd caught?

Fact is I couldn't count. The bucket—ten gallons—was stuffed full of fish, of all kinds. And I'm not saying it was full of fish pushing water to the bucket's brim. I'm saying there wasn't any water left at all. Damn thing was stuffed full of fish. Maybe forty, fifty of em. All stuffed in there, tails sticking up and flipping.

Y'know what I think, Doc?

There I was, reading a strange book about invoking some nature god to help with my crops and my pumpkin patch, and while doing so, I managed—without paying attention—to catch near fifty fish. Something *knew* what I was pondering and it offered me a blessing. Rewarding me, maybe, and promising more things to come.

If only I'd known then what those more things were.

$$\infty$$

When I got home from fishing I lied to Betty, saying I didn't catch a damn thing. Don't know what this says about me or her, but she believed me. She accused me of not fishing at all, said I probably sat under a tree and read my fool head off the whole morning.

Was on the tip of my tongue to tell her about the whole bucket of fish, but I didn't, for some reason. I let her drag me into a row about me wasting time reading "them fool books" and how things was falling down around our ears cause I "wouldn't get off my lazy ass."

After, I slammed out the door, went to the truck

and sneaked the bucket around back to the barn. Knowing Betty doesn't ever set foot near the garden until harvest, I went out and started laying down the fish. I know lots of other farmers do exactly the same thing, so if she did come out and see me, it would be easy to explain what I was doing, though I'd then have to explain why I'd lied about not catching any fish.

Something I'll never understand about laying down them fish, Doc. My garden's fairly big, about hundred feet by sixty or so. Was only planning to lay down fish in the east end, where my pumpkin patch is. Didn't figure on having enough fish for the whole field, not by a long shot.

Here's the thing. You know the story about Jesus and the loaves of bread and fishes? About how He blessed them when He was feeding the five thousand or whatever, and two fishes and a loaf of bread fed them all, and didn't run out?

Same thing happened with this bucket of fish.

When I was finished with the pumpkin patch, I still had over half a bucket full. Halfway done with the garden, still had the same amount. Wasn't until I'd covered the entire garden with fish did I empty the damn bucket.

It was a miracle. Like Jesus and the loaves and the fishes. I didn't feel blessed or joyful, though. Honest to God, felt more scared than anything else.

Well, when you lay fish down on a garden, got to plow them right in or it'll stink up and draw flies. I wasn't hankering for a whole field full of flies. Soon as I lay down the last fish, I hustled to the barn, hitched the plow up to the tractor, fired her up, pulled out and plowed them fish down in my field, working them in, turning the soil over.

Finally plowing the fields got Betty off my back. She acted right friendly to me afterwards. Made some fine venison steaks for dinner (apparently we'd had some squirreled away in the freezer after all) and didn't bother me none when I settled into my study to read more from *The Way of Ah-Tzenul* (which to be honest, I still don't remember much about). Later at night? Well, we got frisky for the first time in a long while.

I can't help but think, Doc. If Betty had known what was coming, she would've sneaked out to my gun closet in the living room after we'd finished, grabbed my thirty-ought and put me out of my misery right then and there. Would've been better all round. Because later on, near midnight?

I went out to the field and called on Ah-Tzenul for the first time.

You ever sleepwalk, Doc? I never did before I read *The Way*. Sure enough, after me and Betty had our relations and we dropped off, I woke and found myself standing at the far end of my garden. And I was—well, this is embarrassing, Doc, cause I'm a private man and don't like talking about such things . . .

Well, the part about the "planter offering his seed?" That's what I was doing. Standing at the far end of my garden, buck-naked under the moon, hand on myself. Working it to beat the band. Again, I don't like sharing all this cause it's private and personal, but you're a Doc, right? Sure you've heard worse.

And maybe you can explain this to me. When I finally got—well, got *there*, a bomb went off in my head. I seized up all over, felt like electricity was shooting through me, snapping my back. I offered my seed, as *The Way of Ah-Tzenul* said I should. It kept shooting out of me onto the ground. My whole body burned. I'm ashamed to say even though some part of me was scared, another part me?

Well.

I kinda liked it.

Loved it, in fact, cause it'd never been so powerful between me and Betty, ever.

Here's the other thing, Doc. Scares me more than anything else. After it all happened I felt tired and woozy, so I'm not sure if what I saw actually happened, but when I looked down to the ground, where I spilled my seed? Damn my eyes if the ground wasn't sucking it down. Minutes passed and the ground at my feet was dry as a bone.

Here's another thing which hit me, Doc, as I stumbled away from the garden and back down to the house, suddenly desperate to get back to bed before Betty discovered I'd left. I came awake standing at the *far* end of the garden. The muscles in my back, belly and thighs quivering, sore as hell. As if I'd worked my way along the garden, spilling my seed the whole way. I'd covered the *whole* field. Now you tell me, Doc.

How's that possible?

The following week was the last time Betty and me was on good terms. Sunday, after I found myself offering my seed, I spent the day mending things around the house. We ain't never been much for church-going, and honestly, Doc? After finding *The Way* and reading it, and the whole fish thing, and offering my seed? The thought of me walking into God's House seemed blasphemous. Like maybe I'd get struck by lightning soon as I walked through the door.

Anyhow, rest of the week me and Betty got along fine, probably the best we have since before the kids. After only having relations occasionally, we was having them every night. And yes, before you ask, every night afterward, I found myself waking up at the far end of my garden, under the light of the moon. When I finished up? Well, words can't explain how it felt. My whole body exploded.

Now, you might think this would wear me out terrible. Sure enough, after each time, I staggered down to the house, feeling sore as hell, and, not to press a joke too far, drained empty. Literally.

But each morning after offering my seed, I felt good. New. Full of life and blazing with energy. Every single day I did what Betty had been after me to do for weeks: Plant the garden. Corn rows on Monday, potatoes Tuesday, lettuce on Wednesday, onions and radishes on Thursday, peas and carrots and broccoli on Friday.

Then, Saturday, one full week after I'd found *The Way* in a dumpster at the landfill, I planted cucumbers and my pumpkins at the far end of my garden, and yep, that night, I found myself up there at midnight one last time, after an especially rousing bout with Betty, offering my seed. I say last time, because after that night it never happened again. I'd offered my seed and planted seed. According to *The Way of Ah-Tzenul*, it was now time for something a bit more *nourishing*.

Ironically enough it was also the last time Betty and I had relations. The new spark we'd been enjoying for a whole week died after I spilled my seed on the garden for the last time.

I know what yer thinking, Doc. Yer wondering if I've gone off my rocker. Probably don't know what to think about invoking the spirit of Ah-Tzenul and all, but trust me, Doc. I ain't lying. I did all that stuff and more.

Why would I?

Why go to such lengths?

Sounds foolish, and I suppose it *is* foolish when you cut to the quick. But that pumpkin contest, Doc. Yeah, being a farmer full-time, I needed the produce for our living, so planting the whole garden was important.

But that pumpkin contest.

Hell, Doc. Growing crops is the only thing I've ever done well. The bad harvest last year? Specially them rotten, lopsided pumpkins? Ain't gonna lie, Doc. It worked on me something fierce all winter long. Not entering the Halloween Festival for the first time in ten years. Not taking at least one of the top three. It was a slap in the face.

And those pumpkins, dead on the vine? Well, must sound awful vain and foolish, but it was emasculating. Like my own balls being sliced off.

Also, I ain't above admitting *The Way of Ah-Tzenul* was working on my head something fierce. *The King in Yellow*, *Long Lost Friend*, *The Traveler's Gate* and some of Lovecraft's books have worked on my head something fierce, too (though I can't bear to throw them out, on account of how much I love books in general), but they wasn't nothing compared to this. I ain't ashamed to admit I haven't exactly been in my right mind since I first opened that damn book . . .

What you say?

How's this got to do with why I called you here? Don't worry, Doc. We're getting to that, directly.

The Sunday after I last offered my seed up to Ah-Tzenul, I got hit by the worst case a let-down. Felt as if some part of me died. After tending to the animals, I felt the need to settle down in my study and read. Hell, I'd spent the whole week plowing and planting. Figured I owed myself. I'd picked up a few new Stephen King novels last month at the used book sale at Bassler Memorial Library, so I figured on starting one of them.

So I was surprised to find myself sitting up in my chair, blinking as if coming out of a long sleep, with *The Way* open in my lap, reading about "invoking the spirit of Ah-Tzenul through the nourishment of the sow's blood." I sat there and stared at *The Way*, wondering how the hell I'd gone and read it when I'd wanted to read something else. Also, how could I sit there for a whole hour and a half reading without remembering *what* I'd read!

But there it was, staring me in the face. Sitting open in my lap. Mocking me with its slanty-sidewise handwriting. Though I had no memory of what I'd read, the last sentence burned in my brain: *Invoking the spirit of Ah-Tzenul through the nourishment of the sow's blood.*

47

I re-read the pages before that bit, and I gotta be honest, Doc. It set me back on my heels. Spreading pig's blood all over my field. I didn't know what to think about that. I understood the fish guts thing. Most farmers do, I suppose. Rotting fish produces nitrogen. Plowing it down before planting's gonna make for lots of nitrogen in the soil. But pig's blood? Not only that, but bitch pig's blood?

How the hell was that gonna help?

Course, I'd just spent the whole week spilling my seed all over the field. How was pig's blood any stranger?

I read a little more to see what else it'd say. Apparently, I couldn't spread the blood on the field during the day. I had to spread it on the field at midnight, under the spring full moon (which was coming soon, according to the Farmer's Almanac). There was another spell I had to chant while doing it.

Now, right there you figure I would've realized, once and for all, this wasn't something I should be messing with, having read *Long Lost Friend*, *The Traveler's Gate* and *The Witch Book of Throop*. But Doc, I'm sure you'll agree with me. Most men wanna keep their own counsel rather than heed the words of others. This was my field, my pumpkin patch and my chance to take top prize. Also my chance to put Betty (lovingly, of course) in her place for a change. Man get in such a state, ain't much he *won't* do.

I slowly closed *The Way*.

Sat there and stared into nothing, thinking hard.

We only ever have two or three pigs at a time, Doc. Takes about six months for them to grow big enough to butcher, about two hundred pounds or so. The pigs

I had weren't only about four months along, not a hundred-fifty pounds. Butchering them then would be a waste, getting us only half the meat. I think, Doc, right then and there, if I'd been left to my own self, I would've tossed *The Way* in the fire pit and burned it.

But Betty had to poke her fool head into my study. She sorta sneered and says, "Lookit you. One week of hard work and here you is, sitting on yer ass and reading more trash. Make a hell of a farmer, you do. Sitting on yer fat ass, reading."

She shook her head, smiling the whole time, and left. Me, however, I was near shaking to rage. Which is kinda strange, when you think on it. Betty had always sorta pissed me off with her talk about books being foolishness and me being lazy for sitting on my ass and reading, but I brushed it off most the time.

Right then?

If I'd had my hand on my shotgun or ax? Think I might have sent Betty right out of the world.

Thinking back?

Might have been for the best, all things considering.

⤬

Doc, does sleepwalking ever happen during the day? Cause after that Sunday when I woke up after reading *The Way,* remembering nothing; after Betty lit into me, I found myself dozing off and then waking up in the middle of doing things I had no plans of doing at all.

Take butchering them pigs. One minute I was getting to my feet, mumbling about Betty sassing me and how she'd regret not showing me respect; next minute, I found myself sticking my first pig in its neck.

49

You grow up on a farm, Doc? Hell now, you did? Don't suppose you ever butchered a pig? No? Well, it's a damn messy job, for sure. First stick in the neck sends a fountain of blood all over. And worse, I wasn't concerned with getting the meat at all, Doc. All I wanted was blood, so I went to extra efforts to drain the blood into buckets as I went. Getting meat was secondary.

So pretty soon, I stood there with them carcasses hanging high from my barn (but it wasn't too long before they was spoiled, Doc, cause spring is the wrong time to butcher pigs), with three ten-gallon buckets beneath, catching their blood. And, though I remember most of what I'd done, I wandered away from the barn and down to the house to wash up in a daze. Even now, I can sorta remember butchering them pigs, but from far away. Like I watched someone else do it. Make any sense to you?

One thing I do remember. Whole time I was talking to myself. Talking, or sorta singing. Chanting, maybe. But I don't remember the words. Even if I did, I don't think they'd make much sense, because from what I do remember?

They didn't sound like no words I'd ever heard in my whole life.

I was washing the blood off my hands in the sink when Betty came roaring into the kitchen, swearing to raise the roof. She must've seen me coming down from the butchering pen and wanted to know what the hell was going on, me butchering them sows so early.

The kitchen door slammed open hard enough to

rattle the pots and pans hanging next to the stove. She says, "Seamus Freely! What the hell you doing, butchering them sows? Ain't more than hundred pounds each! Won't get no meat off them worth keeping! Supposed to be our meat for the winter! You lost yer damn mind?"

I stood there, slowly washing my hands, rubbing them under the hot water. They was glowing red, on account of how hot the water was. Staring at my hands—rubbing, clenching, unclenching—still sorta hypnotized, I mumbled, "Nuff meat there to last us awhile, Betts. Last us just fine."

Betty stomped, rattling them pots again. "Hell we'll be fine! We'll be outta pork by the end of summer. How we gonna get through the winter, Seamus? What the hell was you thinking?"

Right then I started rising from my funk, Doc. Her angry words sent hot flashes up my neck. I grit my teeth harder, washing and rubbing my hands faster under the hot water. I says, "Mind me, woman. Don't you sass me none. We'll be fine. I'm still head of the household round here. If I say it's time to butcher the sows it's time to butcher, and you get no say-so."

I paused and then, in calm, cool words, I says something I wasn't planning on, the words spilling right outta my mouth. "Besides, *The Way of Ah-Tzenul* says to invoke the spirit of Ah-Tzenul in your harvest, you gotta give an offering of . . . "

"Books," she says, grumbling. "Yer damn books. That's where you're getting this foolishness from? Hell, I should've known. You sitting around all day on your fat ass, reading them damn books, stuffing your head with fool ideas about nothing at all. Why, I oughta drag them books out to the burn pit, pour kerosene over em, and burn em up, and another thing . . . "

I can't exactly tell you what happened next, Doc. And I can't exactly tell you why. Betty and me, we've had some knock-down drag-outs over the years, some real screamers. She's threatened to burn my books before. Said worse things, too. So why everything went so hot and red, I don't know. Maybe I was embarrassed, because after all, she was right, Doc. *Was* a waste to butcher them pigs so early, but *The Way of Ah-Tzenul* had called for sow blood, and I couldn't say no. I was invoking the spirit of Ah-Tzenul on my field, on my crops, especially on my pumpkin patch. I had to grow pumpkins this year, Doc. Had to win that damn contest.

Also?

She was disrespecting *The Way of Ah-Tzenul*. I can handle her disrespecting me. Hell, even when things was good between us she was always a smart ass. But she was disrespecting *The Way of Ah-Tzenul* and all it'd taught me. For some reason, that I couldn't abide.

The butchering knife I'd used to stick them pigs was in my hand in an instant, and I covered it in spurting red again. And yeah, Doc. It was this knife, the one I got right here.

Now, Doc, you sit tight. Ain't gonna stick you with this if you sit still. Sure as hell didn't call ya here to gut you in my living room. And no, Betty ain't gone. She's the reason I called ya here in the first place. But you let me finish my story before you judge me. Don't you try getting up and running neither.

Actually, you come this way, Doc. We'll head up to the garden, out back. Only way you're gonna understand everything. You walk before me, and don't make any moves. I been sharpening this knife every day since I butchered them sows and stabbed Betty in the neck.

Every. Damn. Day.

Turned out that night was a full moon. Don't know if I knew or sensed it, but it's why I chose to butcher them pigs. Maybe it was all coincidence, but something inside me says that ain't so. None of this has been coincidence. The frightening thing? I think it was bound to happen the moment I found *The Way* in the dumpster at the Webb County Landfill.

Anyway, that night.

By the light of the full moon.

I dumped them buckets of sow's blood all over the garden, softly chanting them same strange words I can't remember, as *The Way of Ah-Tzenul* said to. Like with them dead fish, somehow the last drop didn't get spilled until I'd covered the whole field. And here's a strange thing. You'd think a whole garden covered in pig blood sitting in buckets since midday would stink to high heaven.

But it didn't, Doc. Smelled a little coppery but mostly smelled of freshly-turned earth and Adirondack pine. The blood soaked right into the soil, just like my seed did. Wasn't a drop left on the surface, except now I don't think "soaked" is the right word.

Drank.

That soil hadn't soaked the blood up. It drank the

blood. Cause I had invoked the spirit of Ah-Tzenul in my garden, and as it says in *The Way of Ah-Tzenul*, when Ah-Tzenul's been invoked to bless your crops . . . Ah-Tzenul is always hungry, and apparently thirsty, too.

Watch your step there, Doc. Up this little rise, and here we are.

Yep. Ain't it a beaut, Doc? Best garden I've ever had. Gonna be able to can and freeze enough to last me through the winter all the way into next planting season, for sure. And I ain't ever seen such corn or potatoes. Those alone are sure to fetch a fine price at the farmer's market in a few weeks. Fact, I've got no worries about the coming winter at all, Doc. *The Way of Ah-Tzenul* says things about blessing the hunt, starting bee hives, everything else you can possibly think of when it comes to gathering your own food. Got some new young sows and they're already hundred pounds each. By the time I need to make another offering, they'll be plenty large enough for me to get all the meat I need.

What's that?

Oh, Betty. Well, let's come to the far end of the garden, Doc. Here we go, follow this path along the side.

Look at them pumpkins, now. That one there has to be near forty feet round, all shiny orange and near perfect. Definitely take first place in the Halloween Festival in a few weeks. I reckon I can charge a pretty penny selling the rest for jack'o lanterns, too. I don't know for sure, but I wager making jack'o lanterns out of pumpkins grown with the essence of Ah-Tzenul might make for a special Halloween indeed.

THINGS YOU NEED

I see you're looking at the other pumpkin. The one behind my sure prize winner. Yep, yer right, it's the biggest in the whole garden. Guinness Book size, sure enough, if I called anyone up here to see it, but I ain't gonna do that.

Why?

Well, to be perfectly honest, this is where I ended up planting Betty after I stuck her. I been sorta lying and telling everyone she ain't been feeling well and been resting, and I feel sorta bad, but I couldn't tell folks the truth, now could I? It's a real good thing Betty never got along with folks down in town. If she had more friends, I might not have been able to . . .

Hold on there, Doc! You stop right there and don't struggle, or your gonna get this knife right in the belly. See, I wasn't lying when I said Betty wasn't gone. The part about the spirit of Ah-Tzenul taking a treasured vessel when invoked? Well, don't matter what you think, don't matter that we fought and she hated my reading and I stuck her in the neck, my Betty was treasured by me, she surely was. That's where I buried her, Doc. Right in my pumpkin patch, and considering what she thought about my pumpkins and the Halloween Festival it's right ironic . . .

You hold still!

C'mere! See this ridge here, long the bottom of this here pumpkin? See how it's sorta quivering? *The Way of Ah-Tzenul* was right, Doc, it surely was. Once you invoke Ah-Tzenul's blessing on your crops, it's always . . .

Now you stop that! My Betty's hungry and if she ain't fed right quick . . .

Ah, hell, Doc, now ya done it! She gets right mean when her food ain't alive . . .

4.

I STARED AT the reel-to-reel as it fell into a soft hissing *click-click-click*. After several seconds of listening numbly, I reached out and pressed stop.

Silence rushed in, even more oppressive than before. I stuck my hands into my pockets and glanced around the store. No shopkeeper. He *must've* gone, I decided, because there was no way he could still be around and not hear the tape playing.

And what *had* I heard on the tape? At the time I leaned toward an old radio drama of some kind. I'd listened to plenty of those over the years on the road between magazine gigs, on the AM stations. Re-runs of 'The Shadow,' 'Suspense,' and 'Inner Sanctum Mysteries.' They were corny as hell but entertaining. I especially loved how the hosts always shoe-horned their sponsor's advertisements into the show. "Tonight's tale about sex, murder, and revenge will give you a delightful chill . . . just like the kind you get from sipping a refreshing Lipton's Ice Tea on a warm summer day!" Made me grin every time.

Thing was, the longer I stared at the old reel-to-reel, the less sure I felt about my instincts. There hadn't been any theme music, any host introducing the story, no corny sponsor's advertisements. Nor did I hear any voices other than the guy telling the story, or any special effects, though I had caught the sound of scuffling and a shout at the very end, and the weirdness of the story would certainly fit in an episode of 'Inner Sanctum' or 'Suspense.'

I decided not to worry about it. Really, it was the least of my concerns. For some reason I'd been compelled to come back into Handy's Pawn and Thrift instead of going back to my cabin . . .

and the .38

. . . and I couldn't for the life of me figure out why. Or maybe I was still in denial about how much I'd grown to hate my life. Regardless, the urgency I'd felt on the curb outside the store faded. I figured enough was enough. Time to leave and go to bed.

But I think I *knew*, somehow, the only thing waiting for me was my .38. I'd had it for a year or so (maybe longer?), and it had never been anything more than a stray thought in the back of my head. It had swelled, however, into an unrelenting pressure. An undercurrent surging beneath my thoughts. I wasn't exactly thinking, *I can't go back because if I do I'll kill myself*, but subconsciously, I think the option had somehow become a real possibility.

So instead of heading straight for the door, I glanced around the sales counter some more. My gaze fell on the Magic Eight Ball again. I thought what the hell? I picked it up and shook it. "So. Am I stuck here for the night? Is this where I'm gonna finally find what I need?"

I gave the damned thing one more shake. Held it, and watched the milky fluid inside settle.

THE OFFICE

JOHN PINKERTON KNELT before the bookshelf in the rear of his office. He searched the bottom shelf for something to read while toying with his old Magic Eight Ball, the quirky fortune-telling toy recognized by any child of the eighties.

He'd been searching for what felt like hours. This happened often (more so these days), and he couldn't honestly say it displeased him. Browsing his overflowing bookshelves presented him with an infinite selection of journeys waiting to be taken. Every book he'd read represented old friends he loved revisiting. The ones he hadn't, new friends in waiting. Choosing which to read was a pleasing difficulty.

He shook the eight ball with one hand, smiling. "What's it going to be?" he whispered, running his other hand along the spines of books on his tightly packed shelf. "Some ghost stories, today?"

The white polyhedron, suspended in liquid turned murky with age, jiggled as it revealed: Future is Hazy.

John chuckled as he returned his attention to the books before him. "Story of my life," he whispered. "Story of my . . . "

Something whisked along the floor outside his office.

He slowly stood.

Turned and gazed at his office doorway.

Saw nothing but darkness beyond.

Which was strange.

Because he'd left the light in the hall on. His office was in the basement, which consisted of the washroom, furnace, and the playroom. By nature it was dark. A subterranean space with no windows. He always left the lights on outside his office because he didn't like the dark. Never had. Beth fussed about his little quirk (saying it wasted electricity) but she'd long ago resigned herself to his habit, and now offered her half-hearted complaints mostly for show.

He'd turned the hall lights on when he came downstairs. He was sure of it. But he saw only darkness beyond the office doorway.

"Beth? Hey . . . Beth? I'm down here, honey. In my office? Could you switch on the stairs light?"

Maybe Beth hadn't realized he was down here. Frugal as she was, she'd shut off the lights. But that didn't make sense. There were two sets of lights on the way to his office. The stairwell lights and the lights in the hall. Beth would've had to descend the stairs, at least, to turn the hallway lights off. He'd heard a noise, of course, which maybe had been her . . .

But it had sounded different. More like a *swishing* sound. The hem of a dress whispering against the floor. Beth wasn't prone to wearing dresses, even for formal occasions.

"Beth?"

Not a sound. He stood in the middle of his office

and listened for a moment, directing his senses upward, searching for sounds of life. The floor, creaking as someone walked from the den to the kitchen. The more distant creaks of either Marty or Melissa ascending the stairs to their bedrooms on the second floor. The distant murmur of the television in the living room or the radio in the dining room, or water running in the kitchen or bathroom sinks, down through the pipes . . .

Nothing.

Nothing but dead silence. Which was odd, because he'd heard sounds only moments before. Hadn't he? Hadn't Beth called to him, saying they were heading out for a bit? Hadn't he nodded unconsciously as he searched for something to read?

It wouldn't have been the first time. Over the past few years (especially since the kids had turned into teenagers and therefore strange aliens from distant planets who wanted little to do with him) his office had become his refuge. He'd spent increasing hours there channeling his youth building car models, or relaxing in his old recliner, reading.

He'd always been an avid reader, showing little discrimination in his diet. He loved all genres. He'd majored in Business Communications at Webb Community College and now worked as a Customer Service manager at Dine-a-Mate—a small company which published a yearly coupon book—but he was rarely without a novel. Whenever he had a spare moment, he was always reading. A novel during breakfast. A different one before bed. Another sat propped open on the exercise bike in the kids' old playroom (long unused, as they now preferred to hole up in their rooms with their WiFi tablets, watching God Knew What on Youtube). In fact, it was hard to think of a time when he wasn't building models or reading.

Something whisked down the hall.

John stepped toward his office door. A mild chill rippled across his skin. He was certain he'd heard something.

Sudden inspiration struck him, and he chuckled aloud. Of course. It was probably the family cats—a calico named Pebbles and a tomcat named Peanut—batting something across the basement's concrete floor. They were notorious for waking everyone at night with similar shenanigans. Most likely they were batting around a piece of cardboard or something.

In fact, an entire scenario formed. Beth had probably yelled down her plans to run an errand and he (as always these days) had called back "Sure, see you later!" without realizing it. He'd done it several times before, after all. Beth had probably sent one of the kids to turn the hall light off in addition to the stairwell light. This had happened to him on several occasions, too. They'd gone their merry way while he'd browsed through his voluminous book collection, lost in a bibliophile's paradise.

It had to be the cats making the swishing sound along the floor in the hall outside his office. He'd go out there now, flick on the hall lights and herd them upstairs. Tossing the Magic Eight Ball hand to hand, John stepped toward the door leading to the hall . . . and stopped.

Something twitched in his gut.

A feeling. A strange, skin-crawling sensation. For

whatever reason (though it was ridiculous), he didn't want to enter the dark hallway beyond.

Why?

Having no logical basis for his fear, John figured he felt uneasy from abruptly realizing he was alone in the house. He returned his attention to the bookshelf at the rear of his office, the one he'd been browsing when he'd first heard the strange sounds outside, only being made by the cats, after all.

The top shelf held purely "literary works." Poetry collections of Blake, Yeats, Robert Frost, and Shakespeare. Prose collections of Zora Neal Hurston, Hemingway, Nathaniel Hawthorne, Flannery O'Connor, and folktales collected by the Brothers Grimm. Novels, from *The Man in the Iron Mask* to *Madame Bovary*, to *Villette* and *Jane Eyre* by Charlotte Bronte, to *A Passage to India* by E. M. Forster.

The second shelf held old pulp novels from the thirties and forties. When he was fourteen years old his great grandmother, recognizing a hungry reader, started giving him one novel a month. They bore such outlandish titles as *The House of Darkness*, *The Tree that Screamed*, *The Strangler Fig*, *The Devil's Mansion*, *Crimson Ice*, *The Undying Monster* and *Heads, You Lose*. He'd consumed those books one after the other, a new junkie mainlining his first fix. Grandma White promised him when she passed, he could have them all. Those books were older than any of the others in his office.

The bottom shelf (the one he'd been searching when he'd first heard the cats playing in the hall) held his collection of horror anthologies. The famed

THINGS YOU NEED

Whispers series, edited by Stuart David Schiff, featuring the varied works of Ramsey Campbell, Stephen King, Charles Grant and so many others. *The Mammoth Book of Best New Horror* from England. *The Shivers* series, published by Cemetery Dance. *Masques, Borderlands, Shadows, Stalkers, Dark Forces, October Dreams I & II, Corpse Blossoms, Horror Library Volumes 1-5*, and *Prime Evil*. Classic horror anthologies jammed next to paperback collections of slightly lesser repute with titles to match; *Shock Rock, Walls of Fear, Tales by Midnight I & II, Hardshell, Post Mortem, Zombie Nation, Zippered Flesh* and *A Taste for Blood*.

John stopped and frowned, noticing something odd. Among the horror anthologies was a black leather-bound book he'd never seen before. It was a strange size, looking more like a journal, jammed between *Whispers 2* and his hardcover edition of *Dark Forces*.

He touched the book's spine, fingers trailing down its pebbled surface. He was about to pull it out, had his finger hooked on the spine's edge, but he figured it was probably a collector's edition he'd bought at Arcane Delights, the used bookstore in town. That's all.

Scanning the shelves unsuccessfully for something else interesting, John brushed off his knees and stood.

Something swished down the hall.

He wasn't concerned, however, because he'd already identified it as the cats playing. He ignored the sound, dismissing the slight chill running along his skin. But as he stood, he noticed several things shifted around on top of his bookshelf. Die cast metal figurines of Marvel characters: Hulk, Wolverine, and

Spiderman in particular. Which didn't make sense. The kids weren't allowed in here. Touching anything on his shelf was absolutely forbidden, because this was the accumulation of twenty years collecting odds and ends. He'd started it shortly after moving in, when Mom and Dad had sent him several boxes of his things they'd stored while he'd attended college. In one of the boxes, he'd found old action figures, a Slinky, some fuzzy dice, the Magic Eight Ball in his hands, and several of his old car models. Some of them intact, others missing wheels, hoods, or engines.

He'd unpacked the contents of the boxes onto the top of his shelf. Over the years, he'd added bits and pieces of whatever caught his fancy. In particular, a few old fashioned soda bottles (Pepsi and Mountain Dew) he'd found alongside the road. Also, the die cast Marvel figurines Marty had thrown away a few years ago when he'd declared them "baby toys" and "could he finally get an iPhone, please?" Last fall, John had come across a set of wax Halloween figurines—a grinning grim reaper, a ghost, a skeleton and a jack'o lantern—at Handy's Pawn and Thrift. It was love at first sight.

From the looks of it, someone had been in his office messing around with the Marvel figurines. Scattered in a pile were Hulk, Wolverine, Spiderman and also, he saw now, Magneto. He frowned; holding his Magic Eight Ball close to his chest with one hand as he gently re-set the figurines with the other.

Who could've been down messing with his things? It had been years since either Marty or Melissa had tried to sneak in here.

Replacing Hulk to its original position against a

dark green Mountain Dew bottle from the seventies, John hefted the Magic Eight Ball, wondering if either of the cats was to blame. Not Pebbles, he supposed. She was too big and old to be jumping from the floor to the shelf. Peanut, however, was still young and also small, more than capable of not only launching herself up to the shelf but small enough to walk along its edge while causing only minimal disorder.

Another oddity: Usually he shut not only the basement door at night but also his office door, to keep the cats out. Perhaps he'd been preoccupied last night and had forgotten to close them? Unlikely but it was certainly possible, seeing as how he was the only one in the house so concerned about shutting both doors at night. If he'd forgotten, it was more than likely the others hadn't worried about it at all.

Speaking of the cats, they were really going at it out in the hall. He should herd them upstairs, but again, for some reason he couldn't put his finger on, he didn't want to leave his office right then.

On a whim, John shook the Eight Ball. "So. Were my cats responsible for this mess?"

Out of the murk, the faded letters on the polyhedron read: Ask Again Later.

John chuckled, but as he examined the arrangement of figurines on his shelf, realization struck him. One of them was missing. He gazed at the little superhero tableau until it came to him. Cyclops. The X-man with laser eyes. He'd been there with the others. Now, John noticed, he wasn't.

He thought for a moment, working the eight ball in his hands. A creeping unease tickled the back of his neck. *Who's been messing around in here*? He dismissed the question, realizing Peanut had probably knocked Cyclops onto the floor, where she'd then batted him under the shelf.

To dispel the faint unease over his shelf's mysterious disorder, John shook the eight ball again. "Did Peanut knock Cyclops under the shelf?"

The polyhedron slowed its spinning. Faded letters resolved into: Answer Is Unclear. John grunted. "Figures."

Regardless, he didn't want to root under the shelf for Cyclops at the moment, the way his knees were getting these days . . .

knees?

my knees are fine

. . . so he'd search for Cyclops later.

The familiar itch of wanting to read something flared again. It pleased him, but also struck him as a little odd. Normally, he wasn't so indecisive. He turned to scan the old, pressed-wood shelf to his right, the kind found at K-Mart or Wal-Mart and not requiring any real skill to assemble.

He unconsciously rolled the eight ball in his hands as he scanned the shelves. These books offered a trip down memory lane. His teenage collection of Star Wars novels. At one time he could've made the proud declaration he owned every one. Even the hard-to-find Han Solo novels from the late seventies. He'd stopped collecting them halfway through college, though. Now he owned only a fraction of the franchise's backlist.

He wasn't sure he wanted to read one of these. He mostly enjoyed their nostalgia. He'd arranged his old Star Wars action figures on the shelves, along with several commemorative *Empire Strikes Back* soda glasses his parents bought when he was a kid. A final touch was a plastic but realistic lightsaber hilt Marty had discarded when he'd declared himself "too old for space stuff."

This shelf was a time portal. It transported John to an era before his children had grown away from him. A time when Beth had shown him more than the dutiful obligation she offered now, as she filled her days following Rachael Ray's advice for weight loss or trendy but affordable home interior ideas, found on some website called Pinterest. She was always "pinning" things (whatever that meant). Recipes, sewing patterns, and hairstyles. Even when she was in the car with him, *alone*, she focused on her iPhone, listening to him with only half an ear.

John frowned at what appeared to be a black leather-bound book, similar to the one he'd seen on his horror anthologies shelf, between *Heir to the Empire* and *Dark Force Rising*. He couldn't fathom why it'd be here or why it looked so similar to the other one.

He reached out to touch it but figured it must be some sort of Star Wars novelty book he'd recently purchased and forgotten about, which happened often. He'd buy books either at rummage sales, used bookstores, or online, shelve them, then forget about them. It wouldn't be the first time.

Working the eight ball in his hands, he dismissed the strange black leather-bound book and re-focused on the reading itch he couldn't seem to scratch.

As he kicked something across the floor.

John glanced down, puzzled, and saw something which only confused him further. The animatronic tarantula (about the size of his hand) which usually sat on his Ramsey Campbell shelf. But there the toy spider was, on the floor a few inches from his foot, obviously what he'd kicked.

John stood still.

Staring at the tarantula sitting in the middle of his office floor, as something whisked along the concrete in the hall outside his office. For one surreal moment, the tarantula appeared real. Poised to scuttle under his desk or turn and attack his foot, which was why Melissa hadn't wanted it, of course, despite badgering him for weeks to buy one after seeing an ad for it on Animal Planet. Remote controlled, life-like except for its larger-than-actual-scale, it was all Melissa had talked about for weeks until John broke down and finally bought it from the Toys R' Us over in Utica.

He'd had his doubts from the moment he saw it at the store (he'd thought it neat himself), but at the time he was happy he'd found something his mercurial, ever-more-complex preteen daughter wanted, something he could actually provide.

Which was why (though he'd suspected her reaction from the start), he felt let-down (disappointed as hell) at her immediate rejection the instant he'd removed it from the box. Her eyes had widened (at first he'd hoped in excitement); her mouth had worked silently until she finally whispered, "Ew. Get it away from me. It's *gross!*"

He'd done his best to swallow his disappointment and what remained of his pride, hoping maybe Marty would show some interest. It had been a remote control animatronic tarantula, for God's sake, and it obviously frightened his little sister. As a kid, John would've begged for such a treasure. Marty, however,

68

had barely spared a glance from whatever game he was playing on his iPhone, muttering with barely concealed scorn, "Whatever. Thing's totally fake. Lame, Dad."

He'd liked it, however, so into his office it went to stand guard over his Ramsey Campbell novels, which seemed appropriate. There it had sat for the past four years.

Until now.

He juggled the eight ball, happy for something to keep his hands busy as he stared at the toy tarantula sitting on the floor. He couldn't explain how it had gotten there. It hadn't been there when he'd come in earlier this . . .

Morning?

Afternoon?

He caught the eight ball in his right hand and held it there, considering. It was odd. He'd certainly lost track of time in his office before. Hours of reading had passed him by, leaving him fuzzy as to the time, especially since he'd retired.

Retired.

He frowned. He wasn't retired. He had ten or fifteen years left before he could even consider it, which all depended on whether or not Melissa would settle for a few affordable years at Webb Community or if she'd insist on something more prestigious and, more importantly, far more expensive.

But he wasn't retired yet.

was he?

No, he wasn't retired. His mind had just slipped, thinking about how much time he'd probably spend down here when he *did* retire, when the kids weren't around. Not that he saw much of them these days, anyway.

He chuckled and shook the eight ball. "Getting daffy before my time, thinking of retirement and all. That it? Am I losing it?"

Out of the milky fluid, the words read: Future Is Hazy.

For some reason, the eight ball's continued ambiguity troubled him, which was stupid, of course. The eight ball was a toy, nothing more. It wasn't purposefully offering him vague answers.

He tossed the eight ball into the air, caught it and was glancing back to the floor when Beth peered around the corner and into his office, face blank. John straightened in surprise, having not heard her steps in the hall . . .

only that whisking sound

. . . and was about to ask her if she needed anything, but before he could speak, she reached in and flicked the office light off. Plunged into darkness, he didn't see her leave but heard her footsteps this time, which sounded quick and agitated as they sped down the hall, away from his office, and up the stairs.

"Beth! What the hell?"

A shrill kind of panic filled his chest. He crossed the floor as quickly as he could in the darkness. He slapped at the wall, searching for the light switch. Rationally he knew it was silly to fear the dark. It couldn't hurt him, right? But his heart was throbbing triple time as he groped for the switch, his panic escalating with the irrational belief he was dissolving into the dark, and soon there'd be nothing left.

He found the switch and flipped on the light, banishing the darkness and instantly easing his throbbing heart. He took a deep breath and massaged his chest with one hand (it felt heavy, the pain spreading to his left shoulder, which scared him in a completely different way), squeezing the eight ball tightly with the other.

What the hell was Beth doing? Shutting the lights off without a word? John wondered if maybe he'd done something to anger her, but Beth addressed her complaints head on. She didn't play passive-aggressive games. Besides, he'd thought the house was empty, her gone for the day.

His mind swirling, he glanced to the floor, searching for the animatronic tarantula.

It wasn't there.

John stared at the floor. The toy spider had been there a moment ago. He'd kicked it and then wondered how it had gotten there. Then for some inexplicable reason Beth had reached into his office and flicked the lights off. After he turned them back on . . .

The toy spider was gone.

John glanced at the bookshelf standing next to the writing desk he never used. There the toy spider was, where it was supposed to be, but facing the wrong direction. Also, like his knick-knack shelf, his books were in disarray. Several had been knocked over.

John's throat tightened.

His chest felt heavy again as an icy dread washed over him. It became hard to breathe, as an aching pain radiated out into his left shoulder. All the hours he'd spent in his office over these years, he knew every nook and cranny, fastidiously dusting and organizing his books and making sure everything was just so.

"Who's been in here? And . . . how? When?"

Maybe it had been the grandchildren. Marty's kids

were okay. He and Marty had never enjoyed a close relationship but at least he kept his kids in check, unlike Melissa. Her brats ran wild all over the place. They were always getting where they didn't belong. It figured, with the way she let them do whatever they wanted in compensation for ditching her husband. He remembered the time he'd come in here and her little brat Dillon had been pushing the animatronic tarantula along the floor making *vroom* sounds.

A spike of real fear lanced his heart.

He gripped the eight ball hard enough to hear its plastic shell creak. "Who's Dillon? What grandchildren? What the *hell* is happening?"

Instinctively, he glanced down at the eight ball. Floating letters spelled out: Ask Again Later.

There were those damn cats again, whisking down the hall, though instead of sounding like Fluffy and Princess knocking around pieces of cardboard on the cold concrete floor . . .

no, it's Peanut and Pebbles

. . . it sounded more like the hem of a dress or a robe dragging across the floor outside the door to his office, where it was still so dark.

John rested a slightly shaking hand on his aching chest and rubbed in slow circles. He was ill. Confused. Was he having a stroke? A heart attack? He was far too young, at age 45 . . .

60?

. . . but he'd heard stories, of course. Of healthy men dropping dead from heart attacks in middle age. He had to admit he'd been feeling more stress than usual these days. Melissa had turned from his darling little tom-girl who loved to play with garter snakes into a high school senior with the painted-on face and clothes of those barely dressed girls in all the rap videos she watched.

He was too old to know her anymore. Too old and from a foreign era, the rules of which no longer applied. His worst fear was not Melissa turning up pregnant and unwed, but that he'd push her there, leaving her adrift by fleeing to his office and seeking shelter in the pages of the stories which had become more important to him than real life.

He massaged his chest harder, trying his best to ignore Peanut and Pebbles . . .

Fluffy and Princess?

. . . whisking something down the hall. Yes, stress. Both Melissa and Marty had become strangers to him. Melissa, a startling feminine creature who scared him because she was developing curves out of nowhere and didn't at all resemble the little girl he used to take fishing and hiking. Marty had morphed into a sullen malcontent. Hanging around those dropouts from the Commons Trailer Park every weekend, drinking, probably also smoking dope and laying with loose girls.

Wait.

What was he worrying about?

Melissa was only 16. She'd only recently started dressing in short dresses and shirts with low-plunging necklines which sent him scurrying to his office. Marty was only twelve. Getting a little surly, but still doing okay in school and toeing the line, if only barely. They hadn't gotten into any trouble . . .

Had they?

Again, unbidden, John's mind toyed with thoughts

of a stroke, a heart attack, or some other ailment affecting the mind. Hadn't the former owner of Arcane Delights, Brian Ellison, recently passed away after Alzheimer's and dementia had stolen his mind?

No.

Brian Ellison still owned and operated Arcane Delights. Didn't he? John had bought several old Stephen King novels there, only last week.

Hadn't he?

Drawn by the memory of the Stephen King novels he'd purchased (he swore only last week), his gaze slid to the huge, handmade wooden shelf next to his office door, which of course was his Stephen King shelf. He owned nearly every one of King's books and multiple paperback copies of his favorites: *It, Salem's Lot, Pet Semetary, Christine* and *The Dead Zone.*

He paused, frowning at the black leather-bound book stuffed between *It* and *Salem's Lot.* It looked familiar, but he couldn't place from where. He shrugged and passed it over, searching for the model of *Christine* he'd built about six or seven years ago . . .

8 or 9

10 or 11?

. . . when he'd taken up modeling again over the cold winter months. Since then he'd been spending more and more time alone in the comforting solitude of his office. Delicately assembling cars with airplane glue and tweezers, trimming parts with an Xacto knife, escaping into memories of his youth instead of facing the strange realities of today's world. Obamacare (thinly veiled communism, anyone could see). Marriage equality (he didn't hate gays but marriage had always been between men and women and such cataclysmic changes made him uneasy in ways he couldn't explain). The increasing violence he saw on television, like the awful story of two men who'd broken into a family's home, killed the father and son, tied the mother and preteen daughter to the bed and raped them for hours before setting them on fire. Down in his quiet office he felt protected from this changing world as he channeled his youth through car models, plastic glue and Testors paint.

There it was. The model he'd constructed of King's famous Plymouth Fury. Sitting on a book club edition of *Christine*, right where it should be. The relief he felt at the familiar sight nearly buckled his knees. The longer he gazed at it, however, the more something appeared off. The model car sat crookedly, the left front tire leaning inward. Tentatively, John picked up the lovingly assembled 57 Plymouth Fury.

The left front tire fell off.

It hit the original-printing book club edition of *Christine*, bounced, and fell to the floor with a plastic rattle.

John's hand began to shake so badly he feared he might drop the model and damage it worse. With forced care, he gently replaced the crippled car, cringing at the way the model's front end dipped at its missing wheel. Somehow, he forced himself not to drop to his knees to search desperately for it, especially with the way his arthritis was bothering him these days . . .

but he didn't have arthritis yet

his knees felt fine

. . . and instead took several slow steps backward until he once again stood in the center of his office, as the swishing sound in the hall grew closer.

Those damn cats.

Feeling strangely infantile in the way old people sometimes do and hating himself for it . . .

but I'm only 45

50?

. . . John Pinkerton clasped the Magic Eight Ball in two hands and raised it as if in supplication. Feeling equal parts foolish and desperate, he shook it and whispered, "Am I going crazy?"

Faded letters emerged from the murk inside the ball: Answer is Hazy.

He shook it again, rasping, "Am I going insane? Having a stroke? Am I dreaming?"

The polyhedron turned slowly until it revealed: Ask Again Later.

John licked dry lips. Ran a hand through his hair and rubbed the back of his neck. Scattered thoughts bounced around his mind. *Why did Beth stare at me like she didn't see me and turn the lights off? Who's been sneaking into my office? Who's moved things around? What's happening to me?* Feeling lost, he glanced helplessly at the desk next to his Ramsey Campbell shelf.

There, sitting upon it, was a black leather-bound book.

The whisking sound out in the hall . . .

the hem of a robe dragging across the floor

. . . drew closer.

Ignoring the sound, John approached he black book sitting on the writing desk he never used. He finally admitted to himself—though it made about as much sense as the toy spider being misplaced or Beth staring through him and turning the lights off—he'd seen the book all over his office. Jammed in with the horror anthologies, with the Star Wars novels, the Ramsey Campbell novels, and on the Stephen King shelf. Somehow, John knew if he turned away, he'd find it elsewhere.

On his Charles Grant shelf.

Next to *Boy's Life*, with his Robert McCammon novels. Nestled between *Dune* by Frank Herbert and *Foundation and Empire* by Isaac Asimov. With his modest collection of Nero Wolfe mysteries. No matter where he turned in his beloved office, his quiet sanctuary against a mad world grown increasingly alien, somehow he knew he'd continue to find it, hiding in plain sight, waiting for *him*.

A strange sort of resolve hardened inside John, a kind he hadn't felt since high school . . .

middle age?

. . . and with an amazingly steady hand, he flipped open the black leather-bound book sitting on the writing desk he never used.

Names.

An entire page of names. A list. He read them off silently. They were men and women's names (or in some cases, perhaps boys' and girls' names) and for the most part unfamiliar. Written in a clear, moderately ornate script. He flipped several pages and saw more. Names and more names, all written by the same hand.

After the fifth page, a name jumped out.

Elizabeth Kinner.

He knew right away who she was. His Kindergarten teacher from 39 . . .

50? 60?

77

. . . years ago. A wonderful woman whose tireless love for children had touched everything she'd done in the classroom. She'd been near retirement age when he'd been in her class. If memory served him correctly, she'd passed away quietly in her sleep his freshman year at Webb Community College.

A spark flared deep in his consciousness. He didn't dare consider it directly as he studiously ignored the whisking sound moving closer to his office.

He flipped another page. More unrecognizable names until he reached the bottom of the sixth page and, predictably, another familiar name appeared: Bob Cranston. Bob would've graduated high school with him, had he not been hit by a drunk driver walking home from football practice. The name below, Al Moreland. The boy who'd been hit by a train while riding his four wheeler on the tracks, John's tenth grade year. They never found Al's body. Only his demolished four wheeler.

He flipped another page.

And another.

More and more names he recognized. Mr. Drake, the farmer who'd unfortunately flipped his tractor onto himself trying to free it from mud in one of his fields. Sam Perkins, a hunter who'd disappeared in the woods one winter. Eddie Bannister, a two-bit high school dropout who'd been killed, most believed, by his partner in crime Derek Barton (who'd since fled to parts unknown) in a botched robbery at Handy's Pawn and Thrift. Bud Hartley, local simpleton but gentle giant, who'd died of complications in Clifton Memorial Hospital after a pile of burning garbage at the landfill fell on him. Lizzy Tillman, who'd died when the

NYSEG payment center flooded in that awful storm a few years ago . . .

Decades?

And on.

More and more names he recognized as he turned the pages. Names of people he knew, all of them dead and gone. Their names, written on the pages he kept turning, as a robe dragged down the hall toward his office.

He kept turning until he saw nothing but blank emptiness. He flipped back a few pages until he found the last page of names, ran his finger down them—seeing Art Finely's name, part owner of Henry's Drive-In, who'd died of a heart attack two years ago, Brian Ellison of Arcane Delights . . .

but I saw him last week

. . . and several others which appeared familiar, but he couldn't place.

He stopped at the last name.

"No," he rasped, throat feeling tight and dry, skin cold and clammy. "No. It can't be. It can't . . . "

He stepped away from the black book full of handwritten names of people who'd died, sitting on the writing desk he never used, gripping the Magic Eight Ball so tight his knuckles ached. He backed away and kicked something on the floor again. He spun, glanced down, and saw the animatronic tarantula on the floor. A gasp, not from him but from a blonde little boy he didn't quite recognize . . .

Dillon

her brat son Dillon

. . . who'd been on his hands and knees pushing the toy spider across the floor but had jumped up and was now staring at the toy with a wide-eyed expression crossed between fear and awe.

The boy . . .

Dillon

. . . opened his mouth but before he could say anything a middle-aged woman with a tight narrow face, straight hair and gray-dishwater eyes ducked around the corner and into John's office . . .

Melissa

. . . and grabbed the boy by his shoulder, fingers digging into the meat so badly John winced in sympathy. She spun the boy around to face her, scowling, eyes flashing darkly. "What are you doing in here?"

The boy's mouth trembled; he stuttered, but couldn't get anything out.

John stepped forward, sad desperation surging through him. Why did she treat her son this way? He was a pain in the ass sometimes and he did sneak into his office and mess with his things but it was okay. She didn't have to hurt him. Is this what he'd passed on? Was this his legacy? No one should ever touch his things? "Melissa, it's all right. He was playing, he was . . ."

His middle-aged divorced and bitter daughter didn't listen, only squeezed Dillon's shoulder harder. "Answer me! You know Grandma doesn't want anyone in here messing with Grandpa's things! You already broke one of his cars as it is!"

The boy swallowed and finally managed to blurt out, "The light was on! It was on, but I didn't turn it on, I swear! Grandpa said someday I could have the toy spider, after . . ."

Something twisted in John's head.

Had he said that?

When?

And who was this child? And this strange older version of Melissa?

someday I could have the toy spider, after

after

The strange-familiar middle-aged woman shook the boy. "I don't care. You're not supposed to be in here, do you understand? Grandma will decide when and if you can have the damn spider. Let's go."

She grabbed the boy's hand and jerked him from the office. The boy protested with, "But Mama, the spider moved! I was playing with it and it moved all by itself!"

The strange-familiar middle-aged woman slapped the light switch on the wall as she left, plunging the office back into darkness. Panic thrummed through John as he scrambled for the light switch, slapping desperately until he flipped it back on.

Relief flooded through him, but it was short-lived, because as he stepped back from the light switch, he glanced up at the bookshelves against the far wall—two blue shelves normally filled with miscellaneous horror, science fiction and mystery titles, with everything from William Hope Hodgson to Bentley Little to Agatha Christie—and gasped: They were mostly empty. A few paperbacks lay forlornly on their sides, but the two blue shelves which had formerly been stuffed full of books was now empty.

Except another black leather-bound book, lying on its side, on the middle shelf.

"No," he muttered, the word gushing out of him in a frenzied litany. "No, no, no, *no*."

He spun around again and saw the Star Wars shelf in disarray, many of the action figures lying sprawled on their sides, the commemorative glasses gone. His knick-knack shelf was likewise in disorder, empty where things had been taken. On the floor sat several cardboard boxes. On the sides, written in neat, precise handwriting in black marker—Beth's handwriting—he read *John's Things*.

The whisking sound hovered beyond his door.

"John."

He spun, clutching the Magic Eight Ball in front of him. There, standing in the doorway to his office . . .

Beth.

But not the Beth he knew. This one's hair was white, cut cruelly short in an economical bob. Her face looked much the same, with the exception of lines around her mouth and at the corners of her eyes tired eyes. Weary eyes, and inexpressibly sad.

"John," she whispered. "John. I don't know how the lights keep turning on. But if you *are* here, please stop. I can't take much more of this. I'll sell the house soon, John. Swear to God. Please stop it with the lights. Please."

Frantic, mind crumbling, John stumbled forward. "Beth. Beth, I don't understand. Please don't go. Don't turn off the lights. Don't turn them off!"

Beth turned and, as she left his office, flicked the lights off, plunging the room back into darkness. Outside, the whisking of the robe against the cement came closer.

And into the office.

John stumbled back to the far corner where his old recliner was, or should be. His recliner, found at the

82

Salvation Army in Utica, where he'd spent countless hours (more and more as the kids found him old, useless, and irrelevant, and Beth considered him less interesting than her flower gardens or her cross-stitching or her Methodist Ladies Society meetings) reading Rod Serling, Ray Bradbury, Flannery O'Connor, Stephen King and Poul Anderson, sometimes poetry, in his recliner, his seat of dreams.

John lurched backward in the darkness and collapsed, crying out when his backside struck nothing but hard cold cement, not his recliner. It was gone. Everything was gone, *gone.*

He gazed through eyes blurred by tears. The lights were still off, but a soft glow had seeped into his office, through the door, and he could see the empty shelves, bereft of every single book he'd collected and read and had hoped to read. Gone, gone, all of it gone . . .

Light filled the doorway of his office, a soft glow and a strange sensation of overwhelming peace, of contentment and rest, of kindness and . . .

"NO!" The scream ripped from his guts. "GET AWAY FROM ME!"

Despite the fact he felt nothing but acceptance, John Pinkerton screamed with all his might and threw the Magic Eight Ball at the soft glow filling the doorway of his office. The air of benevolence faded, leaving him with nothing but cold emptiness, crushing loneliness, and worst of all, despair.

He slid to the cold concrete, lying in the fetal position, knees pulled to his chest, sobbing at the loss of something he couldn't define, couldn't grasp but also couldn't bear. He blinked his eyes . . .

. . . as if waking from a deep sleep. He found himself kneeling before the bookshelf in the rear of his office, trying to decide what book he should read next. He shook the Eight Ball with one hand, smiling. "What's it going to be?" he whispered, "Classic literature, today?"

The white polyhedron, suspended in liquid turned murky with age, jiggled as it revealed: Future is Hazy.

John chuckled as he returned his attention to the books before him. "Story of my life," he whispered. "Story of my . . . "

Something whisked along the floor outside his office.

5.

THE WHITE POLYHEDRON, suspended in old, milky fluid, jiggled as it revealed: *Future is Hazy.*

"Story of my life," I whispered. "Story of . . . "

A chill hand gripped my heart.

My throat tightened. I had to swallow hard to open it again. A rush of *something* filled me. Dread, and fear. I felt lightheaded. I dropped the Magic Eight Ball and it bounced off the counter to the floor. It rolled away into the dark. I sagged forward and barely caught the edge of the counter with both hands, leaning on it for support as my stomach clenched and my knees buckled.

I closed my eyes and took several deep breaths. "What the *hell* was that?"

An answer wasn't forthcoming, but honestly, I didn't want one. What I wanted was to get *out* and back to my cabin at The Motor Lodge. I didn't care what I might do with my .38. I wanted out.

Bracing myself against the counter, I twisted at the waist and glanced over my shoulder at the door. I blinked several times, trying to clear my vision, but the aisle leading past the shelves stretched out forever. The floor shivered under my feet and the door seemed miles away, and tilted sideways.

The skewed perspective played hell with my senses. My head pounded harder as I tried to focus on the front door; my guts clenching, threatening to send my dinner everywhere.

I closed my eyes and whispered, "It's not real. Not real not real not real not real . . . "

The clenching in my guts eased. I took one more deep breath, pushed off the counter, and lurched down the aisle toward the front door.

The floor tilted with every step. I lumbered ahead, however, with the grace of a drunken mill worker (no disrespect to mill workers who drink, mind you). I narrowed my eyes so all I saw was a bit of the front door and not how crooked it was, how it tilted back and forth, back and forth . . .

I slammed into it, hand scrambling for the knob. My vision of the skewed aisle and door had obviously been an optical illusion or something. But I didn't care, I wanted *out*.

I grabbed the doorknob and twisted.

Nothing.

No click.

Not a sound.

I used both hands and yanked with everything I had. It didn't budge. I pulled harder, but my hands just slipped off the knob. I flew backwards and slammed into the nearest shelf of junk.

I'm not gonna lie. I yelped like a kid when the shelf's metal edge jammed into the small of my back. I rolled to the floor in a shower of toys, ceramic mugs (a few which shattered), keyboards and an upended box of old floppy disks.

THINGS YOU NEED

Something *dinged*. An electronic device had switched on in the fall. But my brains were too frazzled to worry about it. I closed my eyes and grabbed my head, took several deep breaths and sat still.

Silence.

Which meant I *had* to be alone, for sure. No way the shopkeeper was out back and didn't hear the tape player, and then everything crashing down. I was alone, the door was locked, and I felt my grip on reality slipping.

Something happened. When I picked the Magic Eight Ball up and shook it. Something happened.

I pressed the heels of my palms into my eyes and rubbed. My head no longer pounded, and my stomach felt more stable, too. I rubbed my face and tried to piece my wits back together.

Something.

I heard something.

A voice. Whispering from far away. Actually, whispering wasn't it, exactly. It was quiet, low and hissing, but the tone sounded excited about something.

my life, going to change my life

"Hello? Anyone back there? Mister? Listen, I'm not trashing your place, honest. I could use some help, though."

I hated the way my voice sounded. So weak. Afraid. Hell, *old*. But I've got to admit, I was shook up. All my snark blown away. I was tired, scared, and I wanted *out*.

"Hey! Anyone there?"

ssssss

this is it

going to change
my life

Static. I was hearing something through static. I remembered the *ding* when things hit the floor, so I scanned the items I'd knocked off the shelf. Next to my foot I saw something which stood out from the junk: a brand new digital camera. A Nikon. *That's* what dinged. Apparently it had switched on.

The viewfinder was glowing, the camera playing back a recorded video. Dark flickers passed over the screen. Something moved, or the camera panned. It was running on a loop and between snatches of dead air I heard a whispering voice.

going to change my life

I sat and stared. Then, on impulse, I reached out—my hand amazingly steady—and picked the camera up, to the hissing tune of: "*This is it, going to change my life . . .*"

OUT OF FIELD THEORY

B RIAN PALMER SHIVERED in spite of the warm noonday sun. "This is it," he muttered, staring at the picture he'd taken. "This is *it*. This picture is going to change my *life*. This. Is. *It*."

It was about time. All the other pictures he'd taken with his Nikon hadn't been worth a damn. The first was out of focus. Couldn't see the barn on Bassler Road for shit. Another was framed wrong, cutting the top off the old gazebo in the abandoned koi garden down the road. As for the brilliant yellow and orange koi swimming in the old pond next to the gazebo? Red and yellow blobs.

Some of the other shots? Of Bassler Road curving into the distance? Of an abandoned old truck sitting by the railroad tracks? They were okay, but he knew what Professor Spinella would say: They looked like stock photos in Adirondack guidebooks found in tourist novelty stores everywhere.

Which wouldn't cut it if he wanted his final project for Philosophy of Photography to pass. He needed something unique to analyze through any one of the philosophies they'd studied this semester. Philosophies he'd struggled to understand from the start.

But as he'd examined his pictures, nothing clicked. Not the water flowing under Black Creek Bridge, or the abandoned factory on Black River, or the bandstand next to Raedeker Park Zoo. Every. Single. Picture. *Sucked*.

Except one.

Something in it caught his eye. He'd taken it only a moment ago, of an old Victorian farmhouse everyone in Clifton Heights called Bassler House. It was in the middle of a fallow cornfield. He'd snapped several wide angles, then on a whim zoomed in on the front door and the window next to it. He snapped the shot instinctively.

And he'd created a striking effect. The area around the doorway had endured the years passingly well. Cancerous, mottled damp rot had riddled the siding around the window, however, spreading rash-like toward the door.

"Geez," he muttered, tapping the zoom button. "That's not bad. In fact, it's . . . "

He trailed off.

In the window, at the edge of the image's frame he saw a smudge. A shadow. Of . . .

Something.

He couldn't tell what because his framing had cut the rest.

Brian gazed over his shoulder back at the old house, thinking. Dimly, he remembered a theory they'd studied this year, by some guy named Deleuze. He raised the camera and examined the cut-off shadow in the window. He recalled a snippet from an essay written by Deleuze, assigned early in the semester:

. . . the out of field phenomenon occurs when literal framing of an image leaves elements and actions partly out of frame, implying their continuation past the frame . . .

The philosophy part of his class had sucked. Brian hadn't understood much of it. He loved taking pictures of things. Who cared *why*?

Like the other philosophies they'd studied, he'd struggled to understand Deleuze's ideas. Professor Spinella had explained it this way: Anything cut off by the framing of a picture didn't actually end but continued outside the frame somewhere else. Photographing images created another reality. A reality of the image, which wasn't limited by the artificial framing imposed by the photographic device. He'd thought the whole thing a bunch of bullshit when they'd studied it, but . . .

He tapped the image on the Nikon's small screen, his stomach tingling with excitement. Maybe he'd found at least *one* photo that would help him pass his final project. Maybe he could take similar shots and use them for a presentation of Deleuze's theory.

He glanced at his watch. 2:00 PM. Plenty of time for him to take more pictures. Maybe even jimmy his way inside the old house, see if he could find something interesting to shoot. He should be able to get enough pictures before evening. Because who wanted to muck around an old house after dark?

He slipped his hand into a small satchel slung over his shoulder, digging for another memory card he could use for the camera, intent on filling the whole thing with pictures of this house. The prospect of actually taking pictures that meant something to him, for a change, was exciting.

So long as he got his ass out of there before dark.

A year ago Brian had never imagined he'd become so desperate to take a "unique" photograph. Everyone liked his pictures then. His parents had indulged his hobby, sacrificing their meager savings to buy him the Nikon for his 16th birthday. He'd served as president of Old Forge Academy's Photo Club for three years straight. Was one of the lead photographers for the school journal and yearbook. The summer before and after his senior year, he'd done some freelance work for the Webb County Courier (paid in contributor copies only, but a byline was a byline.) Then to cap it all off, right before graduation, his picture of a sunset over Black Bear Mountain won first prize in Old Forge Academy's Penny Harper Scholarship Contest. The scholarship paid his way through two years at Webb Community College to study photography. His future career behind the viewfinder was assured. At least in his mind.

But a year into his studies had given Brian a new, depressing perspective. He freelanced for the campus newspaper, but his photos were hardly ever used, apparently not "fresh" or "original" enough. His old spot with the Courier had been handed over to a high school successor. He'd eagerly tramped through the countryside all summer after graduation, taking scenic pictures of waterfalls, creeks, lakes, old cabins, mountains, and sunsets. He'd submitted to every contest and journal he could find. All of them rejected him by form letters stating: "Thank you for your interest but at this time, your photos don't meet our needs. Please submit again in the future."

As the semester wore on, his studies and various class projects ate into his free time. His own personal photography shrank to a third of what it had been. Complicating matters: His scholarship paid for tuition, room and board and a limited meal plan. He was on his own when it came to gas, groceries, the laundromat, textbooks, and photo supplies. His father worked construction; his mother was a nurse's aide. They barely met their own needs, and he could expect no extra money from home.

So he reluctantly found work as a checkout bagger at The Great American Grocery down the road from campus. Working nearly twenty-five hours a week on top of his schoolwork left little time to take pictures for himself.

Brian stopped about five feet from the old house's front door, wrestling as always with his future, his dreams, and their slow, painful death this past year. All the ideas in his head were breathtaking, but when he had the rare moment to actually get behind his camera, the results seldom matched his daydreams. His professors, so far, had felt the same way. Best he'd managed in any of his classes the past year was a B.

It would be incredibly convenient to blame his mediocre grades on how tight his schedule was. He always felt so tired, unable to focus, with little time to develop his technique. The truth of the matter? In his gut he knew none of his excuses were valid. Several of his classmates were only carrying B averages, but their photos possessed something his lacked. Their photos had a kind of shine. A *vitality*. His were lifeless things in comparison.

Everything he'd shot over the last year had been the same. You could see all the different angles, focuses and lighting techniques he'd learned. Could tick them off a freaking checklist. But when viewed as a whole, his photos fell flat. Didn't match the visions in his head. They had no life of their own.

The truth of the matter, then, was far simpler, and a lot more depressing. He had enough talent to turn photography into a nice hobby, if he continued to pursue it, and nothing more.

The picture of this house, however.

Something felt different about it. A vibe he'd not sensed in his work for a while. If the image he'd just shot hadn't been a fluke, if he could take more like it, maybe his dreams weren't dead after all.

He paused before stepping forward, checking the batteries on his Nikon, wondering about the history of the place. He wasn't a Clifton Heights native. His cousin Rich lived here, had suggested a month ago Clifton Heights would be a good place to take pictures. Said it was a "unique" town, "kinda scenic'n shit." When he saw Rich again, he'd have to ask him about the history of this old place.

Satisfied with the camera's battery levels, Brian approached the front door. Whatever its history, the house felt long abandoned. As if no one had lived in it for years. Decades, maybe.

Brian stopped several paces from the crumbling remains of the house's front porch. There it stood, tottering, like every abandoned house he'd ever seen. Paint largely peeled away, several windows without glass, roof sagging in places. He imagined it had once been a stately old home.

His gaze traveled over the decayed face of the house. As he settled on the window and door he'd snapped a picture of, an uneasy thought occurred to him: the shadow. In his excitement over the picture he'd never considered what had thrown the shadow.

A brief chill passed through him.

He shivered, but shook it off. There hadn't been a real shadow there, of course. An angle of the light was all, something formed in the 'reality' created by his camera, nothing more. In fact, it was an excellent lead-in for his project, the shadow having been created by his framing, created by the reality *he* had created in taking the picture.

Bolstered by this idea, he continued. As he neared the front door, he saw (with the faintest relief) no shadow looming in the window. *C'mon. You want to be a photographer? For real? Suck it up, Nancy.*

He placed a hand on the door, pushed it open and stepped inside.

A foul odor assaulted his nose as he entered what remained of the home's foyer. Brittle wallpaper flaked away from the walls. Grit crunched beneath his shoes. He hadn't expected such a rotten smell, but of course it made sense. Empty for years, no one living in it, heating it or taking care of it; everything moldering in the damp, freezing through winter, only to thaw into rot again every spring. Probably nothing here had escaped the creeping decay. He realized if this house had a basement or a crawlspace beneath the floor, he'd need to be wary of his footing.

Also, the dark. Not pitch black but definitely something he needed to account for. He held up his camera, toggled to 'lighting options' on the digital menu and selected 'night portrait,' adjusting the flash settings for optimal exposure.

Something scuttled across the floor, from left to right.

Brian stiffened, goose-flesh rippling across his skin. Adrenaline surged and his heart pounded.

Instantly he felt stupid, though his heart still thumped and it took considerable effort to shake off his jangling nerves. A mouse. A squirrel, a chipmunk, or God forbid, a rat. It had only been a rodent of some kind, scurrying for cover. Place was probably lousy with them, and he didn't need to be—

His eyes fell on the hallway receding to the back of the house. Clearly the main hall, which opened into a large room. A den or perhaps a dining room. Off the hall on both sides, several doors led to other rooms, and as he stared down the hall, something clicked in his head. A switch flipped. Possessed by an inspiration he'd not felt all year, Brian raised his Nikon, focused on the hallway, stepped sideways so his framing caught the hallway at an angle, partially cutting off its opening, and he snapped a picture.

In the flash, his fancy took over, papering the rotten walls with wallpaper, installing polished wooden floors and a stucco ceiling. He imagined what this room must've looked like years before.

The image faded, replaced by the moldy reality of now. A feverish excitement filled him (tainted by the faint worry that, as always, the finished product wouldn't match his imagination) as he thought how he could use these photos for his final project. Filled with enthusiasm, Brian gave himself over to the camera as he hadn't since high school. He lost himself in the process as he moved and shot, moved and shot. His eye became the camera, his mind using the camera's flash to wash away the decay with images conjured from his imagination of what might have been.

Brian returned to himself.

Dazed, breathing heavily, and clutching his Nikon as if his life depended on it. He took a steadying breath and blinked his eyes. Suddenly aware of the room's chill and the sweat gluing his shirt to his chest, he shivered and glanced around.

Sunlight filtered in through a smudged, gritty window. Leftover furniture—recliners, kitchen chairs, end tables—had been strewn around the room. The recliners were in tatters, the end tables and kitchen tables in rotten pieces. Also, wooden crates had been stacked against the wall, full of unidentifiable matter.

His thoughts seized as he gazed upon a yawning black rectangle before him. A doorway, its door long since gone. The wall surrounding it was made of cinder-blocks, splotched with black-green mold.

He had no way of knowing, but he didn't think the doorway led to another room. The darkness beyond looked thick and absolute. A dank, cold, earthen smell wafted from it. *Basement*, his mind whispered. *Maybe root cellar.*

He lowered the Nikon, closed his eyes and rubbed

his temples with his fingertips. How long had he been in the zone?

He'd shot 'in the zone' before, of course, but not since high school. He supposed other creative types experienced something similar. At a peak moment of creative excitement, the conscious mind faded while intuition took over. It used to happen a lot. When he was shooting woodland trails, lakes, mountains, sporting events in high school, he'd slipped into the 'zone' without noticing. He'd pointed and shot, pointed and shot. When he reviewed his pictures after coming out of the zone, they *were* good (they always were back then) and many of them he didn't remember taking at all, so deeply immersed he'd been.

Going into the zone had never felt like this, however. Back then he'd slipped in and out of the zone easily, smooth as silk. This, with his heart pounding, breathing as if he'd run a marathon, sweating rivers, he felt as if he'd been *sucked* into the zone, and almost hadn't made it back out again.

He held up his Nikon with trembling fingers. How many pictures had he taken?

He glanced at the digital screen, which showed the looming black doorway to the basement, but also, in the right bottom corner, a little red 15. Fifteen pictures. He'd taken only fifteen pictures.

It felt more like fifty.

The next question: fifteen pictures of what? He couldn't remember. As his thumb hovered over the review toggle, a strange compulsion gripped him: *Delete them all.* He should go back to the main menu, select 'batch delete', wipe the whole memory card clean, and get the hell out.

On the heels of this, rationality kicked in. *Why? It's only an old house.*

He pressed review. A spread of thumbnail images replaced the basement door on the Nikon's screen, the first thumbnail outlined in yellow. He pressed review again, bringing up the first image.

He had to squint at first to make out anything, because not only was the back room dim . . .

why aren't you looking at these outside?

. . . but the room in the image was, much as the rest of the house, badly damaged by damp rot, the wallpaper blackened with water damage. No furniture was readily apparent in this shot, so he kept searching for something interesting . . .

There.

In the corner, mostly out of frame. A head. A horse's head? With a handle sticking from its cheek. A rocking horse. A child's room?

He peered closer. Couldn't see the rest of the rocking horse because it was mostly out of frame, but he figured it was similar to most rocking horses.

He sucked in a deep breath.

A shadow.

Like the one in the window, from his first picture. It was also mostly cut off by his framing, but from this angle, it looked like . . .

The shadow.

Was riding the rocking horse.

His damp T-shirt suddenly felt ice-cold. He shivered. A handful of feeble explanations offered themselves, but most of them fell flat, if only because he now dimly recalled the window in that room facing *away* from the sun. No light streaming through it,

99

throwing his or other shadows on the wall behind the rocking horse.

What was it, then?

Nothing.

An odd coloration of the wall.

A smudge on the lens.

Nothing.

But he quickly dismissed the notion of hitting the zoom to see if the shadow extended over the handle on the rocking horse's head, forming the barest suggestion of fingers. He toggled to the next picture, instead.

why aren't you looking at these outside?!

The room in the next image was more easily identifiable, if only because of the bookshelves—warped, crooked, several shelves broken—and an old rocking chair in the far left corner, also mostly out of frame. A sitting room of sorts. There were probably more bookshelves out of frame, maybe a table and a few recliners.

He zoomed in on the bookshelves, a cautious admiration replacing his uneasiness. It was a stirring shot of books—knowledge, understanding, intellect—destroyed by something so basic as time and the elements. Some of the books were intact, while others were swollen with damp, pages likely stuck together, ink smudged and unreadable. This was a *good* picture. He could already imagine the narration for it (a whole bit about time and nature overcoming knowledge) in his final project.

"Hell yeah," he whispered as he panned left. "In the zone again, finally . . . *shit!*"

A streak of ice raced down his back, arrowed

straight to his guts. His fingers failed. His precious Nikon tumbled from his fingers and landed with a dull *thud* at his feet. He blinked, and in a flash, he thought he saw the same thing he'd just seen in the camera floating in the yawning blackness of the basement door.

His neck tingled, heart pounding in his chest. He closed his eyes and counted to ten, squeezing his hands into fists so tightly his knuckles ached and his fingernails bit into his palms.

"Nothing," he rasped, his voice sounding thin in the suddenly oppressive silence. "Nothing there."

After a ten count he swallowed and opened his eyes, gazing into the emptiness of the basement doorway.

Nothing.

Except impenetrable darkness. But the ice still rippled across his shoulders and down his back. His heart still pounded away. Slowly, he knelt and picked up his Nikon without taking his eyes off the black doorway. He stood slowly, thought about turning and striding out, but opted instead for slowly back-pedaling one step at a time. For some reason, he didn't want to turn his back to the doorway. He retreated slowly, as if afraid of waking something up.

Which was stupid and ridiculous.

There was likely nothing down there except mold, cobwebs and spiders, maybe a few garter snakes or rats. No ghostly face—which he thought he'd seen sitting in the rocking chair, peeking around the edge of the frame—was going to float out of the dark basement doorway any time soon.

so long as you don't turn your back to it

Stupid.

But he kept backpedaling away from the dark, empty basement doorway. He didn't see anything there, he *didn't.*

His right shoulder thumped the door-frame leading out.

He yelped, spun, and scrambled out of the room. He reached with his free hand, grasped the rotten edge of the door and slammed it shut.

He stepped away from the closed door, telling himself he hadn't seen darkness rushing across the room after him. *No,* the doorknob did *not* jiggle for an instant. It was only the residual vibration of him slamming the door shut.

Still, he felt much better with something between him and the yawning basement. Because shadows couldn't grasp and turn doorknobs, could they?

but they can seep under doors

He shook off the foolish thought. Dammit, after a year of frustration he was *finally* taking good pictures. He wasn't about to let a stupid case of the willies ruin it. As if in defiance of this, he ignored the bottom of the door . . .

which shadows could *seep under*

. . . held up the Nikon and looked at the next picture.

He sighed. It was the kitchen, what remained of it. He'd taken a picture of the sink. As he examined the photo, his fears subsided. A narration ran in his head about how everyday life had most likely centered around this now abandoned kitchen sink. Washing hands before dinner, dishes after. Getting a cool drink on a hot summer day . . .

His gaze slipped to the image's bottom left-hand corner. He squinted and zoomed in on something that looked triangular and metal, lodged into the counter-top's edge.

An axe?

He couldn't tell.

And the dark stains on the blade and counter-top, were they shadows, or stains?

Of what?

He shook his head, closed his eyes and pinched the bridge of his nose. "Geez. I'm goin buggy. I gotta get out of here."

When he opened his eyes he noticed two things which brought his goose-flesh rippling back. One: It was getting dark, harder to see.

Two: He didn't recognize the room he was in at all. Empty, floor littered and gritty, wallpaper moldy, doorways to his left, right, and before him. The door to the backroom and the basement directly behind him.

Also, maybe it was a trick of the fading light, but he couldn't see very far down the halls. Which was crazy, of course. How big could the house be?

He swallowed down his unease. It was only an old farmhouse. Didn't matter which hall he took. It would eventually lead back to the front door.

Right?

Still, he couldn't make himself step into one of the halls. He raised the Nikon and toggled to the next picture. Maybe there'd be a landmark he'd recognize, some image which might jog his memory.

out of frame

you're out of frame

"Hell with that," he muttered, holding up the Nikon.

The bathroom.

He'd centered this shot on the toilet. The sink next to it and the mirror above the sink were cut off at the frame's edge.

He opened his mouth. To swear or gasp, he wasn't sure, except he suddenly struggled for the breath to do either. In the mirror, along the frame's edge, he saw a shadow.

Like the one in the outside window.

what lies cut off by the frame still continues off the frame in a reality created by the photographic device

He cleared his throat and said in a voice more whiny than defiant, "Screw it. I'm getting out of here."

Which way, though? Which hallway? He could keep paging through the rest of these photos . . .

he didn't want to because he thought maybe in each one the shadow of the thing hiding past the frame would get closer

. . . but he didn't think looking at them would help him remember the way out. It hit him, then, with the force of lightning: The backroom. Where the empty basement door was.

and the shadow rushing toward him

He'd seen trees outside the one window. Maybe he could jimmy the window open, crawl through it and get out?

Maybe. Problem was, he'd have to face the basement door again, and whatever was waiting in the darkness below.

Click

Click-click-clickity-click

Icy fear flushed down his spine. The doorknob. Of the door leading to the backroom. Something was jiggling it on the other side.

No. It was something else, *had* to be.

But as he forced himself to glance over his shoulder, he caught a glimpse of the doorknob turning all the way with a final-sounding *click*.

The door cracked open.

Brian plunged forward, sprinting down the hall. His feet pounded on the old wooden floors, sounding strangely dull, underscoring how alone he was, that there was no one to hear or help him.

something crackled after him, like crisp autumn leaves skittering on concrete

He pumped his arms and ran harder, and yet, impossibly, the end never came. As if he were running on a treadmill, the end never got closer. Countless, innumerable open doors to infinite rooms flashed by and he couldn't help seeing them from the corner of his eye.

shadows rushed toward him
lay on beds
dangled in nooses from crossbeams
swung axes
danced, flitted, cavorted
rocked on wooden horses and sat in chairs
lay in bathtubs

Shadows spun and twisted in those rooms while Brian pounded down the never-ending hallway, his breath roaring in his ears, his lungs aching as a stitch burned in his side. He wasn't going to make it and the cold behind him was rushing closer.

With an explosion of breath he launched through

the doorway at the end. He whirled, grabbing frantically at the door. In his desperation, his sweaty hands slipped on the old, greasy brass knob as something skittered and hissed down the hall.

His fingers closed on the knob.

He glimpsed wide black eyes and a wrinkled, snarling mouth rushing toward him.

Brian slammed the door shut.

Silence.

Except a high-pitched keening sound which, as he backed away from the door, he realized came from him.

He breathed air in sobbing gulps, backing away from the door. "Shit. Shit, shit, shit. Gotta get outta here."

He spun, eyes frantically tracking the room. It was a den. Old, unused fireplace against the far wall. Three sagging couches facing the fireplace, what was probably once an ornamental rug on the floor between them. In the far left corner, a door. To his immediate right, a staircase curving away to a second landing. To his immediate left, the foyer.

Yes.

He recognized this room now. He'd started here, which didn't make any sense at all, because he distinctly remembered a hall leading to many rooms, not a den, but he didn't care because there was the foyer and past it the front door.

His relief morphed instantly to panic as his shoulder thumped against the foyer door. It wouldn't open. The doorknob clicked uselessly in his hand. No matter how hard he twisted or turned it, laid his shoulder against the door, it remained closed.

Locked?

No, idiot. Stuck. Old house warped by the damp. It's jammed, is all.

The window.

The front window. The first picture he'd taken was of the front door and the window next to it. He scrambled to the window, grabbed at its latches with trembling fingers, yanked upward.

Nothing.

The catch was still locked. Cursing, he fumbled with the catch, trying to flip it over—

Frozen. With rust and time, and the window frame was also probably warped, like the door.

"No problem, right?" He muttered. "It's glass. We can break it."

He glanced around. There, on the floor near one of the couches, was an old flashlight, a heavy, metal one. Proof other folks had been in here besides him, right?

but why leave a flashlight here?

He ignored the question and scrambled over to the flashlight and scooped it up. For some reason the cool metal tube felt reassuring in his hand. He leaped toward the window, winding up, but a bright flash stabbed his eyes. The sun? Coming through the glass at the right moment, blinding him?

"Geez! Shit!" Brian's aborted swing fell short as he clapped his other hand on his eyes, rubbing them. His vision wavered and blurred, out of focus. He rubbed them harder. Stepped closer to the window, looked down the drive.

His heart skipped.

Like an engine run too hard for too long, his mind

threw several gears as a black emptiness yawned beneath his feet.

The old flashlight fell with a hollow thud from nerveless fingers.

Outside.

Someone was standing down the drive toward Bassler Road, their back to him.

Brian gaped as he raked trembling fingers through his hair, pulling on tufts *hard*, trying to make himself wake up.

The person at the end of the drive turned suddenly, appraising the house with intense interest and excitement.

Holding a camera.

Brian rasped shallow breaths. He sagged against the window, hands pressed flat against the cold glass. The figure at the end of the drive held up his camera, presumably examining pictures he'd taken of the front door and window.

Brian slowly backed away, legs quivering. All his will leaked out of him and it took every ounce of reserve not to collapse into a huddled pile on the dusty floor.

The shadow.

The shadow in the window. The shadow *he'd* seen in his picture. The shadow was-it was . . .

The door to his left—the one he'd slammed shut on the rushing dark—rocked in its frame. The door knob jiggled once. The door creaked.

Fell still.

And slammed open. Something dark and vaporous and cold rushed into the room. There was nowhere left to run. Brian threw up his arms and screamed.

THINGS YOU NEED

Brian Palmer shivered.

"This is it," he muttered, staring at the picture he'd taken. "This is it. This is going to change my *life*."

6.

THE VIDEO ON the camera's viewfinder dissolved into snowy static. Remembering how it had looped before I picked it up, I frantically searched for its power button. Found it and switched it off before the person in the video could again start whispering excitedly about something changing his life.

The viewfinder fell dark and silent. Like the Magic Eight Ball, I wanted to throw the camera away. Didn't want to touch the damn thing anymore, much less hold it. Instead, I gently turned it over in my hands, my rational mind slowly kicking into gear. There wasn't anything strange about the video on the camera. Not at all. Whoever had owned it must have been making some sort of low-budget student film (although I couldn't imagine anyone filming a whole movie on such a small camera) out at this place called Bassler House. Found footage movies were all the rage these days, right? Maybe they'd uploaded it onto their computer, edited it, added a cheesy horror soundtrack, then uploaded it to Youtube. Or, maybe the kid filming it had gone broke at some point, pawned the camera and forgot to wipe the memory card first. All explainable, right?

Right?

Yeah, I know. Not explainable at all, leaving way too many questions. All I can say is a part of my mind had switched off. From the instant I flipped play on the reel-to-reel, and heard whatever it was that I'd heard, a part of my brain (the part that tries to figure things out) went into sleep mode, like a computer's hard drive does to save energy.

I hadn't seen anything in the Magic Eight Ball. It had been a mirage. I'd just watched a lame experimental student film some college kid made with his camera, nothing more.

Of course, I had good reason not to ask many questions. Honestly, my memory had gotten fuzzy on how I'd gone from holding a .38 in my room at The Motor Lodge to driving aimlessly through this little hick town, with nothing in between. One minute, sitting on the bed, holding the gun. Next minute, driving around, with no memory of how I'd gotten there. I didn't want to ask questions about that, for sure.

Or about the .38.

So this is what I did: I gingerly set the Nikon back on the floor, as if frightened it might somehow turn on. I took a deep breath, pushed myself up on one knee. A wave of dizziness hit me. I closed my eyes and rubbed my face until it passed. When I felt a little better, I opened my eyes and stood, wobbling a little on unsteady legs.

Slowly, achingly, I walked to the door. Placed my hand on the glass, which felt ice cold, and gazed at the street outside, at the empty space by the curb where my rental had been parked.

My rental.

Which wasn't there.

Instead of the panic you might expect from seeing no car where there should be one, several dull questions filled my head. What make had the car been? Model? Year? Color? Had it been a Standard, Automatic, or one of those cool Hybrids? Did it have GPS, or one of those EZ PASS sensors to get through tolls?

Each question bubbled up from the depths of my brain. Numb, directionless, with no answers. They bounced off a blank wall. I couldn't remember.

Of course, I never thought much about the rental cars I drove. You know how many different cars I rented over the course of my old career? I always went with a mid-sized economy, nothing distinctive or unique, all the same. Like the motel rooms I'd slept in, all the cars I'd driven merged seamlessly into each other. Of course I couldn't remember much about my rental. I never paid much attention to them.

Still.

It bothered me in a way I couldn't put a finger on. I tapped the glass and muttered, "Was it a Prius? A Honda? A Toyota Camry? Did I drive here at all? Maybe I walked?"

Again, though I didn't want to, I thought about The Motor Lodge. Me, sitting on the edge of the bed, holding my .38. Then me aimlessly driving a car I couldn't remember through this strange little town. No memories in between of getting up and showering. No memories of getting into the car, starting it, or pulling out of The Motor Lodge's parking lot. Nothing but a black fuzzy transition from the bed and the .38, to sitting behind the wheel of a . . .

Ford? Chevy?

I couldn't remember. I backed slowly away from the door, thighs quivering. I felt as if I'd been ill with a fever for days. I wiped my mouth. My lips were cracked and sore. The lightheaded feeling was returning, black tendrils creeping along the edges of my vision. Something hid behind the creeping darkness besides unconsciousness, however. Something *huge* and I didn't want to see.

Something clicked.

To my right.

Clicked again. Began clicking and whirring in rapid succession. I did as little writing in high school and college as possible, but I knew that sound, recognized its rhythm, which was undeniable.

Printing.

Something was printing. To my right. I turned slowly and approached the sound until I reached it in several slow, halting steps. There, sitting on a rickety nightstand at the end of a row of shelves was a gray word processor. And it was on. Clicking and whirring steadily away, printing words on a piece of paper scrolling out the top, and as I peered over, I read the words *I started sidewalk scavenging for the extra cash* . . .

SCAVENGING

I STARTED SIDEWALK scavenging for the extra cash. I lost my teaching job about a year ago, one year short of tenure and in a way guaranteeing I'd never teach ever again. While Clifton Heights is large enough for several churches, a small hospital, two high schools and a zoo, it's also small enough that news travels fast. The only place willing to hire me was the twenty-four hour Mobilmart outside town, and then only part-time, third shift. I wasn't crazy about it, but paying rent and utilities provided plenty of motivation.

I knew working part time for minimum wage at a gas station wasn't going to cut it, so I had to take additional measures. For example, once a month a food bank visits Clifton Heights Methodist Church. Though it killed me to accept handouts, it lowered the grocery costs, which helped me pay bills and still eat.

I also began collecting cans and bottles along the interstate and side roads, because The Can Man was offering six and a half cents for each. After seeing an ad in the classifieds for Greene's Scrap Processing saying they pay for metal, I decided to start collecting scrap also, because along the roads I often found rusted parts of tail pipes, mufflers, other bits and pieces of steel and iron. Sometimes if fortune favored I found whole mufflers, catalytic converters, aluminum hubcaps, and on occasion aluminum wheels.

That's why I started sidewalk scavenging. Thursday morning Webb County collects trash, so Wednesday night folks leave it on their curbs. The idea struck me on the way to work one night, passing homes and their garbage: Here was scrap metal lying around for the taking.

I did some research first, calling Greene's for a breakdown of the scrap metal rates, and believe it or not you can turn a decent buck scrapping. The most valuable metal, copper, garnered two-fifty a pound. I rarely found much of that, maybe because most folks knew they could get decent money for it themselves. I did collect a fair amount of old brass, though—in doorknobs or exterior lighting fixtures—which went for a buck sixty a pound.

Mostly I found steel—seven cents a pound—and a decent amount of aluminum, forty cents a pound. After a few trial runs I managed to fill my minivan with old metal lawn chairs, filing cabinets, pots, pans and old propane grills, lighting fixtures, aluminum siding, toolboxes, bed frames, you name it. If it was metal, I took it. Depending on how much aluminum and brass I collected, Thursday morning I'd earn anywhere from fifty to seventy bucks. May not sound like much, but even at the minimum, it amounted to two hundred dollars at month's end. Combined with my gas station wages and the cans I collected, this made life bearable.

Which was all I'd wanted. I knew what I'd done. Knew it was stupid, reckless, knew it had destroyed someone's life. Knew it was *wrong*. I also knew I'd gotten off relatively easy, all things considered. I'd wanted nothing more than to numb myself. Pay my bills, eat, and live.

Sidewalk scavenging is legal, too, but I'd already known that. Three years prior to losing my job I'd encountered a scavenger picking over *my* garbage, considering either an old nightstand or a cheap wooden bookcase. He declined both but showed up the following week, looking over some pots and pans before moving on empty-handed. I called Sheriff Baker and he said so long as my landlord didn't care and no one made a mess, it was legal.

The fellow didn't return and I never saw him again. I remember feeling relieved because something in his disconnected gaze made me feel uneasy, as if I'd been offered a haunting glimpse of how *anyone* could fall out of the human race.

It's ironic, how I see his gaze now in my minivan's rear-view mirror, staring back at me.

After several false starts—one week finding only a bent section of an old storm gutter, the next a frying pan— I got better acquainted with most of Clifton Heights' streets, avenues, cul-de-sacs and dead ends. I also learned several things I'd never thought about before, things I might've thought important if I still felt a connection with people.

For example, I found most my scrap in the better sections of town, not in Center Village Apartments or out at the Commons Trailer Park. You need a certain income to buy new stuff often enough to throw old stuff out. Also, folks living in the poorer sections simply can't afford to throw anything away, even broken things. Life has taught them to waste nothing.

Also the poorer sections offered more moving portrayals of humanity, which probably would've meant more to me if I'd still been teaching English, still reading poems, plays, and short stories. I'd quit reading after getting fired. Most of the time, I numbly consumed hours of talk shows.

One night, I drove past an apartment building which almost made me feel something. The worst slum; it had gone unpainted for years. Its exterior was a mottled gray, with no shutters on its windows, out of which hung battered air conditioners. The front steps leaned and the porch sagged in the middle.

The lawn offered the most striking portrait. No grass at all, but someone had raked the dirt with meticulous care. Under a diseased elm sat an oval picnic table, and next to it a charcoal grill. In spite of the apathy I'd cultivated since losing my job, I imagined a small patchwork family of a mother, child, and boyfriend, perhaps interracial, savoring whatever enjoyment they could cooking cheap hamburgers or hot-dogs and eating them under that sickly old elm.

In the middle of this raked dirt lawn sat the most lovingly cared-for flower garden I'd ever seen. It was filled with pansies, black-eyed Susan's and irises. Mulched with black compost, ringed by stones which someone had obviously spray-painted white.

It was breathtakingly beautiful. Someone was doing the best with what they had. I couldn't help wondering if a Mayella Ewell lived there, and what her life was like.

Another thing I learned about Clifton Heights I hadn't known before: Its roads were more complicated than I'd ever realized. Every Wednesday I turned down a road, into a cul-de-sac or a residential complex I'd never seen before. I often lost my way, driving around in circles, retracing a road I'd just taken. In fact, once or twice after taking a wrong turn the premonition struck me: Maybe I'd actually gotten lost.

In short order, however, I encountered a familiar landmark—a sign, a distinct garbage can or porch swing—and found my way again. My dull worry faded, forgotten until the next time it happened.

Turns out, I should've paid closer attention to how easy it was to get lost in your own hometown.

I never ran into anyone I knew, though I'm certain I must have driven by their homes and scavenged metal from their curbs many times. It didn't dawn upon me right away, but soon enough I couldn't help but think of the scavenger I'd encountered. I couldn't help but think of his dead eyes, realizing then the same thing was happening to me. I'd been left at the curb like the refuse I scavenged through, with one major difference.

No one was likely to come scavenging after me.

I'd been scrapping for about six months when I pulled up to a promising pile of junk before a two-story white home with blue trim on Hyland Avenue. After a quick once-over, however, I decided to leave because like many other homes this one had boxes of books on its curb for disposal, which always depressed me. Despite not having read anything since losing my job, it still saddened me to encounter discarded books.

This house had thrown out hundreds of books, neatly sorted in cardboard boxes. For the first time since I started scavenging I felt the urge to rescue them (though I wasn't planning on reading them), so I wanted to get out of there before I succumbed to the temptation. As I rounded the boxes a name jumped out from one of the covers, halting me in my tracks.

Ray Bradbury.

Above it: *The Illustrated Man*.

The cover hit me hardest. It was older, featuring a heavily tattooed man sitting with his back to the reader. Against my will I bent over and with numb fingers picked up the well-worn book. Straightening, I opened the cover and turned a few pages to the blank page after the title page.

Except it wasn't blank.

In an all-too familiar looping script, I read: *To Emily. Live Forever!* And, of course, it had been signed.

By me.

Because impossibly, this was the short story collection I'd given one of my students for her eighteenth birthday. This wasn't her house or her neighborhood, but I felt certain, as impossible as it was, this was the book I'd given Emily Travis about a year and a half ago. Before I'd been fired for sleeping with her. Before she killed herself when she learned she was pregnant with my child.

I remember the first time I saw Emily Travis, during my fourth year of teaching, her ninth grade year. I'd dashed from the school across a rain-pounded parking lot to my car. I was throwing my books into the back seat, struggling with my umbrella when I saw her.

Sitting on a swing in the playground, head hanging, clutching the swing's chains, arms limp, shoulders sagging. Sitting there in the rain, her black hair plastered to her face.

I froze, unable to tear my gaze away. Nothing untoward reared in my head then (and nothing would for several more years), but I couldn't shake the heartbreaking poignancy of the moment: This girl slumped over on a swing in a downpour, oblivious and uncaring of the cold rain pelting her shoulders, head and arms.

Today, I know what I should've done. I should've shaken the moment off, resolved to alert the guidance office to what I'd seen. After, I should've left well enough alone.

I didn't do that.

I popped the umbrella up and walked over to the playground to see if she was okay.

Then I gave her a ride home.

As I stood outside the house on Hyland Avenue holding that impossible Ray Bradbury collection with its impossible inscription, the memories of Emily and I tumbled through my head. I'll never share those with anyone. I'm not going to pretend what happened between Emily and I was 'special'. I'll not defend nor justify my actions, because they were wrong. Though

I never meant any harm, I'm an adult. I *was* a teacher. A figure of authority and responsibility. I failed that responsibility. I destroyed her life and mine in the process.

When we slept together, I was only twenty-eight and she was eighteen, bearing the weight of double those years on her shoulders. However, we were first linked after that rainy day on the playground. It took several years for it to manifest into life-destroying proportions, but I should've been more aware. More cautious. I should've seen it coming and headed it off. If I had, I might still be teaching today, (at another school far away), and Emily Travis would still be alive.

But she's dead.

And I'll never teach again. There's nothing which can change this, no matter how hard I search for it.

Doesn't mean I can stop looking.

I left *The Illustrated Man* behind, explaining its existence away. Emily's father more than likely donated all her books to Arcane Delights, a used book store on Main Street run by Kevin Ellison, (where I still have over a hundred dollars trade-in credit I'll never use). Whoever lived in the house on Hyland Avenue had purchased it, ignorant of its origins. When they'd finished it, they had discarded it.

A logical and rational explanation.

So I dropped it among the others. Climbed into my minivan and drove away. Forgetting it, hoping to come across a large gas grill or something else nice and heavy.

I left it there.

Only now realizing I shouldn't have.

That night it was harder getting home than usual. I took wrong turns down streets I'd never seen before. Retraced my routes, driving in circles before finding my way back to Main Street. When I finally did, I sighed, my anxiety seeping out of me.

Over the next few weeks, however, finding my way home got harder.

The following Wednesday night rolled around as if no time had passed. I was again cruising for scrap metal. I didn't think anything unusual at the time because it wasn't as if much had happened since the previous Wednesday. I worked Thursday, Friday, Saturday and Sunday nights at the Mobilmart, 11 P.M. to 7 A.M., which meant I slept most of Friday, Saturday, Sunday and Monday morning and early afternoon. Monday evening I usually walked one of Clifton Height's many back roads to pick up cans and bottles. I spent Tuesday watching whatever talk show was on. Tuesday night I'd go to The Stumble Inn, order a plate of hot wings, sit, and quietly get myself as drunk as I could afford. Then, the next day was Wednesday, which meant more talk shows and then later, scavenging.

My social schedule didn't offer much in the way of milestones to mark passing time, and I'd become accustomed to 'slippage'. It didn't seem strange I couldn't recall what I'd done since the previous Wednesday. That's the way things were, and my memory of finding the impossible copy of *The Illustrated Man* had hidden itself behind the blurred scenery of my colorless existence.

THINGS YOU NEED

Everything changed when I found the next thing, in front of a small white Colonial with red trim on Novak Street. Soon as I stepped out of my van and saw it, several connections fired in my head. I remembered how hard it was getting home last Wednesday, how afraid I was of being lost. I remembered with a shiver *The Illustrated Man* I'd given Emily before she died.

A gray Texas Instruments 8010 electric word processor. Sitting atop a box of old TIME magazines.

It was mine.

I knew this because of the round sticker on the keyboard's cover, of a robot—I think from the cover of an Issac Asimov novel—sitting on a cliff, watching a sky turning purple-orange at sunset. The sticker came in the mail with my subscription to *Asimov's Science Fiction Magazine*. One of the many speculative magazines I'd consumed during college (along with *Cemetery Dance* and *Twilight Zone Magazine*) as I pounded out stories on that gray Texas Instruments 8010 electric word processor in my attempts to become a writer.

I forgot to mention writing, didn't I? I'd grown up in love with science fiction, fantasy, and horror. During college all I'd wanted was to write, my degree in English Education a half-assed fallback plan.

Right then I realized I couldn't possibly explain away the word processor's presence. I'd destroyed it twenty years ago after receiving my thirtieth rejection. I'd gotten drunk and tossed my word processor out our third-floor dorm room window in a fit of rage. Luckily I didn't hit anyone but I still got written up by the Residence Director and fined.

Twenty years later there it sat on a box of moldy

TIME magazines in front of a red-trimmed white Colonial on Novak Street. As I stared at it, something broke inside of me. A door opened and loosed the real reason why I'd hurled my word processor out my dorm room window. At the time I'd told myself I'd gotten fed up with writing, disgusted with the endless toil and the sting of rejection, angry I didn't have the necessary talent.

Maybe all those things were partly true. I realized, however, standing on the curb, it wasn't the whole truth.

I'd been afraid. Of my father. Afraid of his continued scorn of my dreams. I'd grown tired of weathering said scorn. Upon receiving my thirtieth rejection letter, I hurled my dreams out the window with my Texas Instruments 8010.

I'd always assumed my rage had come from the bitter realization I didn't have enough talent to write. Staring at that impossible word processor, however, I understood my rage had come from knowing I didn't have the courage to stand up to my father's scorn. The rage had come from giving up my dreams.

Then I remembered how I'd left behind Emily's copy of *The Illustrated Man* the previous week. I gathered up the Texas Instruments 8010 and took it to the van. A piece of paper fluttered from its wheel to the ground but I didn't stop to inspect it. The masthead appeared terribly similar to the kind on my last rejection letter, from my college literary journal, *The Oswegian*.

That would be too much, seeing the same letter twenty years later.

THINGS YOU NEED

Emily had loved all the speculative genres as much as me. She'd grown up reading Bradbury, Poe, Matheson, L'Engle, Lewis, Tolkien, Dahl, and so many others. She'd escaped from her fractured childhood into those mesmerizing tales.

Like I'd escaped from mine.

I did manage to find some scrap metal. Three rusted lawn chairs and a crooked folding chair. I missed a lot after collecting the Texas Instruments 8010, however, numbly cruising the streets. Buildings, houses, telephone poles and garbage piled on curbs blurred past.

I also had a hard time getting home. Got lost in the poorer section of town, only blundering by pure happenstance onto Old Barstow Road and the NYSEG Utility Payment center to find my way back to Main Street.

For some reason, however, I wasn't as afraid of getting lost. I kept driving, ignoring the garbage piled on curbs in front of houses . . .

Because they didn't have what I needed.

Something inside kept pushing me to drive, drive until I found something I did need.

Another numb week of working third shift at the Mobilmart passed by. I slept, walked for cans, and drank at The Stumble Inn. Then, once more, with seemingly no time passing, I found myself blinking awake as I pulled off Main Street onto a side street I didn't recognize. Apparently I'd been sleep-driving into another night of sidewalk scavenging.

My scalp prickled with unease. My heart pounded the way anyone's does when they jerk awake at the wheel. I nearly slammed on the brakes when, glancing out the window to see which street I'd turned onto, I saw the Texas Instruments 8010 sitting on the passenger seat. For some reason, I'd lugged it back out to the minivan for my Wednesday night scavenging.

Or, more disturbing: I'd never taken it out of the minivan at all. Which made me think maybe all my blurry memories of the past week were nothing more than echoes of other weeks playing themselves over in a loop. Maybe I'd never left the minivan at all, never stopped driving, and had been driving ever since.

I tried to remember what I'd eaten last night for dinner.

Did I have luck in collecting bottles and cans on Monday? What road had I walked? Had anything unusual happened at the Mobilmart the last week?

Nothing. And the kicker? I had no idea what talk shows I'd watched all week, either.

I felt close to losing it, then. Close to slamming my foot on the gas and sending my minivan careening down the street into whatever came by, be it another car, truck, or kid on a tricycle. Anything to snap the colorless, unbroken stream my life had become.

In all the time before I started finding these things, I never once allowed myself to wonder why my life had fallen apart, never let myself ponder where things had first gone wrong. I had repressed those questions, too scared of facing the answers, and where those answers would lead.

Even though that was what I needed the most.

∽

A sudden urge tugged at my brain, heart, and soul. I pulled over to the curb, braked and parked the minivan. The pile of garbage before a yellow Concord with black trim had something I needed. Slowly, feeling distant and far away, I got out and stood before the refuse piled on the curb and *saw* what I needed. Two things, actually.

One: A wooden crate full of smashed vintage soda bottles, circa 1960s. Shards of Coke, Dr. Pepper, Pepsi bottles and the emerald green bits of a few 7UP bottles. Two: The wreckage of a homemade, cheap plywood comic book rack, littered with torn and crumpled comic books, all the classics: Batman, The Astounding X-men, Superman and ROM: Space Knight, shredded into ruin.

I stared, my face rigid, when a brisk, non-confrontational but stiff voice asked, "Can I help you?"

I glanced up and saw a middle-aged man wearing a white-dress shirt and tan khakis, easily upper-middle class, probably disturbed in the middle of dinner by me pulling up to his curb. Sharp, clear blue eyes weighed me, his stance casual, but poised and wary, regardless.

I opened my mouth but remembered the scavenger I'd encountered on my curb years ago, realizing this man wouldn't see the broken soda bottles and destroyed comics. He *couldn't* see them. Only I could.

Because I needed them.

I swallowed thickly, cast my eyes down and whispered, "No, I'm fine." Got back into my minivan and pulled away from the curb as quickly as possible while retaining some shred of dignity.

I waited until nightfall, driving and turning down an endless variation of streets with no names until I somehow returned and collected those smashed bottles, destroyed comic book rack, and ruined comic books.

Because they were what I needed.

When I was only twelve my alcoholic father came home from another Saturday night with the boys, drunk and raving about the usual: Liberal hippy democrats ruining the government. Blacks, Hispanics, and welfare ruining the economy. How his shrewish, spineless hag of a wife undercut his God-given right to run the household by letting his faggotty son read comic books and write stupid stories and collect those stupid soda bottles.

The routine Saturday-night run-through. It usually ended with Mom reluctantly letting Dad man-handle her into the bedroom to keep his hands off me. It usually worked well enough.

But not that night.

She said something different. I never discovered what because she packed her bags and disappeared for good the next day. Whatever it was broke the routine because I heard Dad roar. Heard the smack of a calloused hand on flesh. Mom screamed. Then his heavy Timberlands pounded their way to my room. I was, as usual, sitting on the bed writing in a black and white marble notebook, surrounded also by several issues of Spider-man, Superman, and The Incredible Hulk.

He kicked my door in so hard it slammed against the opposite wall. Without a word he hauled back and decked me with a hay-maker I can still feel ringing in my jaw when I'm tired or stressed.

I sprawled onto the floor, head spinning, bleeding from my mouth and nose, then everything dissolved into a medley of pain, curses and punches, a few kicks. How I came out of it without broken ribs I'll never know.

I don't remember much, save two devastating sights which came back to me the instant I saw those broken soda bottles and ruined comic books lying on the curb. At the height of his rage Dad attacked my flimsy, cheap comic book rack—made by him in a moment of kindness, from lumber mill castoffs—and ripped the comics from their plywood slots, tearing and crumpling their pages, screaming and cursing. Then he snapped each shelf and tore the whole thing from the wall.

Afterward, the coup de grace. He grabbed my Louisville Slugger (which he'd bought for my tenth birthday despite knowing I hated sports) from where it leaned against the wall. He wound up and in one swing cleared my knick-knack shelf of those carefully collected, cleaned and arranged vintage soda bottles. Their shattering sounded as shrill cries in my ears.

I passed out to the sight of Dad swinging up and down, pounding those broken bottles into dust. The torn pages of my comic books fluttered around us, dying butterflies of my youth.

My father abused me off and on in similar escapades until I fled to college, leaving behind a man who eventually got knifed to death in a drunken bar fight. I want to say he only abused me physically and emotionally, but that would be a lie.

I can't defend what happened between Emily and me. But the pattern is clear now, isn't it? Two scarred souls who tried—despite the consequences—to heal each other of their festering wounds. And of course I don't know for sure because she kept her plans secret, but I think Emily killed herself less because of shame but more because she feared her father's jealous reaction if he discovered her secret.

How do I know she wasn't ashamed of us?

Why else would she address her suicide letter to me?

I'm still driving. I've found lots more things since the broken soda bottles and ruined comic books. A box of my G. I. Joe action figures Dad threw away when I turned nine because I was "too old for baby toys. Boys don't play with dolls." Also, some of my stuffed animals. One of them my beloved Pound Puppy, which Dad had insisted on throwing out when I'd turned five, because "how can you stop wettin the bed when you act like a damn baby?"

Lately I've been finding my old black and white marble composition notebooks here and there. I haven't looked in them (afraid to see what I wrote years ago), just piled them in my minivan with all the other things I've found.

See, I don't collect scrap metal anymore. I collect things I need. I drive all the time, now. I have no memories of stopping for food or gas, or ever going home or back to work at the Mobilmart. It's always Wednesday night. I'm always turning down yet another street I don't recognize, searching for what I need and while I keep finding things, I haven't yet found what I need the *most*.

A dog-eared copy of *The Illustrated Man*.

The one I gave to Emily, with an inscription which is dreadfully ironic now: *Live Forever!* I think I'll be driving around forever until I find what I so desperately needed and should've accepted the first time around. Maybe if I had, I wouldn't still be driving.

7.

I LAID THE last page down on the pile strewn at my feet. I slumped where I sat next to the word processor—a Texas Instruments 8010—and covered my face with my hands. The instant darkness made me sleepy.

So tired.

Of everything. My job. My life. Driving from school to school. Doing my shuck and jive to get kids selling magazines, kids who half the time didn't give a rat's ass. Tired of them, tired of the same motels, the same cars so alike I couldn't remember anything about them, the same old bar whores. I was tired of the whole damn game.

That's why I'd bought the .38, of course. I'm sure *you* saw that coming a mile away. How could I have missed it? It was right in front of my face. Had been for over a year. How many times can you sit in your motel room—or cabin—and cradle the gun you bought for "personal protection" before you get the message, loud and clear?

Anyway, sitting before a pile of paper spit out by a Texas Instruments word processor, on which was written a story about a guy as lost as me, I was starting to get the message. I had to face *why* I'd bought the gun. Had to admit *why* I felt compelled to hold it and stare at it for hours, why I'd been doing so for months now. I was tired of everything. Right then, sitting there cross-legged on the cool, wooden floor, I knew what I needed for me not to be tired anymore.

needed
we have
things you need

This is nuts, my fading rationality protested. *So I've got a little lost time between The Motor Lodge and here. So what? And that weird shopkeeper, babbling about things we need or whatever. He set me up for this, sure enough. And the lock on his door* must *be broken. It was unlocked when I tried to get back in; it's locked now because it's broken. The lock is broken, or something in the door-handle is, for sure. And what I saw in the Magic Eight Ball? I'm tired. Hallucinating. And on the camera? Some guy messing around making a low-budget ghost story, and word processors have memories, right? You could type something on them and save it, print it out later. So yeah, this story was already saved and an electrical short or something turned it on, printed it out. That thing on the reel-to-reel was just an old radio show. That's it, that's all.*

But where's my car?
Why's it gone?

"I don't know," I rasped. "Someone stole it. Or towed it. Something."

Which of course made no sense whatsoever, but you gotta understand, part of me was facing for the first time the reality that I wanted (*needed*) things to end. In response to the shock of my realization, my brain was flailing to come up with any and all rationalizations to explain my situation.

make? color? model?

do you remember anything about the rental?

was there a rental?

I licked my lips, brain sluggish. I had no answers. I didn't want to think about them, or about the blank spot between me holding the .38 and then driving around town. I scrambled for something else to focus on, anything, my mind whirling.

An idea struck me.

"The telephone," I whispered. "I can call the police. 911. Did Patchett give me his number?"

Odd, huh? I remembered dinner with Mr. Patchett, the English teacher from Clifton Heights High. Remembered how great the food was at The Skylark Diner, but I couldn't remember much after holding my .38.

I didn't think about it, however, as I scrambled to my feet, suddenly energized, digging into my pants pocket for my cell, kicking myself for not thinking of it sooner. I'd call the police, 911, someone, explain how I'd accidentally got locked in this old junk shop, and they could roust the shopkeeper (forgetting, of course, how I never got his name, but figuring in a small town like this everyone knew everyone) or maybe the store's owner to come get me out.

I suppose I should've expected what came next. I mean, given the circumstances and all the crazy things happening, it was the most logical thing. Still, I felt my heart *thump* when I tried to swipe-unlock my phone and nothing happened.

THINGS YOU NEED

The screen was dead.

"What the *hell*? I charged it back at the cabin. Didn't I?" I grabbed my hair and barely stopped short of pulling it out. "It was charging in the car . . . "

what car?

do you remember?

" . . . I know it was!"

The store phone. The store had to have a phone, right? I stuck my dead phone (it shouldn't have been dead; I *had* charged it) back into my pocket and spun on one heel. Powered by a manic desperation, I strode down the aisle toward the sales counter. Of course, there had to be a phone somewhere, and a store phone directory, or at least emergency numbers tacked on a board.

There it was: I could see it as I neared the counter. An old black phone. Not a rotary, at least, not that old. I reached the counter, grabbed the receiver off the cradle and was already finished punching in 911 and waiting impatiently with the earpiece pressed against my ear before I realized there was no dial tone, no busy signal, no static, nothing.

All the purpose in me faded, replaced by a dull emptiness. I felt useless, directionless, hopeless. What was the use? There was no point in doing anything, or saying anything, or trying to.

Something trilled. An electric warble.

A cell phone.

An old school cell, by the sound. One of those early low-tech jobs, on which you could only call, text, and maybe play basic games. And sure, yeah—a junk shop these days probably would have a box of old cell phones, or Tracphones or whatever.

135

It trilled again.

I spun away from the desk, scanning the shelves filled with clutter. To my right, somewhere. The row against the wall? Two strides and I was there, and heard the trilling again, several steps down the aisle. About halfway down on the bottom shelf was an old wicker basket full of cell phones. Flip phones, bulky Tracphones, one or two slide-out phones . . .

One on top lit up and trilled. An iPhone, surprisingly new-looking. Its screen flashed: *Unknown Caller*. Not wondering even for a second how or *why* a newer iPhone in a basket of old phones in a thrift store could suddenly power up and receive calls, I grabbed it, swiped my thumb to unlock the screen and put it to my ear. "Hello? Can you hear me? Listen, I don't know who this is, but you've got to . . . "

"Please! Omigod, can you help me? I need help! I can't-I can't find-Oh, God, I can't . . . "

A PLACE FOR BROKEN AND DISCARDED THINGS

THE SHEER SIZE of Save-A-Bunch Furniture impressed Shane Carroll the most, initially. He hadn't expected it to be so large and sprawling. Also surprising, it was a re-tasked high school, which was unexpected in itself. Such a modestly-sized town as Clifton Heights not only having two in-use schools but also an unused high school on its outskirts. Converting it into Save-A-Bunch also impressed Shane in its utilitarian efficiency.

It hadn't taken long, however, for another feeling to impress itself upon him as he and Amanda strolled through its labyrinthine hallways, past recliners, sofas and armoires. He couldn't name the sensation, exactly. A nagging sense of unease? Discomfiture? An odd displacement which made everything feel slightly out of place?

He didn't know what it was. Something about the old school's halls—now lined with refurbished and used furniture of all kinds—set him slightly off kilter. He didn't know why. Everything looked clean and orderly. Recliners and sofas neatly pressed against lockers, allowing ample space in the halls for patrons to peruse safely.

The lobby likewise had impressed Shane. It had been arranged professionally and with meticulous care. A massive cherry wood desk greeted customers upon their entrance, serving as a front counter and customer service area. On it sat a sleek laptop computer, a corporate telephone with extensions, a fax and small copy machine, and two neat piles of various purchase forms. Behind the desk stood two cherry wood bookshelves full of binders, no doubt an inventory of the store's offerings. No one had been there to meet them, but Shane figured a store this size kept all its workers busy.

Finishing off the lobby was a waiting area featuring a voluminous brown leather couch, two matching leather recliners facing it, separated by an ornate glass-topped coffee table, scattered with several magazines. All the pieces had price-tags attached to them. A nice touch: A ready-to-purchase waiting area.

All throughout, the ceramic tile floors were swept clean and polished spotless. Walls gleamed with fresh coats of paint, as did the lockers, which impressed Shane, too. Though not in use any longer, the lockers appeared neat and brand new, rather than battered and chipped by time.

Still, something about the lockers nagged him. Especially the ones with furniture pressed against them. He'd struggled to pin down his feelings as he and Amanda browsed, but the best he could determine was a vague restlessness spawned by a *trapped* sensation. The furniture wasn't pressed against the lockers to provide walking room. They kept the lockers *closed*, keeping something inside them. As if the lockers were apt to open on their own . . . .

It was a silly notion, to be sure. One he banished from his thoughts almost immediately.

Almost.

Because as they rounded corner after corner, Shane become more intrigued with what might be in the lockers. Surely, when the school closed and was then refurbished, every locker couldn't have been cleaned out completely. What might remain, shut off from the world, coated by layers of dust and time? An old love note, discarded and long forgotten by its author and intended audience? A ball cap? Maybe an outdated textbook, or an empty soda bottle? A box of cigarettes and a lighter?

Shane's curiosity mounted when Amanda, without saying anything (no surprise there; she hadn't said much of anything to him lately) wandered into a classroom filled with end-tables. Compelled by his curiosity (and his nagging unease), Shane sidled up to the row of lockers and casually (glancing around, as if he were sneaking past an *Employees Only* barrier) triggered the latch. He'd figured it might stick, but to his surprise it clicked smoothly. He pulled the locker open.

He expected its interior to be cobwebbed and dusty, full of bits and pieces of years gone by: Broken pencils, crumpled paper balls, candy bar wrappers. As the locker door yawned open, however, he saw nothing but a clean, spotless interior. At first glance it appeared empty.

And then he saw the old, bulky cell phone lying far back in the right corner. It was gray and blockish, a rectangular shape. Obviously outdated, but it appeared brand new.

Shane stared at the cell phone, wondering how it had gotten there. According to Amanda (where had she heard about this place again?) the school had been closed since the seventies. Maybe one of the store's elusive employees, still using an old phone, had dropped it? But if so, how had it ended up in a locker?

Shane stood there, one hand on the locker door, staring at the old cell phone. It appeared mundane, innocuous, trivial even. Who knew how it had gotten in there, or why? There it was, though. A gray, blocky old cell phone, probably a Nokia, the heavy ones you could use to knock out a mugger, if needed.

He should close the locker and find out what Amanda was doing. Last thing he needed was for her to see him standing here and staring into one of the old lockers. Best case scenario, she'd rake him over the coals for being nosy, saying she couldn't take him anywhere, so why did she bother, anyway?

Of course, that would require she show some life. Worst case scenario? She'd say nothing and continue to ignore him as she had the last seven months.

He grasped the top edge of the locker, about to close it. Instead he bent over, reached out, scooped up the Nokia, and stuck it in his pocket. Then he closed the locker quietly as he heard Amanda's heels clicking toward him.

He turned, stuffed his hands into his pockets and assumed what he hoped was a neutral expression. Neutral was the safest expression to wear around Amanda these days. A literal survival technique.

"Find anything good?"

Amanda didn't look up, scrolling on her iPhone (as she always did lately, anything to avoid looking him in the eye), no doubt comparing prices of the end-tables she'd found to those she'd bookmarked on the Internet. "Not really," she said. "A few of them were okay, and would probably fit into the den, but compared to what I could get online, not such a bargain."

She glanced up briefly, favoring him with a blank expression of her own. "Let's go up front, ask where the sofas, recliners, and beds are. This place has so many hallways I can't remember half of what I saw on the way here."

Of course he'd agree with her. He didn't care one way or the other. He certainly had no other plans for the day, which didn't matter, either. Amanda had planned it, which meant they would do it. Period. His acquiescence was merely a footnote, and as a lot of things in their marriage lately . . .

is this a marriage?

. . . not of much concern to her. At least, so she acted. Which, of course, begged the question, as he dutifully followed her down the hall and around the corner in search of the front lobby, why he was so willing to follow along.

It certainly wasn't the sex, of course. There hadn't been any, lately. He instantly felt ashamed at the thought, wondering how he could possibly think of *sex* first, after everything they'd endured.

no

don't go there

As a seemingly endless procession of freshly-painted locker doors streamed by, Shane admitted the only answer that made sense: He still loved her. Despite her rejection of him, holding him at arm's length, despite everything that had happened, he was still here, with her. Helping her pick out furniture for their new house in Eagle Bay. He was here, because he loved Amanda Carroll. Couldn't imagine ever walking away from her, or waking up in the morning without her. He felt all this, despite her casually dismissing him as part of the scenery (ironically, like an old armchair you can't bear to part with). He felt a deep chasm open beneath his feet whenever he thought maybe things would be better if he left. Or worse, when he thought maybe if Mandy in accounting (a lithe redhead who'd been flirting for months) asked him out to lunch, he'd accept, because at least *someone* wanted to have lunch with him. Maybe he'd see where things would go.

He cut himself off, a stinging sense of betrayal twisting his guts, because he still loved Amanda. Couldn't live without her, and thought he might actually kill himself if he tried to cheat on her, temptations regardless. Unfortunately, those things had become a footnote also.

As they turned right and proceeded down a hallway lined with coffee tables and lamp stands—pushed against the lockers, again reinforcing the illusion they were keeping the lockers closed, keeping something inside from getting out—Shane thought for the hundredth time he wasn't being fair to Amanda. It wasn't as if she'd gotten bored with him and wanted to trade up. She hadn't done anything wrong. Yes, she'd held him at arm's distance for months. Had retreated behind a cool exterior, but all through their move, him coming with her had never been a question. Divorce or separation wasn't an option, not even a casually whispered aside. So she must still want him in her life, too . . .

like an old armchair you can't throw out

. . . even if he'd been put on an indefinite holding pattern. He only hoped he'd be allowed to land before he ran out of fuel.

She didn't do *this*, he reminded himself as they came to another intersection. *She didn't ask for this, and you can't blame her for it.*

And he didn't.

He wouldn't leave, either. He loved her, and though they hadn't slept together in months, (the last time had been a joyless, mechanical affair), though she had retreated emotionally and treated him as part of the scenery, he wouldn't leave her. He wasn't happy but he wasn't exactly unhappy, he just *was. Be*ing without her was nothing but a recipe for madness and despair.

What if she asked him to leave?

Told him they were done, and she didn't want him around anymore?

He didn't know.

It's not her fault.

But it wasn't his, either.

He pulled away from his thoughts as he came to Amanda's shoulder at the intersection. She stared ahead, eyes glazed and distant.

"Everything okay?"

His voice broke her out of the trance she'd fallen into. She pursed her lips and narrowed her eyes. "Place is a damn maze. I thought for sure this led to the main lobby."

Shane looked ahead. Bean bags filled the hall on the other side of the intersection, of all kinds, shapes and colors. It was also a dead end, its doors probably leading to what was once the school's playground. He couldn't tell for sure because they were behind rows of bean bags, heaping piles reached for the ceiling.

This was the nature of Save-A-Bunch, so far as Shane could tell. The front sales area appeared neat and professional, and the halls and classrooms had been arranged with orderly rows of furniture. But around the edges—like at the end of this hall—the order crumbled a bit. In this case, bean bags piled haphazardly to the ceiling. Though it was stupid, he didn't like those piled bean bags. Hulking, lumpy, and bulbous. Like the gelatin clumps of tadpole eggs he'd seen floating in an old water hole at the edge of his parents' property, growing up.

Shane glanced down the hallway to his left, which stretched to a corner turning right. This hall featured bookshelves, clothes bureaus and armoires, pressed against the wall, lined up neatly next to each other. For some reason, these pieces hadn't been pushed against the lockers, and though it made him feel weak and silly, he didn't want to walk down that hallway at all.

The hallway to their right led to another intersection too far away to see clearly. And lining it were perhaps two dozen recliners of all shapes and sizes. "Hey, look. Recliners."

Amanda stared down the hall, speechless. Shane frowned and peered at her face. She wore the same empty expression he'd become accustomed to over the past few months, but her eyes trembled with fear. He couldn't tell exactly *how* he knew she was afraid. A shimmer there, a trembling, a glimmer he hadn't seen since It happened.

No.

"You okay?"

Amanda shivered, as if shaking herself from her fugue, literally pulling her wits together. She blinked, and the fearful shine he'd glimpsed there faded. "I'm fine. It's just—"

Just *what*?

She shook her head, sounding puzzled. Did he see fear flickering in her eyes again? "I thought, when we walked through the lobby, the recliners were in the hall to the *right* of lobby. I can't see from here," she pointed to the dim intersection ahead, "but that doesn't look like the lobby."

"Oh. Well, maybe they have lots of recliners."

Amanda's hand lowered to join the other clutching her red purse before her, in an oddly frightened gesture. "I suppose. This place is so big and confusing."

She wasn't looking at him, but he nodded slowly. "Yeah. It is." He wasn't saying it to humor her. The store's layout meandered and branched off into numerous halls and intersections, with many blind alleys stacked with furniture.

and those lockers someone doesn't want opening

Disconcerting, yes. It would be easy to lose your bearings and get all crossed up. Still, he didn't quite understand the fear he saw in Amanda's eyes.

"Well." Amanda's tone still sounded doubtful and hesitant. "Guess I'll check them out. Haven't found any good recliners online yet, so why not?"

She set off, and again, Shane noticed a marked hesitancy in her stride, as if she were a child proceeding down a dark alley at night. He stepped after her, *Are you sure you're okay?* poised on his lips.

He closed his mouth and came to a halt when the Nokia he'd found vibrated.

He clapped a hand over the Nokia's bulge in his pocket, nervous guilt coursing through him, which was ridiculous, of course. Yes, his inexplicable urge to pocket the old Nokia—which he'd forgotten about completely— didn't make sense. Also odd; he'd immediately forgotten about it. Of course he'd made the mistake of allowing himself to think about Amanda, their relationship and the null zone it had fallen into. He'd almost allowed himself to think of *that*, too. Then he'd gotten sidetracked by Amanda's strange unease over this sprawling store.

He had no reason to feel guilty about the Nokia. No reason to suddenly fear Amanda knowing about it or to worry she'd be angry at him for taking it, no need to hide it from her.

The phone vibrated again.

And again.

Unsure why he felt so guilty, Shane glanced at Amanda's slowly receding back as she hesitantly made her way down the hall, examining the recliners lined up on *both* sides . . .

keeping those lockers closed

 . . . in furtive, sweeping glances, as if she were afraid, for some reason, of stopping at one recliner too long.

The Nokia vibrated again.

Struggling against a strange sense of betrayal and a surreal unreality, Shane slid his hand into his pocket, withdrew the phone, and without looking at the screen, he pressed the answer button and put the phone to his ear. He turned away from Amanda, again stricken by a guilt he didn't understand. His whisper sounded harsh and furtive in his own ears. "H-hello?"

A quiet hissing. Not exactly dead air, but not static, either. Then, a clearing of a throat, and a tremulous, feminine whisper, "*M-Mike? Is that you?*"

Shane glanced over his shoulder at Amanda's receding back, sure the woman's voice had echoed in the hall, and would catch Amanda's attention. He glimpsed her red-jacketed form standing before a classroom door, most likely another showroom for furniture lined up in neat rows, appearing eerily like diligent students sitting at attention. She didn't act aware of his presence, or hear his whispering. He turned away and replied, "No. I'm sorry. Who is this?"

A tired, wretched sob. A gasp, and then a murmured, "*No, no, no, this can't be, this can't!*"

The Nokia clicked off.

Shane pulled the old cell away from his ear and stared at it, regarding again how out of date it was. It could still be used, of course, being a Tracphone. All you needed was to buy a Tracphone card with a serial number to get minutes. So maybe whoever had owned the phone had simply wanted basic communication, without all the frills and complications of a smartphone. And of course, it certainly didn't *look* old, but brand new, out of the package. So he supposed it was conceivable that, however the phone had come to be in one of the lockers, it had done so recently, and had some battery life remaining.

But now the screen was dead. He pressed the power button. Nothing happened. Maybe whatever spark of power had remained was gone?

Who was Mike and the woman asking for him?

Had this been Mike's phone? People switched numbers all the time and got new plans with a newly assigned number, and they often received wrong calls. Maybe that's what happened, here.

Shane shook his head and glanced up to see that Amanda was gone.

An irrational fear flooded his heart. Of course, she'd stepped into the classroom to examine whatever she'd found in there. Nothing to worry about. Still, she'd done it so quietly. He'd been occupied with the strange Nokia when she'd disappeared, which made him feel strangely responsible. As if she'd vanished when he should've been watching over her.

Gripping the now-dead Nokia in his hand, Shane walk-trotted down the hall toward the classroom Amanda had been standing near. He forced himself not to run, feeling his shoes threatening to slip on the glazed and polished ceramic tile floor. He knew it was stupid, she was only browsing used furniture for their new home, but by the time he reached the classroom his heart was hammering and he was breathing heavily, clutching the old Nokia so hard his knuckles ached.

He stopped at the classroom door, almost slipping again on the weirdly slick tile floor. He sighed in relief, seeing Amanda's red coat, seeing her standing there in the middle of the room, but his relief was cut short as an entirely *different* kind of fist clenched his heart. He opened his mouth to speak, to call out to Amanda, to say *anything*. Nothing came but a choked silence, his throat clogged with thick emotion. He felt, vividly, as if he'd been punched in the stomach.

There Amanda stood, back to him, rigid and

still, hands dangling at her sides, in the middle of the classroom, which didn't feature recliners, but cribs.

Baby cribs. Rows of them, lined up perfectly, as if with a square and compass. Another invisible punch to the gut: It looked like a ghostly, abandoned post-natal ward in a hospital, but filled with empty cribs bereft of infants never to be.

Amanda turned stiffly. He met her frozen gaze. Mouth working, but he couldn't speak. He groped for something, any words of comfort, but everything inside of him wilted in the face of the raging grief he saw blazing in her eyes.

"What . . . " she paused, looking slowly around her at the neatly ordered rows of empty baby cribs. "What the hell? What. The. *Hell*?"

The paralysis which had silenced him snapped. "Amanda. Listen. It's a furniture store. Right? A *used* furniture store. New parents are gonna be broke, right? So of course a used furniture store is going to have used baby cribs, because parents starting out will need quality used ones for cheap. Right?"

She ignored him, glancing around the room, eyes bright and wide, shining with unshed tears. "No," she rasped, pointing indiscriminately around the room at the cribs, as if they were to blame for her pain. "No. This is *wrong*, Shane. All kinds of wrong. What about- what about—"

Shane cocked his head, frowning slightly. "What?"

Amanda stopped pointing and squeezed her hand into a fist, her jaw clenched. He figured it was his imagination, but he imagined he could hear her teeth grinding together as she rasped, "All the babies. Who used to sleep in them. It's disrespectful, Shane, disrespectful to them."

She gasped.

Shut her eyes.

Grappled with her purse, digging through it frantically, and withdrew a pink inhaler. She stuck it into her mouth and triggered it, drawing in deep, wheezing breaths.

Shane stepped into the classroom-turned-showroom, hands up (exposing the old Nokia, he realized belatedly, but Amanda couldn't see because her eyes were still closed), in a gesture of peace, or submission, or surrender, he wasn't sure. "Amanda. Honey. Please. It's not . . . " his voice cracked. He swallowed and tried again. "It's not . . . "

Amanda took one last breath. Her chest eased. She removed the inhaler, dropped it back into her purse, opened her eyes and glared at him.

Shane felt as if time itself stopped. For a moment, he couldn't breathe, as if all the air had been sucked out of the room, and he almost felt like *he* needed an inhaler. He'd almost mentioned *it*, hadn't he? Had almost brought up That Which Should Not Be Talked About, Ever.

"No," Amanda muttered in a dull monotone, her rage fading as she shook her head in short, jerky sweeps. "No, no, no, *no.*"

She marched stiffly forward. Hands clenched into tight fists, swinging at her sides. Staring straight ahead, past Shane. She would've bumped shoulders with him if he hadn't sidestepped as she plunged out the door into the hallway.

"Amanda. Hey. Listen, I'm sorry. It's okay." He

started after her, ashamed he'd come close to mentioning *it*. Especially in the middle of such a freak thing as a room full of used baby cribs, lined up in such neat, orderly rows.

Amanda turned left, out of sight, down the hall.

The Nokia buzzed in his hand.

A kind of unreasoning anger surged in him. He had no cause to be angry at the person calling, searching for her husband or whatever, and Amanda walking out certainly wasn't the woman's fault. Also, why was he answering? He should ignore the call and go after Amanda. However, he figured maybe she needed some space, so instead he let his curiosity get the better of him, pressed *answer* and put the phone to his ear. "What?"

"*Mike! Oh, God-Mike, is that you?*"

"Listen, lady. I'm not your husband and I don't know where he is. I found this phone in a locker at this old furniture store outside Clifton Heights, in what used to be a school, and I have no idea how it got here, and my wife stormed off all pissed at me and is God knows where by now, so if you'll excuse me . . . "

A sharp intake of breath, the woman's voice vibrating with fear. "*You here. At Save-A-Bunch?*"

"Yes," Shane snapped, slightly ashamed at sounding so peevish, but mostly annoyed as he stepped for the door to track Amanda down. "My wife and I are moving to this little town called Eagle Bay because we're not doing well, and we're trying the whole 'change of scenery' deal so we can maybe save whatever's left of our marriage, but she stormed off because I said something stupid . . . "

almost talked about it

" . . . and I don't have time for . . . "

"Find your wife. Do it now. *Is she there? Can you see her? Don't let her wander off, for the love of God. Don't!"*

Though it irritated him more, something in the woman's tone unnerved him. He found himself striding toward the door in a quickened pace. "Listen, I know it's confusing to walk around in here, but c'mon. It's not like I'm gonna *lose* her."

He stepped out the door, glanced left, down the hall.

It was empty.

He saw nothing but the dark intersection ahead.

He stopped and stared, mouth hanging open. A white noise filled his head, and for several minutes, he couldn't manage a single thought.

"Wait. Where'd she go?"

"Oh God," the voice whispered over the Nokia. *"Oh God, it's too late. You'll never find her now, you'll never . . . "*

The Nokia hissed and crackled.

And died in Shane's hand.

Shane stared down the hall of receding recliners, dead cell phone pressed to his ear. For the first time since entering Save-A-Bunch, he became acutely aware of the silence. How it pressed in from all sides, making the air feel heavy.

"Amanda?"

His voice echoed harshly against the walls and ceramic tile floor, bouncing back to him. The fluorescent lighting—apparently the same from when the building had been a school—burned a harsh white which somehow didn't do much to dispel the shadows in the corners and ends of the halls, especially in the intersection ahead.

With a start, he realized he was still holding the dead Nokia to his ear. He lowered it and started walking toward the intersection, each step a little more urgent, his stride lengthening, pace increasing until he was nearly running, shoes clicking against the tile. In his head, the voice of the woman on the Nokia whispered.

you're at Save-A-Bunch?

Maybe it was an optical illusion produced by the sudden spike of adrenaline, maybe his mind was playing tricks on him, so suddenly consumed with such an unreasoning fear, but he felt as if he was standing still, the intersection ahead moving *away* from him.

find your wife
can you see her?
don't let her wander off!

A small part of Shane felt disgusted as he gave in and broke into a run, but as something icy and fearful crested inside him, he didn't care. How could this hallway be so long? How could she have gotten down it so quickly? Who the hell was this woman on the phone, and what did she mean?

don't let her wander off!

After what felt like forever—but also, somehow, bare minutes—he reached the intersection. Shane slid to a stop, slipping on the tile. He breathed in deep, fighting the urge to spin around wildly and scream Amanda's name. Instead he peered ahead, scanning the hallway stretching away from him. Like the bean bag hallway, this one ended in double doors leading outside. Presumably, anyway, because twenty feet into the hall, Shane saw ottomans and foot-stools stacked haphazardly to the ceiling.

To his left, a hallway led to another left turn. Along this hall (which had no lockers, thank God), were more lamp stands and nightstands, arranged neatly against the walls, and two classroom doors he assumed led to more showrooms.

To his right, bookshelves ranged the hall, pressed against the lockers.

thank God

And this hall ended in an orderly stack of boxed bookshelves reaching to the ceiling.

Shane stood still and closed his eyes for several seconds, trying to recall their progress to this point. For some reason, instinct told him he'd be wiser trying to retrace his steps to the front lobby rather than following Amanda in the only possible direction she could've gone after fleeing that weird room full of baby cribs.

not that

don't think about that

He tried to remember what they'd seen before the recliners, then had it: Another room full of nightstands. Right where he'd found the old Nokia. But they'd taken several turns between there and the hall of recliners. He opened his eyes, turned and looked down the hall of nightstands. Maybe, because of the nightstands, this hall looped around to where he'd found the Nokia? Or maybe . . .

His thoughts screeched to a halt.

There.

Something lying on the floor, in the doorway of the first classroom/showroom. A red strap to a purse.

Amanda's purse?

a trap

The thought surfaced from nowhere, a free-floating idea which popped when it hit the surface of his brain.

It was a trap. A more insidious version of the string-yanked dollar, or a Venus fly-trap, or an angler fish . . .

Venus fly-trap
angler fish

The last two metaphors stuck for some reason. A completely random memory came to him, of watching an Animal Planet documentary while making dinner (Amanda was sleeping off her pain and guilt, back in those dark and terrible days right after *it* happened), a documentary about animals and plants which used various tricks to lure prey. It was a ridiculous notion. This was a used furniture store in an old high school building, nothing more.

really?

where are the employees? sales people? stockers? other customers?

you're in Save-A-Bunch?

find your wife

don't let her wander off!

He stood, transfixed, staring at the red strap, thoughts and memories of the documentary on angler fish and Venus flytraps luring hapless victims into carnivorous, snapping jaws and Amanda muttering *no, no, no.*

Of their own volition, Shane's feet shuffled

forward, dragging his legs after him. He lurched, marionette-like, down the hall lined with lamp stands to the first classroom/showroom door. When he reached it, he turned and bent awkwardly.

A red leather purse.

Amanda's, he felt sure.

He reached trembling hands down and picked it up. It felt too light. Empty. Fearfully—not sure he wanted to—he opened the purse's main compartment. Nothing but emptiness yawned. Feeling panic stir in his guts, spreading icy, breathless tendrils out into his chest, Shane unzipped and unsnapped all the smaller compartments, rifling through them with shaking fingers, searching for a dollar, a paperclip, a scrap of paper, hell, one of her Tampons, anything which might indicate the purse belonged to her.

But he found nothing.

With an explosive sigh, Shane turned the bag over in his hands and shook it. Maybe it wasn't Amanda's purse after all. He remembered her saying the gym had been full of clothes, shoes, and accessories, with probably a whole *bin* of purses, so maybe some other customer picked this one up, then dropped it by accident.

what customers?

He couldn't remember seeing any.

The Nokia vibrated again.

In a daze, Shane answered. "Hello? What the *hell* is going on? Who is this?"

"Did you find your wife?"

"No." Shane held up the empty red leather purse which could be Amanda's or simply one a customer had dropped by accident. "I might've found her purse.

I mean, I *think* it's her purse, but it's empty." He turned the purse over and shook it out again halfheartedly, thinking maybe keys would fall out, or something.

"*I found Mike's wallet,*" the woman on the Nokia said. "*I found his wallet, but it was empty. No driver's license, credit cards, social security card. Nothing.*"

"And this was his phone?"

"*It's his number I'm calling. Is it a gray Nokia? Light green screen, black numbers?*"

Shane, still staring into the empty purse, nodded slowly. "That's the one. A little outdated. No offense."

"*Well, it's what he wanted, and . . .*"

clink

And Shane wasn't listening anymore, the woman's voice fading as he glanced to the floor and saw what lay at his feet, what had finally fallen out of the purse. Seeing it tightened his chest, because it confirmed, for him, anyway, this *was* Amanda's purse, and not one from a half-off bin.

Amanda's asthma inhaler.

Lying at his feet.

He squatted, reached down and picked it up with weak fingers. The Nokia had fallen silent. He kept it pressed against his ear anyway, but the hand holding the Nokia might as well not be attached, because his entire being was focused on the inhaler he turned over in his fingers.

Amanda's asthma had gotten worse since *it* happened. The stress, the guilt, the self-loathing, the low-level tension which had festered between them. All factors, Shane figured. However, he'd wondered increasingly over the past few months if Amanda's asthma was, in some weird way, self-inflicted. Maybe she was somehow making her asthma worse, because she felt deserving of it. Her reaction to the room full of crib's seemed to be evidence of that.

Shane slowly stood; his knees sore and achy, as if he'd aged ten years. The longer he stared at the inhaler in his hand, the sicker he became. Lightheaded, and woozy.

He closed his eyes.

Dropped the purse on the floor. Squeezed the inhaler once, then stuck it into his pocket. Amanda would need it when he found her.

When he found her.

Shane breathed in deeply and opened his eyes, for the first time seeing the classroom/showroom's contents.

Baby blankets.

Baby pillows.

Piled and folded on rows of tables. Pillows of all shapes and sizes, blankets of all colors and materials, linen to fuzzy. Baby blankets, at a used furniture store.

Rows of cribs.

The inhaler.

Piles of baby blankets and pillows. All different colors and kinds. Oddly enough, they looked like Benjamin's.

Shane turned slowly away from the mounds of pillows and blankets which reminded him of the ones his dead son had slept with, and walked out of the classroom, into the hall. Again, the heavy oppressive silence pressed down upon him.

He stood, motionless. Feeling nothing at all.

The Nokia vibrated.

He pressed answer and said in a dull monotone which sounded lifeless in his ears, "What is this, lady?"

"*I don't know. My husband—Mike—and I wandered off from each other hours ago. We were fighting. We've had troubles. Well, honestly, we're on the verge of divorce. Anyway, we were traveling through the Adirondacks and stopped at a diner in this little town called Clifton Heights.*"

"The Skylark," Shane murmured.

"*Yes! While we were there, we overheard someone talking about this unbelievable used and antique furniture store. We were trying to get away—trying to distance ourselves from what was dividing us—so we figured because we had a few hours left before closing, we should visit this furniture store.*"

Shane blinked. Something the woman said stirred the mental fog clouding his mind, but he couldn't put his finger on it. "Where is everyone? I mean, we didn't see anyone in the lobby and I figured the folks at the front desk where busy in the office. We didn't think twice about it."

"*I know! There's no one here! I mean, I know it's Friday, but when we called the front office from The Skylark, they said . . .*"

Realization struck him. "I'm stupid," he whispered, "stupid, stupid, stupid." Digging his hand into his coat pocket and pulling out his iPhone, he said to the woman, "The number. To the store. Do you have it on your phone? I can call the office, the front desk, tell them I'm lost, you're lost, that I'm searching for Amanda and you can't find your husband."

"*Yes. Let me check. 315-222-5555.*"

"Okay." Shane slid his thumb across the iPhone's screen, unlocking it. He tapped the phone app and started dialing. "Okay, hold on. I'm calling the store, the lobby, the main desk, whatever. Where are you? What, uh, stuff is on display?"

"*I'm near the auditorium. Or, at least, I think so,*" she whispered, sounding frightened.

"I think we passed it right after the lobby."

"*No.*" Her voice a low, harsh rasp. "*I already checked both ends of the hall outside it. It just leads to more and more halls.*"

"Okay, hang tight. I'll tell them you're by the auditorium," Shane reassured, purposefully not thinking about those blankets and pillows which all looked like Benjamin's, Amanda's purse, and the inhaler which fell out of it.

The number Shane had dialed started ringing. "It's ringing," he again reassured the woman on the Nokia, who had started to cry softly, sounding ready to break apart, "it's ringing right now."

The Nokia fell dead and silent, cutting off the woman mid-sob.

"Damn it," Shane whispered, but right then he heard someone pick up on his phone and say cheerily, "*Hello, you've reached Save-A-Bunch, the biggest, most comprehensive used and antique furniture warehouse in Webb County!*"

"Hello! Hey, listen—thank God. This is going to sound crazy, but my wife got upset at me and sorta stormed off and now I can't find her, she won't answer her phone, and this place is kinda crazy, y'know? I'm sorta lost. Kind of embarrassed to admit it but these hallways go on forever, and there's this lady who . . . "

" . . . *hours of operation are Monday through Friday, eight AM to ten PM, Saturday and Sunday* . . . "

Shane trailed off as the recorded voice droned on about the weekend hours, weekly deliveries to the store, special layaway deals, and using the website for its 3D virtual tour, including a full rendering of their weekly specials. Finally, the spiel ended, inviting him to leave a message at the sound of the beep, and someone would return his call as soon as possible.

BEEP.

A hissing silence.

"Uhm." Shane cleared his throat. "Yes. Uh. Anyone there? I . . . I need some help. I need . . . need . . . "

Hiss.

click

A dial tone in his ear.

Shane hung up. Dialed 911. Listened to two rings, then a harsh tone, a *click*, and the same dial tone, repeating in a numbing metronome.

Slowly, as if moving in a dream, Shane dialed Amanda's number again, figuring he'd get the same two-ring disconnect.

It rang.

Over and over.

Shane sucked in a deep breath, not expecting Amanda to answer, but hoping, *willing* it to happen.

He heard a soft warble. Muffled, but Shane heard it: Amanda's phone ringing somewhere nearby.

Frantic energy pulsed through him. Shane darted out of the classroom and into the hall. He stopped, listening. It wasn't ringing from the way he'd come.

He turned right and listened. Took a few steps in that direction, which confirmed it. He could hear

Amanda's phone ringing down the hall, somewhere around the blind turn to the left.

Shane ran that way, heart pounding in his chest. Amanda's phone kept ringing, which of course didn't make sense because it should've gone to voicemail by now, but he didn't care, didn't think about it. He registered the other classrooms in his peripheral vision as he passed. Shapes flickered, shadows, maybe, but he didn't stop . . .

because something was in those rooms
and wanted him to come in

. . . and he ran past them. He reached the end of the corridor and skidded around the corner, shoes sliding on the unusually slick cement tile floor, and he nearly careened into the opposite wall. He caught himself in time.

The ringing stopped.

His iPhone clicked over to hissing, then the same dial tone clanged in his ear.

He stood, panting, staring down an empty hall lined on both sides with freshly-painted, blood-red lockers as far as he could see. His eyes skittered over them initially, peering at the hall's distant end. He thought he saw double doors with push-bars, like the kind on gymnasiums or auditoriums, where the woman said she was. They were open. The gym or the auditorium. He thought for sure one of them was near the front lobby, and the woman on the Nokia said she was near the auditorium.

He had to get past the lockers, first. Two rows of lockers, with nothing holding them closed.

Even though her phone was no longer ringing, he could've sworn he'd heard Amanda's phone ringing somewhere down this hall. Sounding muffled. As if coming from inside something, from behind a door. A locker door.

Amanda's phone, ringing from inside a locker. The thought chilled him.

The Nokia vibrated in his hand.

He answered it and without preamble muttered, "I think it's in a locker."

"What? Were you able to get the store office? Did anyone answer?"

"I think it's in a locker," he repeated, completely ignoring her, "it's in one of these lockers, I think."

"What? I don't understand."

"Amanda's phone. It's not ringing anymore. It cut off soon as I rounded the corner, but I think maybe it was ringing in one of these lockers in this hall leading to the gymnasium or auditorium or whatever. In one of these lockers, where I found your husband's phone."

"What?"

"Y'know. Your husband's old Nokia Tracphone. Thing is heavy as a brick. Could knock someone out with one of these. And there's no internet on these damn things, if I remember right. Thing's gotta be at least seven or eight years old, maybe ten."

"But he bought it last week."

"It looks brand-new, out of the box yesterday. How do you explain that, Ma'am? How?"

"I-I don't know."

"You said something I didn't understand, but I didn't think about it much. Something about you deciding to come to Save-a-Bunch, even though it had 'gotten late'. What time did you come to Save-A-Bunch?"

The woman paused, and when she spoke, she sounded confused he'd ask such a question, as if the answer was completely obvious. "*It's Friday night. We were having a late dinner at The Skylark, and we decided to come out here anyway. It's Friday night, right before closing. I figured that's why there weren't any other customers around, being so close to closing.*"

Shane closed his eyes and breathed in deep, the wheels in his head turning.

"*Hello? Are you still there?*"

"It's Tuesday," he said softly, eyes still closed, hiding in the darkness there. "It's Tuesday afternoon. We had *lunch* at The Skylark. It can't be later than two or three in the afternoon."

"*But,*" the woman sputtered on the other end. "*That's not possible. It's night. Friday night. I know it is!*"

"Have you looked out the windows recently? Y'know, the funny thing is, I can't remember. I thought it was day, but I can't remember if the classrooms' windows were boarded up or not. And there aren't any windows here, and I sure as hell ain't going into any more of those classrooms to find out. So I can't tell you if it's night or day outside. Here's my big question: what's the year? What month is it? Do you know? Do you remember?"

"*What are you getting at? Month? Year? I don't understand.*"

"The hell you don't. What's. The fucking. Year?"

Silence.

For a moment, Shane thought the Nokia had died again. After several seconds passed, he heard a resigned sob. "*2006. It's May, 2006.*"

THINGS YOU NEED

Shane gazed down the hall lined on both sides by blood-red lockers; lockers which could open at any time. It was darker at the hall's end, the lights dim.

"It's 2017," he said, voice sounding amazingly steady and calm. "July 20th, 2017."

"*How can that be?*"

"I don't know. When Amanda and I woke up this morning, it was July 20th, 2017. We had lunch at The Skylark Diner, as I said. She'd found out about this place—where, I can't remember—because we're furnishing a new house in Eagle Bay. Trying to start a new life, right? A new start. Lunch went okay. As good as anything these days. Since Benjamin-our son-died. Before he was a year old. But things were okay today. Sorta. Then we got here. She tensed up a bit. Maybe because shopping here, searching for furniture for our new house, *away* from our old house, *Benjamin's* house, made it more real, y'know?"

On some level Shane knew he was babbling, but he sensed he had to, because he was nearing some kind of break. The woman hadn't said a word. He didn't know if she was still on the phone, but he kept going, regardless. "But we were okay. I guess. Managing. Not fighting, at least, but we never fought. Honestly? Sometimes I wish we would. Sometimes I think we *should* fight. Clear the air. Let it out. She was quiet, y'know? Ill at ease. But we were okay. Until I found your husband's damn phone in one of these lockers. Where I thought I heard Amanda's ringing, just now."

He ran out of words, feeling winded, as if he'd run a race. He listened, and for several seconds there was nothing until, "*Your son died?*"

Shane breathed in and held it. His heart ached.

After a stretch of silence, he rasped, "Yes. SIDS. Sudden Infant Death Syndrome. Died in his sleep. Taking a nap, for God's sake."

"*I'm sorry.*"

"He was at the sitter's," Shane said, reciting a rehearsed spiel imprinted on his brain. "Amanda and I took the day off work and went on a short day trip. Some time for ourselves, right? Benjamin hadn't been sleeping well at night. Colicky. Doctors thought maybe that's why he died. Undiagnosed breathing problems. Anyway, we needed some time for us. We came home after a road trip to Ithaca, the sitter said the day was great, Benjamin active all morning, happy, now taking an extra-long nap. I saw it in Amanda's eyes, right then. She knew. He never took long naps, even if he'd been up the whole night before. She found him face down. Must've rolled over in his sleep. She wouldn't touch him. I had to turn him over. He was still a little warm. But his face was like a mask. His lips a little blue. Always looks like makeup on TV, y'know? Not real. This was different."

"*I'm sorry. Michael and I were doing the same. Starting over, I mean. We were moving to Old Forge, from Utica.*" She paused, sounding oddly embarrassed, considering their bizarre situation. "*I don't want to go into all the details. But we'd both been unfaithful. This was our last chance, I suppose. To move away from everything, patch things up and start fresh. But we argued all the time. It wasn't working. When we got here, we argued over something stupid, like the color of a couch. He stormed off. Said he was leaving, I could come or not, he didn't care. I tried to follow, but I got lost on the first turn. That was hours ago. I've been searching and I can't find anyone, and the rooms where they display furniture, I don't want to go in them. I don't know why. I just don't."*

She couldn't finish and broke down into sobs, but Shane didn't need her to finish. Somehow, he could guess what she was trying to say.

"I wonder where your husband is," Shane murmured. "I found his cell in a locker. Where is he?"

A sniff. *"Maybe he dropped it."*

"But who put it there? That's what I couldn't figure out when I picked this damn thing up. Wish to God I never had. Who knows? Maybe that's what started everything. Hell. Maybe in a few years, someone will find *my* phone or Amanda's or yours in one of these lockers, pick it up, and get lost. Maybe they'll be folks trying to start over like us, too, but they'll get lost instead."

"Is that why we're here? Why this is happening? Because we're lost?"

Such a wonderful, pat little solution. A nice Twilight Zone-twist, the kind which wouldn't make any sense in any other context. It made Shane think in strange, new ways. How many people got lost over the years searching for direction and purpose? How many eventually threw up their hands and walked away or slammed their phones down, or shut their cell-phones off? Dropped off social media, or, even more drastic, pulled their car to the curb, got out and walked away into the mists, leaving their car running? How many folks every year did any of these things, and then disappeared? Never to be heard from again.

What if someone simply gave up, or simply couldn't take any more and *wanted* to get lost?

The next leap, of course, was simple. Her husband's phone, discarded in a locker. Amanda's phone, also in a locker?

The wheels in Shane's head turned. After standing in one place for so long, he took a tentative step into the hallway. And then another. Followed by another, until he walked slowly and steadily down the hall toward its end, past both rows of lockers, with nothing holding them closed.

nothing holding back the things inside

"Hello? Are you still there?"

Shane walked slightly quicker, now. "I am. And it makes sense, because here's another thought. I don't know where your husband is, or where Amanda is. But we're still here, searching. Why?"

"Because we're lost," the woman said in a plaintive, little-girl voice.

Shane walked faster. Oddly, something akin to excitement mounted inside him. "But maybe we don't want to be. Honestly. Who fought harder to save your marriage? You or your husband?"

Silence.

Shane imagined he could *feel* her reluctance through the phone, until she whispered, *"Me. He agreed to try, but I had to beg him, and I think he only agreed because he thought it would make things easier on him in our eventual divorce, because it would seem like he 'tried.'"*

A tremulous hope blossomed in Shane's chest, along with something sharp and bitter as the end of the hall got nearer. A strange mixture, indeed. "Amanda never said anything out loud. Not in so many words. But I don't think she wanted to move on."

He realized dimly he'd referred to Amanda in the past tense, but he kept talking, moving forward. "For a while I thought she didn't love me anymore. I still wonder, honestly. Struggle with it. Who knows, maybe she doesn't—maybe she has stopped loving me. Maybe the only reason she's stayed with me is because she can't move on. Benjamin's death *stopped* her. I think she felt it was our fault. For going away and taking some time for ourselves. She mentioned once, after—in a causal, off-hand way—she'd never thought to have Ben checked for infant asthma. It's rare to be found in someone so young, but I guess it happens. So I wonder. Maybe she doesn't want to find her way. Or can't. I don't know. Maybe that's why your husband and my wife got lost. Because they *didn't* want to find their way out."

"But why did you find my husband's phone in a locker? Why do you think your wife's phone might be in one?"

"I don't know," Shane admitted, walking faster, trying to reach the hallway's end, which suddenly appeared miles away. "Sounds crazy, I know, but ever since I walked into this place I've thought that something is *in* the lockers. In so many of the halls the furniture's pushed back against the lockers. To keep them closed. Or to keep something inside. Again, commit me to the nuthouse, but I think those lockers can open. Maybe for the right people. People who are lost, and don't want to find their way home. And you know what? Maybe I wasn't sure until now. Maybe I needed this to convince me. I loved Ben dearly, and it *kills* me he's dead. It *kills* me he died while we took a day off for ourselves. I know it's not our fault, but I still kinda blame us. Blame myself for convincing Amanda it'd be good for us to get away. I love Amanda and I'm going to do my damnedest to find her, and pull her out of this place. But—"

He paused.

Drew in a deep breath, and exhaled, "I don't want to be lost anymore. I want to get out of here, *now*."

As the words left his mouth, Shane experienced a strange optical illusion. As he'd walked down the hall, the end had appeared further and further away, as if the hall was made of taffy, and someone was stretching it. But the instant the word "now" left his lips, it felt as if the hallway snapped back. He found himself standing at the end of the hall, the lockers behind him.

To his left were closed double doors, chained and padlocked shut. What little he could see through the rectangular windows appeared abandoned, unused and cluttered with debris. An unused wing of the store, perhaps.

is *this a store?*

To his right, a hall lined with coffee tables, all of them, mercifully, pressed back against the lockers. Before him were open double doors leading to the auditorium.

The auditorium.

Where the lady said she was near. "Hey—you still there?"

"*Yes,*" the woman whispered, sounding faint.

"Okay. I have no idea what the hell this is. How you're here in 2006, and I'm here ten years later. But I want out. I'm not leaving without trying to find Amanda, but I want *out*."

Again, maybe it was his imagination, but at the

word "out" he thought the walls, floor and doors ahead of him shimmered, momentarily as insubstantial as a desert mirage.

"I don't know. I need to find Michael. He's here somewhere, I know it."

"Listen. You're near the auditorium, right? I'm on the other side. There's a hall here full of kitchen tables and coffee tables, but I'm done with these halls. I'm cutting through the auditorium, and I'm coming to you."

"No!" The woman's voice spiked in hysterical panic. *"Don't go in there! I've heard things moving in there!"*

"Sorry, lady," Shane said as he stepped into the auditorium, "I'm coming through."

He entered the auditorium. On cue, the Nokia fell silent. He stuffed it into his pocket and took another step forward, but froze before his next, arrested by the sight. "Oh, shit. You've *got* to be kidding me."

Mattresses.

Stacked higher than him, in maze-like rows. Because the auditorium's floor curved slightly downward, and he was essentially standing uphill, he could see just above the mattresses, rows and rows of them, running the width and length of the auditorium. The other doors were directly opposite, which meant he'd have to wind his way through the rows of mattresses to reach them.

I've heard things moving in there!

He shook his head and slowly descended the slope. Directly before him rose a wall of mattresses. He could only go right or left, and who knew which end left space to get around?

"It doesn't want me to leave," Shane whispered. "Son of a bitch. It doesn't want me to leave."

Again, he thought of Venus flytraps and angler fish.

His iPhone warbled.

He pulled it out of his pocket, swiped his thumb across it and saw the number flashing on the screen.

Amanda.

He stared at it, waves of despair and loneliness washing over him. He couldn't leave here without trying to save Amanda. Everything he'd said about wanting to get out, about Amanda not being able to move on didn't matter. Maybe she was still here somewhere. Hiding. Alone. Afraid. Or maybe wandering and confused.

How could he leave her?

How dare he? He needed to find her. Needed to rescue her, if he could. He could heal her, he knew it, if he could find her, get her to listen, to *think*. Maybe she was calling him, right now.

she's gone

you can't get her back

Bullshit.

His thumb hovered over the answer button, mind weighing options, theories, concepts, thoughts which didn't make sense but still were, anyway. When he'd tried to call Amanda's phone before he thought—though he wasn't sure—he'd heard it ring in one of the lockers in the hall behind him. Which meant wherever she was now—alone, dead, or other—she didn't have her phone.

But *had* it been Amanda's phone, ringing in a locker?

Was this her, now?

Again, the image came to him of a Venus flytrap, along with the realization he'd been standing and staring at his ringing phone, not moving, doing nothing. He remembered another bit from the Animal Planet show, about Venus flytraps stunning their prey with nerve toxins, paralyzing them.

Like he was paralyzed, now.

this place doesn't want me to leave

He thumbed *reject call*. Turned his phone off and stuck it into his pocket, oddly enough, keeping the Nokia out, clenched in his other hand. He descended the sloping floor into the auditorium, to stand before the first wall of mattresses.

The stacks reached about six or seven feet, each mattresses varying in thickness. Each mattress was also affixed with a tag, on which, in neatly printed script, was listed the price and the brand. Each tag was also annotated as either 'new', 'hardly used', or 'used'. The tags themselves more than anything else made the whole situation feel surreal. So utterly prosaic. Mundane. Normal. Neatly printed letters and numbers. Shane wondered, as he walked in either direction, if the neatly hand-printed sales tags would slowly morph into insidious messages of evil and malice, made all the more horrible by their impeccable print.

He glanced to his left. The wall of mattresses extended, so far as he could tell, all the way to the auditorium's wall. He couldn't tell if there was space at the end to slip through to the next row. To the right, same dilemma. He assumed there *must* be space somewhere, to allow customers . . .

what customers?

173

have you seen any?

. . . to walk through this gargantuan maze and peruse all the other mattresses. How would they browse all the mattresses otherwise?

He actually smiled. In the face of the impossibility of what was happening, here he was, wondering about the ineffectual shopping layout of the mattress section at Save-A-Bunch. He shook his head, but a horrible thought occurred to him. What if Amanda and this Mike thought they were still *shopping*? Whatever this was—hell, purgatory, some weird-ass Twilight Zone alternate dimension—what if that lady's husband and Amanda and who knows how many others were stuck in some sort of loop, endlessly browsing, endlessly shopping? Amanda, browsing the store, searching for furniture for their new home, for an eternity. Complaining to herself about the layout, the lack of service, these aren't real deals, where the hell did Shane wander off to? Because deep inside, she didn't want to leave. She didn't want to be found. She wanted to stay lost, and the store was more than happy to oblige.

Shane took a deep breath. Turned left, turned right, muttered, "Hell with it," and started walking right.

Shane was about halfway through the rows of mattresses—there were openings on opposite ends, the paths so far running back and forth, zig-zagging—when he rounded a corner and saw, about halfway down the walkway, a wall of mattresses, and an opening to the right, making the arrangement even more maze-like.

"Oh, c'mon," he whispered, a sick feeling curdling his guts. Inexplicably, the rows, which until this point had followed some sort of order, were now going to feature random turns in the middle of the rows.

this place doesn't want me to leave

"Screw this," he muttered, turning around. "There's gotta be another way out of this."

Mattresses.

Stacked above his head.

Blocking the way he'd come.

"No," he muttered, fighting down a cresting fear which threatened to drown his newfound resolve. "No, no, no. This is *not* happening."

A sound.

Fabric stretching.

Hands, or fingernails, scraping across fabric.

A ripple passed lengthwise along the mattresses barring his way, at eye level, along with the same stretching-fabric sound.

In the midst of his rising fear, a strange fascination nudged him forward. He approached the wall of mattresses . . .

which hadn't been there before

. . . peering at them. Oddly, they appeared less rectangular and more oblong, swollen, a pile of cocoons, or eggs.

Another ripple, along with the sound. Against his will, he took another step closer, part of his mind screaming to run, because he *knew* what was going to happen next. The rippling mattress bulged outward. He could see them clearly: Four fingertips and a thumb, pressing against the mattress's fabric, reaching, grasping from the inside.

like the things inside the lockers

Something larger bulged next to the hand, with the suggestion of a nose and a gaping mouth, opened wide in a silent scream.

Shane turned and sprinted, but skidded to a stop. He'd forgotten how the path had changed angles in the middle of the row, and he'd nearly slammed into a wall of rippling, squirming mattresses bulging with reaching hands and gaping mouths. He turned right, dashed into the next aisle, looked both ways, and saw to his left a wall of mattresses a few feet away—also now shaking and rippling—and to his right the aisle extended all the way to the auditorium's far wall.

He plunged ahead and ran, eyes forward, trying to ignore the flickers of white grasping things on either side of him, faces pressing against fabric, silently screaming. He reached the end of the aisle. Sure enough there was space to pass to the next. He turned left but was going too fast and his left foot slipped out from under him and down he went, hard on his back. He threw his arms out to break the fall but couldn't quite catch himself before the back of his head cracked against the floor.

Pain and intense pressure clamped his head in a cruel vise. His hands flew to the sides of his head— oddly enough, the right hand still clutching the old Nokia—and squeezed, as if he could press the pain away. He felt dizzy, his head was pounding and his breath roared in his ears.

Something cold gripped his ankle.

Shane screamed and kicked out. The hold immediately released. Chest heaving, on the edge of full-blown panic, Shane forced himself to scramble upright onto his feet, throwing up his hands to ward off whatever was coming at him.

Nothing.

He stood, hands straight out, breathing heavily, staring at rows of mattresses stacked evenly and neatly, appearing utterly mundane, not threatening at all. No rippling beneath the fabric, no hands pressing through, no impressions of silently screaming mouths. Nothing.

His hands dropped loosely to his sides, his right hand still, after everything, clutching the old Nokia. He rubbed his face with his left hand. Pinched the bridge of his nose and closed his eyes. Had he seen those hands and silently screaming faces? Felt a cold hand—clothed in fabric—clutch his ankle? Or was this place working on him, as it had obviously worked on that lady, as it must've worked on Amanda.

Making her run in terror, and not answering his calls.

neurotoxins

paralyzing

The Nokia buzzed again, interrupting his jumbled thoughts, which he didn't mind at all. Of course, it was curious and strange, how it kept ringing at these moments, or switching off right when he needed answers. Normal reasons for this offered themselves. Maybe the dying battery kept sending surges of charge through the phone, switching it on. Old phones did that. It sounded logical enough.

He kept thinking, more and more, about who this lady was, and how, for some reason, he hadn't thought to ask for her name.

He pressed *answer* and raised the Nokia to his ear.

"Hello? Are you there?"

"Yeah," he said, trying in vain not to sound breathless and scared. "I made it through the auditorium, about to come out the other side. You're near the auditorium, right?"

A pause, and then, her voice—or the connection, Shane couldn't tell—sounded scratchy. *"I think so. It's not the gym, I don't think. We passed that before Mike ran off. It was full of clothes, I think."*

"All right," Shane said as he neared the auditorium's other set of doors, closed at the moment. "I'm on my way to you. Hang tight."

"What was in there? I almost went in once, but as I said, I heard things moving in there. Something sliding."

Shane pressed down the push-bar on the auditorium door, not thinking about hands grasping from inside mattresses and those gaping, silently screaming mouths. "Nothing. Stacks of mattresses, arranged in a maze. A little creepy is all." The door swung open and he stepped out of the auditorium. "Okay. I'm here, I'm—"

Shane came to a halt, his words dying in his throat as he stared down a hallway lined with blood-red lockers on both sides.

The hall he'd left when entering the auditorium.

"No. Wait. What the hell *is* this? Are there lockers where you are?"

"No, I told you. End tables and nightstands. I stayed in this hall because there were no lockers."

Shane turned to the doors behind him, leading back into the auditorium. They looked exactly like the ones he'd entered, but that didn't mean anything, did it? They'd be uniform, and would be the same.

He faced the hall ahead. So far as he could tell, it was the same hall. Same lockers, with nothing holding them closed. Of course, all the lockers in a high school were going to look the same, especially as all the lockers he'd seen so far had been painted the same bright red. This wasn't the same hall. It couldn't be. Was a trick of the eye.

If he walked down that hall again at a brisk, breathless pace, past those lockers . . .

with nothing holding them closed

. . . when he got to the end and turned right, would he see rows of lamp stands lining the hall, proving he'd somehow ended up right back where he'd been before entering the auditorium? Or would it be full of some different kind of furniture, or more *lockers*, with nothing pressed against them to keep them closed?

Shane again closed his eyes.

Breathed deep. Fighting for control. Quietly, on the edge of hysteria, he rasped into the Nokia, "What's happening.? I'm back to the same place I was before."

"That's why I stayed put. After Mike ran off I didn't follow. I think things move around. *I know it sounds crazy, but not any crazier than anything else, and I think things move around to confuse you, make you get lost."*

On any normal day, or *any* other day, Shane would've taken such a sentiment as signs of encroaching dementia. Now, however?

Some part of his rational mind (albeit, a rapidly shrinking part) fought back. No. He was *not* standing in the same hallway. It only seemed like the one he left. In fact, when he glanced left, down the hall he'd tried to avoid by cutting through the auditorium, he'd see something completely different than lockers.

He turned.

It seemed like the same hall (but of course, the halls all looked the same) except, instead of coffee and kitchen tables, he saw chests. Wooden chests. Chests of all shapes and sizes. Vanity chests. Toy chests.

He felt his stomach drop.

Hope chests.

"Oh, God," he whispered, the words slipping out of him. "Oh my God, no."

"What is it? What do you see?"

The Nokia cut out again.

It didn't matter, because Shane had stopped listening. He stared at the chests, lined up neatly alongside both walls, stretching away to the next turn. He knew if he kept going what he'd find. Despite the quicksilver fear pulsing through his veins, Shane took a hesitant step down the hall.

As with all the other pieces of furniture he'd seen, the chests were lined up neat and square on both sides of the hall. Of slightly different sizes and shapes, Shane had to beat back the image of infant coffins. They were *trunks*, for God's sake. Clothing trunks. Moving trunks, a few of them old Army footlockers, toy chests.

Hope chests.

He kept walking, clutching the Nokia, glancing back and forth between the rows of chests on either side of him. All different sizes, shapes and colors. Old polished cherry, with thick, black metal hinges and latches. Sandalwood, with bright, polished brass trim. A few simple trunks constructed of blond-wood and plywood, probably.

coffins

Toy chests, with simple brass hinges and latches. A green footlocker with faded white numbers stenciled on one end. Another cherry wood chest, this one duller, the hinges tinged with rust. A bright red toy box with white trim.

The one next to the red toy box. Another simple blond-wood chest, with brass hinges and latches. Stenciled on the top of the chest, in bright blue: *Benjamin.*

Shane fell still.

Everything which had happened—even those grasping hands and silently screaming mouths—faded and became unimportant. The hope chest before him, so simple and plain, yet lovingly restored and stained by Amanda early in the pregnancy, was the most impossible thing of all.

"Another Benjamin," he whispered. "Some other Benjamin, from some other family. Not *my* Benjamin. Not *our* boy. Couldn't be, it couldn't be."

His iPhone warbled.

Slowly, numbly, in a dream, Shane slipped his hand into his pocket and pulled it out, not even wondering how it could be ringing, when he'd turned it off before going into the auditorium. He swiped his thumb across the screen, tapped "answer" and, without speaking, held it up to his ear.

Silence.

Shifting.

Whispering.

A slight breath. A sigh, maybe. A *click.* Dead air. Then, the rapid metronome of a severed connection.

Shane canceled the call. Glanced at the screen, saw:

Call ended. Amanda. Pressed the green phone icon to call the number right back. He stood and listened to the call ring, staring at the hope chest with *Benjamin* stenciled on its top, gripped by the conflicting certainty Amanda wouldn't pick up and the fear something *would.*

A ring. Muffled, distant. Shane gazed at the trunk marked *Benjamin*, heart in his throat, as he heard a phone ringing from inside. For several minutes Shane stood there, staring at the hope chest, mesmerized by the weird echo of Amanda's cell ringing in his ear and hearing *something* ring a half-second later inside the trunk.

Amanda's line kept ringing on the other end (which didn't make sense; where was her voicemail?)

Something kept ringing in the trunk.

Ringing.

Shane put the Nokia in his pocket and bent over slowly, reaching for the trunk's clasp, fingers flexing.

Something *clicked* in his ear.

Someone had picked up.

Whatever had been ringing in the trunk fell silent.

Shane stood there. Hand poised above the trunk's latch, other hand pressing his iPhone to his ear, listening to the silence on the other end.

Breathing.

Slight rasping. Someone . . .

something

. . . breathing.

Shane's outstretched hand shook. What would he find inside? All the things Amanda had collected throughout the pregnancy? Pillows and blankets . . .

like the ones which killed him

. . . little onesies and booties, the little baseball player's uniform and the train conductor's outfit? Or the things she'd collected during his first months, in anticipation of his future? Toys and trinkets for when he was older. Matchbox cars and trucks, a Gyroscope, a microscope kit. The small boxed set of Hardy Boys novels or Shane's contribution, a collection of *Choose Your Own Adventure* novels and a crystal radio electricity set.

Would those things be inside? If not, what else? Was this Amanda's phone he was listening to? What was on the other end, right now?

Silence.

Or.

Breathing. Whispering screams, like those silently gaping mouths pressing out from the egg-sac mattresses.

Shane clenched his fingers into a fist. Squeezed it so hard, his arm shook. *Something* on the other end gathered, a sound whispering closer, rushing near.

He thumbed his iPhone off and stumbled back from the trunk. He stared at it for several seconds, fully expecting in some deep, animal part of him that the lid would fly open and *something* would reach out, or something would start thrashing around inside, making the trunk rock and jitter . . .

because it was the right size
Benjamin would fit in there
wouldn't he?

. . . and for a heart-twisting moment he flinched, thinking he'd seen the trunk shiver. He rubbed his eyes, surprised and shaken to find them wet, as if he'd been crying, but no, sweat must be running into his eyes—but the longer he stared at the trunk, he realized it hadn't moved at all.

Still, he felt some presence looming. Something rushing toward him from a deep and dark place. He wondered, had he stayed on his phone a second longer, if he would've heard something speak. He felt it, now. Something rushing toward him up a long, dark tunnel; up from the depths, up to him in the light. If he stayed for one more moment, it would reach him.

Shane straightened, turned on his heel and walked hurriedly down the hall. He had to wipe his damn eyes again with the back of his hand—they were wet and stinging with sweat, and he was huffing because of the adrenaline rush, not sobbing—so he didn't glance either to his right or left as he neared the hall's end. He was still plagued by flickering illusions of the trunks' lids peeking open and something inside them— things somehow part of one *big* thing—watching him as he walked by. As he neared the hall's end, the trunks got smaller, more and more like infant coffins.

The Nokia vibrated in his pocket. He put his iPhone away, pulled out the Nokia and said, "Hello?"

"Where are you? I thought you were on the way."

"Lady," Shane said, his temper and sanity held together by bare threads. "I'm not sure I can get to you. Don't think this place will let me. Think you better start trying to find your own way out."

"*No,*" she rasped, voice suddenly angry and determined. Angry, Shane thought, at him. "*No. I'm not leaving here without my husband.*"

The long hall ahead—somehow, in his blind flight from the rows of hope chests, he'd stumbled through another intersection—stretched out forever, with no lockers or furniture. Shane was walking now, not running, taking his time, as if he had forever. Which maybe he had, because whatever was happening here, time apparently had no meaning.

"Look," he said, forcing a steady voice. "I don't want to leave here without Amanda either. I'm going to do my damnedest to find her and pull her out with me. And I know you want to find your husband. But I found his phone in a locker, and Amanda's phone? First I thought it was ringing in a locker too. Just now, I maybe heard it ringing in a hope chest exactly like Benjamin's. And I think *something* answered my call, but I don't think it was Amanda. Something wanted me to open that chest."

"*Someone put them there,*" she said flatly. "*My husband and your wife have been taken, and their phones put there, and they're trapped here, waiting for us to find them.*"

"No offense, but your husband doesn't sound like the waiting kind. And honestly, in her own way, Amanda isn't either. Both of them are runners. *We're* the ones waiting," he said slowly, "because isn't that what we're always doing? Waiting for things to get better? Waiting for them to come around? They're the runners, and we're the waiters. It's how this place works, I think. Whatever it is. It lures away or chases away the runners, and then tries to paralyze the waiters, keep them in one spot. And here's something else. I think—don't take this the wrong way—but I think what's gonna happen to you has already happened. I don't know how this is possible, but for *me* it's 2016. So I think whatever ultimately happens for you happened ten years ago. Right now, I don't

185

think I can help you, or find you. If I was meant to, if I could help you in some way, I would've found my way through the auditorium to you, instead of being looped right back to where I'd started. So I think we're on our own. I'm sorry. I can't help you."

"*Wait. Wait!*" The lady's voice shrilled, sounding high-pitched, frantic. "*Please. I have to find my husband. You have to find your wife. You can't* leave!"

"Actually, yes I can. I want to bring Amanda with me, I love her more than you can know, and I don't want to leave her here, but maybe she can't come with me. Maybe she can't let go. And as awful as this sounds, I *want* to let go. Have to. *Need* to. And I want to get the hell out of here."

Silence. A fumbling sound, as the phone shifting against an ear, and then a sob. "*I want to find my husband.*"

"Yeah. So you keep saying," Shane said slowly, realization picking at his brain. "In fact, you say it a lot. Like it's the only thing you *can* say. Hey, here's something I've been wondering. What's your name, lady? Y'know, it's crazy, but I haven't thought to ask for your name this whole time. Weird, don't you think?"

"*It's just so confusing, everything that's happening, I don't know where my husband is, and I don't know where I am!*"

"I don't mean to be rude, lady, considering the circumstances, but what's your name? Can you tell me?"

More silence.

"You know what's also interesting? You first called me right when Amanda walked away. Then you called me again, and while I was talking to you, I *lost* her. While I was distracted by your call, she disappeared."

A throat cleared, and then, hesitantly, *"I-I'm not, I can't—"*

"Also, why was *I* the one who thought of calling the store's office? I mean, it didn't do any good, but you had the number. Why didn't *you* try to call?"

"I-I tried, I mean, there was no answer, no . . . "

"Are you even a person?" God, it sounded crazy, something a paranoid schizophrenic would conjure up. "Is this the *store* I'm talking to? This whole time I've been thinking about a special I saw on Animal Planet about plants and animals which survive by luring other animals into their waiting jaws. Like the Venus fly trap, or the angler fish. Is that what you are, lady? The lure? If you're a real person—or better yet, some weird consciousness which *used* to be a real person—you and your husband came here to buy furniture for your new house, in an attempt to save your marriage. *If* you're real. Amanda and I were doing the same thing, only because we lost our baby boy, and were losing ourselves.

"How many? How many couples have come here, and never left? Y'know . . . I don't even remember how we heard about this place."

"The diner," the lady who maybe wasn't a lady at all whispered, sounding far away and not interested anymore at all. *"We overheard someone at the diner talking about it. The Skylark."*

"Amanda got an email, or something. A Tweet. A Facebook message. I don't know. From whom or *what*, I also don't know. Maybe *this* place. Maybe there's a Facebook page for Save-A-Bunch. Amanda 'liked' it, and then she got a message about a sale. Maybe that's how it works."

More silence. Another fumbling sound, and then, a strange sound.

A dull bang.

Against metal.

As if the lady on the other end of the Nokia was calling from inside a—

"*Please. I need to find my husband. Can you help me,* please? *If I could only find him!*"

Shane hit *end*, cutting the call. He stared at the dead Nokia for several seconds, and before the lady or the store or whatever could call him again, he dropped it to the floor, where it fell and clattered with a plastic rattle. As he walked away, he heard its buzz amplified against smooth ceramic tile.

Shane had no idea how long or how far he'd walked since tossing the Nokia aside. He'd taken several left and right hand turns, walking slowly down halls filled with odder and odder mixes of old chairs, recliners, sofas, end tables, lamps, bookshelves, and dining room tables. They were in rougher condition than the other pieces he'd seen, more befitting a Salvation Army or Thrift Store than an antique furniture store. Also, they'd been arranged in a more haphazard fashion, shoved against each other and the lockers . . .

thank God

. . . crookedly, jutting out into the walkway, in some cases tipped sideways, stacked upon each other in tumbleweed fashion, as if they'd been dumped there carelessly by bored workers.

188

As he walked, he saw more open classrooms. From his peripheral, he sensed they lay in similar disarray as the halls, not like the meticulously arranged showrooms he'd seen before. He also again sensed shadows flickering in those rooms, dancing among the jumbled piles of old furniture, but he refused to look at them, somehow resisting the temptation to see them for what they were.

He told himself maybe he'd wandered into a storage wing of the store. These old pieces of furniture were all donations not meant for show or active display, but had been stored back here rummage-sale style. A deeper part of his mind whispered otherwise, however. He'd wandered to a part of the store which was dead. A place where the "glamour" making it so attractive had long since faded. He refused to look at the jumbled piles of furniture directly. Quick, sidelong glances caught layers of dust, cobwebs, jagged ends of broken table legs, and ripped fabric spilling white, puffy innards. Maybe he was finally seeing the store as it was: A graveyard for broken and discarded things. Like the woman on the Nokia (if she'd been a woman at all) and her husband. Like maybe countless other couples.

Like him and Amanda.

This, more than anything else, made him believe everything which had happened to him, despite its surreal, nightmarish quality. This was a cast-off place for broken and used-up things, disguising itself—how, Shane couldn't fathom—in order to lure discarded and broken people desperate for a new future, trapping them inside, maybe forever, if the woman on the Nokia *had* been a person trapped here since 2006, and not part of the glamour.

How, then, was he getting out?

Could he?

He slowed to a stop. Shoved both hands into his pockets, bowed his head, closed his eyes, and thought.

A place for broken and discarded things. What he and Amanda were. No matter what he'd tried, he'd been held at arm's length since Benjamin died. Amanda had been by turns cold, distant, dismissive, passive, empty, and withdrawn. Not crying or raging. Not angry, vengeful, hysterical or depressed.

Dead.

Cut off.

Broken.

He, of course, had felt the same. All his grand gestures—gifts, helping around the house, surprise visits to her favorite restaurants—had felt forced and empty because they were gestures, after all. Reflexes. The things you're supposed to do to support and comfort your loved one.

Still, he'd always loved her. Didn't want to be without her. Therein, of course, lay the problem. He loved her and didn't want to leave here without her. She didn't love him anymore but she couldn't leave him, because then she'd be more lost than she already was.

He didn't want to leave her.

She couldn't leave him.

"But I *could* leave her," he whispered, pain twisting his stomach into broken glass shards, "I don't want to. But I *could*."

A kind of numb peace filled him. Shane breathed deep, opened his eyes and looked up. Where there had been nothing but an infinitely long stretch of hallway cluttered with old and broken furniture ahead now stood two double-doors with push-bars, like the kind which had led to the auditorium filled with stacks of mattresses.

These doors seemed different, however. He couldn't say how. Somehow he knew these doors didn't lead to the auditorium, but somewhere else, perhaps.

The gymnasium.

A strange, quiet determination thrummed through Shane. Pulling his hands from his pockets, he flexed his fingers and approached the gymnasium doors. Grabbed a push-bar, pressed down, pushed the door open, and walked inside.

For a moment, Shane couldn't tell what he was looking at. A wall of different colors and kinds of fabric. After a moment, his eyes adjusted and he understood: Racks upon racks of hanging clothes. Shirts, jackets, slacks, dresses, suits, jeans, overcoats, skirts, sweaters. All kinds of clothes indiscriminately arranged on racks filling the gymnasium. The racks were pressed so close together all the articles of clothing formed one surging entity. They stood abnormally high, clothes hanging slightly above eye level. Walking through would be worse than the mattress maze; it'd be like navigating rows of corn. Shane's increasingly flexible mind wondered if, inside this sea of clothing, it would indeed be possible to wander around for miles and never find his way out.

On a hunch, Shane pulled his iPhone out, swiped the screen, pulled up "contacts" and tapped a thumbnail of Amanda, hair windblown, smiling, from a much happier day long ago. Though he'd heard her cell—or, at least, *a* cell—ringing in the hope chest and maybe ringing in a locker, he had an idea.

It rang, twice.

Distantly, he heard a muffled *ring* in the sea of clothes. Then, the phone clicked and he heard Amanda's stiff voice, the one he'd heard every single day since Benjamin died. *"What do you want? Please don't tell me you're lost, Shane. I'm not in the mood."*

Shane stood at the edge of the clothing racks as a man standing on the shore of an endless sea. He didn't doubt he was speaking to Amanda, however. He recognized the flat tenor of her voice, devoid of spirit, all too well.

I love her

no matter what

"Shane, are you there? You've already called and hung up twice, trying to spook or prank me or whatever. I'm seriously not in the moods. Are you going to help me or not?"

He loved her.

He would try to help her, but not how she meant. He was going after her, even if it meant maybe drowning in the process.

"Sure," he said, doing his best to sound casual and affable as he moved forward, "be there in a sec."

He reached out, parted the clothes and stepped into a fabric sea, dresses and coats swishing closed behind him.

As Shane made his way blindly through hanging dresses, coats, suits and jeans, something whispered among the clothes. He wasn't sure what—clothes rustling as he passed through, or maybe (an unnerving thought) clothes rustling as countless others passed through, all wandering, alone and lost in this sea of clothes, cut off from each other, ignorant of each other, also. Or maybe it was the store whispering, or echoes of all the other lost people talking on their cells about meaningless trivia while they wandered away from everything.

"So like you Shane, to wander off. I swear, I . . . "

" . . . can't take me anywhere," Shane finished as he wound his way through stands of coats and shirts, smiling in spite of the bizarre, frightening unreality of it all. The catch-phrase had been the only bit of levity remaining between them after Benjamin died. Shane *was* a handful sometimes. A big kid, and she couldn't take him anywhere. It was a holdover from better days, when they joked with each other in good fun. It had soured a bit, however. Hadn't it been only a little while ago—hours?—when he'd anticipated her using it disdainfully when he'd first found the Nokia?

"I swear, Shane. You're a large child."

Shane came to a small clearing—again the illusion of walking through a corn field struck him—and glanced around. Before him, racks of suits crowded together. To the left, trench coats and overcoats. To his right, puffy winter jackets. "See. We don't need kids. You've already got one. And I'm never growing up, baby."

He paused, listening. The joke was an old one from before Benjamin. Half a dozen times he'd thought of using it after Benjamin's death (as cruel and heartless as it seemed) if only to shock *any* kind of reaction from her. A response showing some anger, some life. But he never had. Maybe now, it would work, jar Amanda awake.

"Oh, God. You're not one child, Shane. You're like ten."

The dry response mimicked Amanda's pre-Benjamin responses *perfectly*. Not a hitch of sadness, no hint of outrage or anger. Only her usual, sardonic self, something he hadn't heard in months.

And yet, a curious deadness lingered below her words. The mindless recitation of a seasoned actor running through lines memorized long ago. Amanda, trapped and made to forget? Choosing to forget? Or was this the store? Another glamour, a lure, like the lady on the Nokia, leading him deeper into the clothes, so *he'd* get lost too. Then years from now, when another couple fell prey to Save-A-Bunch, some poor soul would find his iPhone—in a locker, on the floor, or in trunk marked *Benjamin*, or some other dead child's name—and then the store would use *his* voice to lead someone else astray.

Screw this. Let's go for the throat. "Y'know. Ah, hell."

"Language. Want our kids to have a mouth like yours someday?"

God. It's like she, it, whatever is reading off a script written by Amanda herself. Now Playing, the Greatest Hits of Shane and Amanda! "Yeah. Sorry. Anyway, I was saying. I've wanted to bring this up dozens of times the last few months. I should've. God knows, I should've. If I had, maybe we wouldn't here, in this situation."

"Shopping for cheap junk to furnish the apartment in Utica? Where else *would we be?"*

THINGS YOU NEED

Shane chewed on his tongue, thinking, choosing his words carefully. The apartment in Utica. Seven years ago, before their house. Either the building or Whatever knew their history or had gotten it straight from whatever was left of Amanda, or Amanda *herself* had fled back to those simpler, happier times.

"It's Benjamin, Mandy. Ben. Our son. Who died. The day we went away to have some time alone. Our baby boy who died. I think—God, I hate to say this—but I think both of us died then, too. Part of us died. I know it. Died, and is maybe never coming back."

Silence.

A slight rustling against fabric, to his left. And then a flat, toneless, "*I don't know what you're talking about, Shane. Bad joke.* Really *bad joke.*"

More rustling to his left, past crowded racks of raincoats. Shane eased after the sound. "I hate to bring this up, Amanda. Here, of all places, now, while—*whatever* this is—is happening."

He turned sideways and slid between two racks of coats, following a narrow path. Ahead—though he couldn't be sure—he thought a red sleeve (Amanda's) slipped out of sight into the sea of coats, jackets and dresses.

"*What's happening is I'm here for deals,*" Amanda—or at least, her voice—said, in an approximation of good humor, tinged by the same strange, rote flatness.

"Yeah. I know." Shane eased between the two racks he'd *thought* he'd seen Amanda's sleeve slip through, and came again to a clearing. Before him, racks of bathrobes, pajamas and sweatshirts. To his right, more suit coats. To his left, sweaters and hooded sweatshirts. "Where'd you hear about this place again?"

The suit jackets twitched, and without hesitation, Shane ducked between the two racks. Ahead, he thought Amanda's black heels flashed into a sea of hanging pant legs. *"I honestly can't remember. One of those deal emails I'm always getting, from who knows how many deal websites I'm always signing up for."*

I bet, Shane thought, brushing aside suit coats of all sizes and shapes, color and material. *Do ghost stores send emails? Tweets? Do they text about their great deals?* "We can't dodge this anymore, Amanda. We need to talk about Benjamin, He died of SIDS. Sudden Infant Death Syndrome. You know how many infants die of SIDS every year? In 2010, more than two thousand, Amanda. *Two-thousand*. I researched it."

Any fake humor vanished from Amanda's voice, leaving only her eerie, robotic flatness. *"I don't know what you're talking about."*

Something silver—her bracelet, the one he'd given her for their anniversary a few months ago?—flashed past coat sleeves. Shane brushed by the increasingly claustrophobic racks quicker, checked from running by a strange fear of slipping, falling, and drowning in this sea of clothes. "Yes you do, Amanda. You've got to face it. *We've* got to face it. I don't want to, God knows. But it's killing us, Amanda. We can't move forward until we put him to rest. Put it behind us. Accept it, move on and try to live."

"Stop it. Stop it. Stop *it."*

Shane thought he saw a flash of auburn hair disappear to his left, through several crowded racks of more bathrobes and pajamas. On an instinctual level he hated the raw desperation hissing in Amanda's voice, the simmering pain. But it also showed a crack in the cheerful, toneless facade, making him think it was her after all, and not the store.

"I want to stop it, Amanda. God, I want to. The pain. The misery. The guilt. The long, awkward silences at dinner, when we can't look each other in the eye. I want to stop it all. But I can't. I can't, unless you stop running away, or I *leave* you here."

Shane passed through racks of clothing to find himself, unbelievably enough, back in the first clearing he'd found. To his left, trench coats. Ahead suits, and to his right, winter jackets.

"It hurts. Stop it."

The trench coats to his right shivered. Shane plunged in, shoving them aside, their hangers rattling on the racks. "I know it hurts. I *know*. But we can get past it. I *believe* it. For the first time, I believe it. But I think we have to say goodbye. We have to say goodbye to Ben, Amanda."

The word *goodbye* sent an image flashing through his mind. Of the trunk marked *Benjamin*, the one about the same size as an infant coffin.

"We never said goodbye, Amanda. We never had a funeral, for God's sake. My parents were so pissed at me for not insisting on a funeral, but I thought it was too much, that it'd break us, figured it would be better to let it go quietly."

He came to another clearing, but this was different. All around him, an insane mishmash of coats hanging with bathrobes and spring jackets hanging with T-shirts and slacks and jeans and shorts. He had no idea which way to go. Panic closed his throat tight, making it hard to breath, but he forced himself to speak, to get it all out, before it was too late, because somehow he knew soon it *would* be too late, and they would never get out of here, ever.

"*No,*" Amanda rasped, her voice a thin, ragged whisper, "*no, no, no, no.*"

Shane turned and, scanning the random swathes of clothes, fought off dizziness and vertigo, blackness spotting the edges of his vision. He forced himself to breathe deeply and slowly, before saying, "Amanda, I was wrong. The funeral wouldn't have broken us. It would've freed us. We would've said goodbye to Benjamin, we would've been freed, but now we're trapped and lost because we never said goodbye, and dammit, I *can't* be trapped anymore. I'm getting out, right now. With or without you."

His final words tumbled from him in rush, and all the energy left him. He sagged, legs trembling, arms weak and rubbery, his iPhone loose in his grip. His thoughts sputtered and came to a stop as he sank to his knees and closed his eyes.

A hush fell.

The whispering stopped.

Something had changed. And yet, he couldn't open his eyes right away, afraid he'd find himself back in the hall filled with blood-red lockers, kneeling, and as he watched the lockers would open slowly, one by one.

"Shane?"

No.

It was a trick.

Another glamour of the store's. He wouldn't fall for it. He wouldn't open his eyes.

"Shane?"

The frantic urgency in his name broke him. Alone,

frightened, imploring. He no more could've kept his eyes closed than he could've stopped breathing.

He opened his eyes.

To see Amanda standing before him. Eyes wide and shimmering, chin quivering, face ghostly white and drawn.

"Shane? What is this place? Why are we here? *What's happening?*"

Somehow, Shane gathered himself and stumbled to his feet. He swallowed and managed, "We got lost. That's all. We got lost."

Amanda's gaze darted from him to something over his shoulder, then back to him. She pointed, her hand shaking. "What's *that?*"

Shane turned, and was somehow not surprised to see the other end of the gymnasium, open double doors leading to a hall beyond. Also, he wasn't surprised to see what Amanda was pointing at, about five feet away.

A hope chest.

And from his angle, he could barely read *Benjamin* stenciled on top.

"Shane. What-what is that?"

Shane glanced over his shoulder and held out his hand. "Our way out, I think," he said simply.

She stared at his outstretched hand. Blinked once, slowly. Then, taking a timid step forward, her lips pressed together tightly and her face a rigid mask of fear, she slowly took his hand.

Her flesh felt cold and dry. Regardless, Shane gave her hand a small squeeze. He turned and led her to the chest. Knelt before it, still holding her hand, as he reached out with his other to the latch on the hope chest marked *Benjamin*. This time, he didn't hesitate, but flipped up the latch. Fit his fingers under the lid's edge and gently lifted it open.

His breath caught.

Amanda stood in silence behind him as he stared at what lay inside the chest. Benjamin's baby blanket. Powder blue, with birds on it. The blanket they swaddled him in since birth. The blanket he'd died face-down on, eight months later.

And it lay over something.

A body.

It could only be a body. He could see, at one end, the vaguest suggestion of a gently sloping brow, depressions which could be eye sockets, and the slight bump of a small nose.

Shane supposed, given everything which had happened, he should be horrified. That was probably the store's intention. One last fatal shock to send him and Amanda scurrying off into its depths forever. But something inside him had reached a threshold. Not only was he done playing games, he'd also realized the truth of things. Whatever this store was, however it got its power to lure people here and trap them, the only power it had was what people like him—lost people like he and Amanda, and maybe the woman and her husband Mike—gave it.

He was done giving it power.

He was taking it back.

A quiet, tremulous peace filled him as he reached for Benjamin's blanket.

"No. No!"

Amanda jerked her hand away. Shane stood and

reached for her, desperate pity and sadness welling up inside. "Amanda! *Please*. This is the only way!"

But it was too late.

Amanda was gone.

Vanished back into the crowded rows of coats, jackets, dresses and suits, with barely a ripple to mark her passing. Shane reached into his pocket, fingers desperately grabbing his iPhone to call her and plead with her one last time.

He glanced down and saw *her* cell lying on the floor, at the edge of the sea of hanging clothes. He stepped toward it.

some people want to stay lost

He stopped and stared at the clothes. His throat closed tight with emotion, eyes blurred. He wiped them with his hand, and choked back a sob. "I'm sorry," he rasped, the words harsh against his throat, "so sorry."

He wiped his face again. Turned, knelt before the chest, reached in and pulled Benjamin's blanket away. As the power blue fabric fluttered upward, he caught the barest outlines of a small, heart-shaped face, bright blue eyes . . .

And nothing.

No trinkets. No baby toys, or Benjamin's favorite stuffed animal—Snoopy, it had been—or his pacifier, or any of the other things Amanda had stored inside for his future. The chest was empty except for dust and small, indefinite particles of debris. It wasn't Benjamin's chest any more, but an old, battered thrift store cast-off. When he held up the blanket, it was no longer Benjamin's baby-blue blanket with birds on it, but a dusty stiff rag peppered with holes.

He dropped the rag to the floor.

Gazed at the open double doors. It tore him in half and made him want to throw up, but still. He dropped his iPhone on the floor. Withdrew Amanda's inhaler from his pocket. Squeezed it once, then opened his hand and dropped it also. It hit the floor with a plastic rattle. A macabre notion: The asthma inhaler rattled like a maraca, filled with tiny bones.

Shane walked toward the doors, away from the sea of clothes.

The glamour of an antique store had disappeared. The hallway outside the gym was dim and the floor coated with grit and dust. Instead of used furniture neatly lined up, the hall was cluttered with overturned school desks, podiums, rolling chairs and bookshelves. Several lockers—old, dusty, tinged with rust—hung open, but for some reason Shane felt no menace from them with the glamour now gone.

He made his way easily to the front lobby. Gone was the professional cherry wood desk, corporate-style phone, computer, and filing cabinets, and the plush waiting area. It was empty, the floor strewn with debris. Through cracked windows he saw desks and chairs in what had once been the main office. It was dark, and for some reason he didn't want to linger, as if something in there . . .

like in those lockers

. . . was watching him carefully, waiting. When he heard the warble of a ringtone—*Amanda's* ringtone—deep within the shadowed recesses of the shattered office, he sped up, trotting to the front doors short of a run. He had a panicked moment when, at first, the push-bar stuck and the door wouldn't open and *his* iPhone warbled Amanda's ringtone even louder in the darkened office behind him, but a frenzied, *angry* flush of adrenaline pulsed through him. He pushed the bar down, laying his shoulder against the door.

It opened a crack.

His iPhone warbled louder.

He laid his shoulder against the door once more, with everything he had, whispering between gritted teeth, "Let me out, damn you! Let. Me. Out!"

The door screeched open a crack. Turning sideways, he slipped through, for one awful moment thinking he might get stuck, the door pinning him, crushing him against its frame.

Then he was out.

His momentum carried him forward several steps. He stumbled, nearly fell, but he caught himself in time. He stood, heaving in deep gulps of air, turning around, astonished to see the door now standing wide open.

He could hear it, dimly.

Ringing inside. His iPhone playing Amanda's ringtone, over and over. He thought how easy it would be. The door was wide open. He must've pushed it all the way as he stumbled through. He could slip back inside, find his phone in the office—it hadn't been so dark in there, not really—and he could answer it. Guide Amanda out, because maybe she was ready to find her way, ready to beat the store.

He blinked. For an instant, he saw it. Shivering, mirage-like over the ruined lobby. The spotless, immaculate lobby of Save-A-Bunch Furniture. He stared at it, mouthing *Amanda* silently. He'd taken two steps toward the illusion before he cried out and flung himself away.

Whatever compulsion had attempted to draw him back faded. He ran to their car, a black Tahoe, parked all alone on an overgrown parking lot long in disrepair. As he neared the car, however, his stomach sunk.

Amanda had driven them.

She had the keys.

In a movie or maybe a television show, or a thriller novel, someone in his position would break the windows and hot-wire the Tahoe. He had no idea how to do such a thing, didn't know if you *could* hot-wire modern cars.

He placed both hands flat on the hood, bent his head and closed his eyes.

Amazingly, he could still hear his iPhone, faintly ringing Amanda's ringtone.

He shook his head.

Pushed off the Tahoe's hood and set out toward the parking lot's exit. He didn't know where he was, and didn't remember much about getting here. Also, he didn't know how far the store's illusions reached. He didn't know how far he had to walk to reach town or in what direction, and he had a strange feeling even if he hadn't tossed away his phone, he wouldn't have gotten service out here anyway. The only calls he would've received would be from Amanda, or the store using Amanda's voice to lure him back.

Had they eaten at The Skylark Diner? Did it even exist? And when he got to town—if there ever was a town in the first place—how could he explain any of this? Explain where his wife was to the police, to his parents, to her parents . . . to anyone?

THINGS YOU NEED

Glancing at the darkening sky, however, he pushed those unanswerable questions aside. Wherever he had to go, he had a long way to get there.

The sun hung low on the horizon.

Night was falling.

Somehow, Shane knew he didn't want to walk these roads alone under the pale light of the moon.

8.

"**P**LEASE! I DON'T *know where my husband Shane is! That's all I know! That's the last time I saw him! You have to help me!*"

At that point my circuits were nearly fried for good. Forget the fact I was locked in a weird-ass thrift shop whose clerk had vanished. Forget my rental car being stolen or towed or whatever. Forget the .38 I couldn't remember putting away back at The Motor Lodge, and forget the crazy hallucinations I kept having. Here was the impossibility of an iPhone coming to life (when mine wouldn't work at all) connecting me with some hysterical lady who in the space of ten minutes or so (though it felt much longer) told me some crazy story about being lost in a high school-turned furniture store where

there were things in the lockers

. . . she'd somehow gotten separated from her husband. It was a crazy story, but the thing is, I *remembered*—sorta—passing a sign reading SAVE-A-BUNCH furniture on the way into Clifton Heights, with the impression of a large building set back from the road. And I couldn't get over the image of her husband walking forever on a dirt road at night, where instead of things hiding in lockers, things hid in the bushes, watching his every step.

But I couldn't tell her that, right? There was no way I could help find her husband, not locked in Handy's. And I wasn't sure if she could help *me*, though I tried to get a word in, anyway.

Yeah, I know.

Here's this lady screaming about being lost, she can't find her husband and she's completely frantic, and all I could think about was how to get her to help *me*. Selfish to the core, for sure.

"Listen, lady. I'm stuck in this godforsaken old thrift shop in town, the door's locked, my phone won't work and someone stole my car. *Your* phone works. Think you could try and call 911 or something, get the cops over here? If I can get out I'll try and come get you."

"No! This is the only number which works, and it's my husband's number! How do you have Shane's phone?!"

"Lady, I have no idea how his phone got here. I'm stuck in this crappy junk store, and your husband's phone was in a wicker basket full of all these other cell phones, and it turned on and started ringing."

"Please. Please help me! I can't find my husband!"

That's when the iPhone died. Cut off right in the middle of her sentence, never to turn on again. Maybe it was a good thing too, because she was falling back into her mindless litany about not being able to find her husband. It was unlikely she could've helped me at all. Still, I kind of freaked out. She may have been crazy and telling nutso stories about being lost in a big furniture store with no exit, but she could've been a lifeline, right? My connection to the outside. So when that iPhone fell dark I flipped out, bad. Swearing and pawing through the pile of cellphones on the floor, searching for an AC adapter to plug the phone in somewhere, maybe get it some juice, but wouldn't you know? No chargers.

"DAMMIT!"

I wound up and threw the iPhone the length of the store, where it cracked against the front glass window. Didn't make a mark, of course, but it gave me an idea: *Hell*, yeah. Break the windows!

Why hadn't it occurred to me earlier?

Maybe, even as I was losing it, I was still trying to be law-abiding or whatever, but by then I figured: Screw the law. Whoever jacked my rental sure hadn't cared about the law, had they? And if that weirdo shopkeeper hadn't vanished and left me stuck in there . . .

but I'd wanted to get back in, hadn't I?

. . . then he wouldn't have had his windows broken, now would he?

Swearing and muttering, I scrambled to my feet and dashed to the front window, scanning the shelves along the way for something I could use to smash the glass. At the end of the aisle to my right, I found a baseball bat. A Louisville Slugger. I grabbed it, planted my feet and swung at the store's glass window hard as I could.

I've never made any claim I was an athlete or anything of the sort. I played baseball in high school but I wasn't any good. Never got on the field, was hardly used in practice, and to be honest: I was an orphan boy who lived in a foster home. Not one of the popular townie boys all the coaches loved. So mostly I stood on the sidelines and watched everyone else do their thing.

But I hit the glass *hard*. The bat *thwaked* against it.

And bounced off.

It *bounced*. Which, given how hard I'd swung, totally threw me off balance. I spun, and for the second time ended up crashing into the shelves of Handy's Pawn and Thrift.

I landed onto the floor, stuff raining down around me. The bat fell from my hand and clattered away. I'm not gonna lie. I started bawling. Crying my eyes out. It was all too much, y'know? My life was a waste. Not ever having a mom or dad. Not growing up in a normal home. All I could think about was the .38 back at the Lodge, because right then I wished I had it.

Tears poured down my face. I wiped my eyes with the back of my hand, and that's when I saw it sitting between my legs in all the clutter I'd knocked down.

A black paperweight of some kind. A pyramid. About six inches wide at the base and six inches tall, and it didn't look plastic. More like highly polished stone. With engravings on it. Etchings.

I grabbed it and picked it up, squinting, trying to read the writing. Foreign, maybe Latin, only I never took Latin in high school, so how would I know?

Here's the crazy part. Considering all the weirdness of that night, I sure wasn't planning on reading those words. At all. Farthest thing from my mind. Regardless, I found myself slowly whispering them, trying to make the weird-sounding syllables fit in my mouth while I rubbed this pattern with my thumb, three hooks spiraling around a dot.

Yeah.

Crazy. Damn near insane. There I was, rubbing a stone pyramid paperweight, muttering this nonsense language, acting crazy, out of my head. But I gotta be honest with you. Hitting the window with the Louisville Slugger, hard as I could, and not even cracking it? That took a lot out of me, I've got to admit. Sent me around the bend.

That's why—honestly—I'm still not sure about what happened next. Not sure if it actually happened, or if I was so close to losing it completely I dreamed the whole thing up. Anyway, I was sitting there, see? Muttering gibberish and rubbing that black pyramid, when the damn thing *vibrated*. It quivered in my hand. Then a tiny hole or something must've opened in the pyramid's tip, because this gas, or black smoke, or *sand* burst into my face. I didn't mean to but I sucked in a huge gulp and started hacking and choking.

Again, I was half crazy at the time, so maybe I imagined the whole thing but as I was running out of air and blacking out, I swore it wasn't smoke or dust but flies, thousands of tiny flies filling my eyes, ears and nose and crawling down my throat as I gagged and tried to puke them up as everything went dark, and I thought, *Oh my God I'm dying . . .*

THE BLACK PYRAMID

REVEREND NORMAN AKLEY perused a table of odds and ends in front of Handy's Pawn and Thrift, which offered its eclectic collection as part of Clifton Heights' Monthly Sidewalk Rummage Sale. Norman's right hand flitted from object to object, never quite touching but considering each as if his fingertips could judge value by intuition alone.

Norman loved rummage sales, but only occasionally did he find anything worth consideration. When he did, he picked it up and examined it, wondering if it would plead to be taken home. Most often, however, he shook his head, noting a slight imperfection here, a stain there. He'd replace the item, offer the table's curator a polite smile, and move on to other tables, their contents varied, sublime, ridiculous, amusing, or simply odd.

The items on Handy's table were varied indeed. A pewter beer stein, its embossed Viking bust glaring. Neat rows of used but polished tobacco pipes. Not-so-fine, yellowed china. A felt-lined box of tarnished silverware and stacks of dusty board games.

That wasn't all.

There were action figures, Legos, Lincoln Logs, and the ubiquitous Magic Eight Ball, which answered every question with: *Ask Again Later.* An old Nintendo Gameboy, and a Texas Instruments word processor. A pleather cowboy gun-belt. Wax Calavera skulls for the Day of the Dead. A Nikon digital camera, in decent shape. Rusty old tools. Tins full of assorted colored beads, marbles, rubber bands, and, oddly enough, a basket full of used cell phones. But nothing interested him until a black shimmer caught his eye among rows of dented matchbox cars and piles of jacks.

He squinted, bent over, and peered closer.

A pyramid.

A gleaming black pyramid unlike anything he'd ever seen. He found himself picking it up and turning it over in his fingers before he fully realized it.

With three sides and a triangular base measuring approximately six by six by six inches, the pyramid was also about six inches tall. As he peered at it more closely, he felt enthralled by its uncanny symmetry.

"Wonderful," he whispered, without understanding why. "Absolutely wonderful."

He rubbed the pyramid harder. Definitely not plastic, judging by its heft. Maybe ceramic, though a voice in his head whispered, *hand-carved stone.*

He hefted it again.

Tapped a side and felt a strange resonance.

Hollow?

He rubbed the pyramid with his thumb, detecting several fine scratches. A curious sense of dreadful anticipation filling him, Norman felt all around it with his fingertips.

Scratches.

Carvings?

A strange excitement stirred within him. He held the pyramid up for closer inspection and saw whirls, lines, and geometric shapes etched over every inch of the pyramid. It was the work of a medieval artisan. But he felt strangely repulsed, also, and two clashing thoughts arose.

Put it down. Go home, pour a scotch, sip it while finishing tonight's sermon notes, forget about it.

Or.

Take it home where it belongs.

He stared at the black pyramid, tracing with a fingertip the designs etched into its surface. Perhaps it was the clouds passing over the sun, but those etchings appeared to be moving. Writhing and wriggling. One of them in particular, three hooks spiralling around a dot in the center, looked like it was slowly spinning.

With great effort, he glanced up and down the sidewalk. Odd. The other tables hummed with would-be buyers but he stood alone at Handy's table, no one minding a cash box, even.

A strange sense of relief filled him. The table's vendors had stepped out, so he couldn't buy the pyramid right now. He reached down to deposit it back onto the table . . .

And saw something he swore he hadn't moments before.

Next to the jumbled piles of forgotten toys, propped against an old tin can full of marbles, a rectangular cardboard sign proclaimed in scrawled black marker: *Take What You Need!*

Free?

He supposed it made sense. Yard sales often gave away items they couldn't sell, a last-ditch effort at passing along things no one wanted before they were thrown away. Not strange at all, except for two things.

One: He hadn't seen the sign moments before. He felt sure of it.

Two: Unthinkable, something so odd, unique and strange . . .

exquisite

. . . would be free on a pawnshop's rummage sale table. Unthinkable.

Impossible.

He clenched the pyramid, savoring how its cool edges pressed into his palm. How his hand throbbed with its wonderfully strange pressure.

A sudden moment of clarity.

If he returned the pyramid now, he'd never see it again. Even if he scoured Handy's shelves for months or years, he'd never find it after today. All he had to do was return it—*relinquish* it—and he'd be free forever.

Free.

Forever.

Ridiculous. Free of what, exactly? A six-by-six-by-six black ceramic pyramid covered with odd etchings? What was there to be free of?

He squeezed the pyramid harder.

Its throb spread through his wrist, up his arm to his shoulder, mingling with his heartbeat. He glanced at the small sign on the table again.

Take What You Need!

"Well then," he said, "today's my lucky day."

Thank heaven for that.

He'd enjoyed precious few of those, lately.

So, with the black pyramid clenched in his still-throbbing hand, Reverend Norman Akley moved on, whistling a jaunty tune, knowing even as he'd enjoy browsing the remaining tables he'd window-shop only, for he'd already found what he wanted.

Found what he *needed*.

He had to force himself not to sprint so he could take the black pyramid home where it so rightly belonged.

❦

"Norman. Back from your expedition? And how were your precious little junk sales?"

Mildred's quietly snide voice dissipated Norman's pleasant fog. He stopped on the walk leading up to First Methodist's modest parsonage (their home for the past seven years, though it had felt much longer) and glared at Mildred where she reclined on her haunches at the edge of the flower garden she devoted more time to than him these days.

"Fine, Mildred," he replied. "And how's the gardening? Those weeds of yours look so very healthy."

Unfazed, Mildred brushed dirt from her thighs. "Well," she said with an ironic smile, "at least *something's* growing around here."

Norman stiffened but offered no comeback. Clifton Heights First Methodist hadn't shown any growth since the Utica-Rome Bishop had assigned him here seven years ago. Instead, its congregation had dwindled to a mere forty or so of the church's most loyal (and most ancient) members.

He sighed. Things hadn't worked out the way he and Mildred had dreamed. Instead of First Methodist's congregation growing because of a combination of sound Biblical preaching and a seeker-friendly atmosphere, it had withered like the posies Mildred tried to plant every year. Their hopes of him impressing the Utica-Rome Bishop into assigning him to a larger church in Utica had died, and now Mildred found herself stuck in a sleepy Adirondack town with two other churches besides her husband's, where she'd never be anything more than the wife of the pastor of "that small church hardly anyone goes to."

When the Bishop indefinitely reconfirmed Norman's assignment two years ago, whatever Christian love remaining in their marriage had hardened into a leaden ball of resentful discontent. This disheartening occurrence had not only disillusioned him but also weakened his faith, leaving it crippled and dry. He'd never thought he would dread every Sunday's message, wanting nothing more than to give the whole thing up and walk away.

But this was his duty.

It was expected of him.

So he preached half-hearted messages on Sunday morning. Met Wednesday nights for prayer meeting with the First Methodist Prayer Warriors (terminally infirm POWs was more apt), listening with a poker face to prayer requests for relief from a dizzying array of physical ailments. He nodded in fake sympathy to lamentations for wayward children who'd committed the ultimate sin of deciding to pursue their futures elsewhere.

And he'd smiled dully through it all.

During monthly potluck dinners of burnt mac and cheese and rigatoni. On countless shut-in visits. He listened with distant compassion to stories of ill and woe, then lightly patted Mabel or Bertha or Willa May on their withered wrists, offering a "peace which passeth understanding."

"Fred Savage called from The Farmer's Market," Mildred said as she bent down and began—fruitlessly—attacking the weeds choking the life from her posies. "Said he's got a whole box of day-old pastries and bread for the Food Pantry tonight."

Ah, yes.

How could he forget?

"Fine. When's he bringing them over?"

Mildred spoke without raising her head as she dug into the dry soil which had proven as barren as her womb, yet another thing she'd blamed him for (not in so many words) the past few years. "I didn't ask. The Food Pantry is one of your projects. Handle your own affairs. I'll handle mine."

Norman's hand tightened around the black pyramid. It must've been an illusion, but it felt as it were throbbing along with his heartbeat.

Mildred's sole duty had been the First Methodist Ladies Ministry Society. It ended after one-year when their only church-supported missionary (an eighty-year-old woman who distributed tracts around mobile home parks in Boca Raton, Florida) died in her sleep. Now, all she did was mess with her damned garden and sit around on her ever-widening ass all day drinking too much wine while reading Amish romances. Of course, it'd do no good to point that out.

He walked past her toward the church (which badly needed a new coat of paint and new roofing). "I'll be in my office, working on tonight's message, if anyone needs me."

"I'm sure you'll be safe from that."

Norman didn't respond. He walked away, barely suppressing the thought of how much he wanted to drive the black pyramid into the back of Mildred's head, point first.

After setting the black pyramid on his desk next to a white ceramic statue of Jesus on the Cross, Norman seated himself behind the desk to compose a message about Jesus raising Lazarus from the dead, and how everyone could enjoy new life through Christ's eternal compassion.

It proved hard going.

He couldn't focus. His mind was cluttered more than usual with cynical doubts about his faith (because Christ's eternal compassion felt more like amicable neglect lately) and also the harsh reality of the Food Pantry ministry: He could deliver the greatest message ever spoken in a church and it wouldn't make a difference.

At first, he'd approached this monthly ministry with as much zeal as he'd felt for everything else. It had been one of his ideas, after all. An effort to reach out and become an active member of the community, enriching people's lives.

But the Food Pantry had failed miserably.

It had taken about two years for Norman to catch on. After contacting a charitable food distribution program in Utica and appealing locally to The Great American Grocery to donate produce, Norman had instituted a monthly Food Pantry on Friday Nights. The only two requirements were listening to a half-hour exhortation on the Godliness of Industry, Hard Work and Perseverance, and a private counseling session with him, so he could be aware of their needs and praying for them.

His intention?

By combining mercy and compassion with encouragement and exhortation, he'd make a difference in people's lives. Eventually he'd see them make something of themselves. After a helping hand from him, they'd learn to stand on their own and move on, to be replaced by new faces in need.

However, instead of a ministry that picked people up and put them on their feet so they could walk on their own, he'd created a handout center which attracted the same group of people every month. When he'd finally understood this, he'd also realized discontinuing the Food Pantry was nearly impossible. Nearly twenty people a month had become accustomed to their free food. Irrationally, he actually *feared* their reaction to closing the Food Pantry.

He didn't imagine a riot, exactly. Only a dreadfully disconcerting image of them clustered outside the church while he and Mildred cowered behind the church's front doors. Them advancing up the walk. Reaching out, begging, like mindless zombies.

So the Food Pantry continued on. Norman delivered forced messages about faith, love and charity. One by one, the Food Pantry Regulars visited his office, sobbing about how their no-good spouse or boyfriend had been fired again, or how their daughter had gotten pregnant and was now living with them, or how their monthly welfare check was late, how they'd fallen off the wagon, gotten fired and they wanted to turn over a new leaf but the Good Lord knew how hard it was living in a bad old world which never gave the little folks a fighting chance.

Over and over again, world without end, amen.

Then of course he'd encourage them in the name of Jesus, Whose grace was eternal, because, "Blessed are the meek and the downtrodden." They'd beg for forgiveness, promise to get right with God, quit the juice and stop throwing their relief check away at The Stumble Inn or The Golden Kitty, then they'd pray in weeping sighs.

The following transformations never ceased to amaze Norman. Once their prayers ended they became all business, ready to accept their handouts and return to their lives, with no intention of changing their ways whatsoever.

So it had gone on.

For the past four years. Tonight it'd be the same. Deep down, Norman again felt the urge to walk out of the church, down the street, never to return. He felt the urge to give up his ministry in exchange for something else, *anything* else.

Something rattled.

Several objects thumped onto the carpet, clinking.

Norman glanced up and saw the black pyramid had fallen from where he'd placed it on his desk, taking Jesus with it. Frowning, he stood, leaned over the desk and saw the black pyramid lying on its side among the remains of the broken ceramic Jesus.

Fallen?

Knocked over, jostled . . .

Or jittered off the desk, of their own accord?

Which was ridiculous, of course. He must've bumped the desk with his knee, lost in thoughts about the dreariness of his life and dead ministry. Certainly that was it.

Certainly.

Yet as he watched, a tremor shook the pyramid, and it quivered.

Rippling.

He was around his desk and bending over to pick it up without thinking, so shocked at what he'd seen, or *thought* he'd seen, he reminded himself as he picked up the pyramid with trembling fingers. It wasn't possible. He hadn't seen the black pyramid ripple.

How had it fallen?

He was tired, frustrated and under stress.

He stood, turning the pyramid over in his fingers, tracing those strange swirling etchings. It felt warm. Warmer than when he'd picked it up at the Sidewalk Sales. It was probably an echo of his pounding pulse, but the black pyramid felt as if it was throbbing.

How had it fallen?

He held the pyramid tight. Something different about the etchings. Something carved into one side, though when he'd examined it earlier he'd seen no such thing.

There.

Turning it over once he saw it, where he'd swear no writing had been only an hour or two before. In a small rectangle below the strange spiraling-hooks design, he saw words which made no sense. He knew Latin—an elective he'd taken in college—but this wasn't Latin, or any other language he recognized. Squinting, he peered closer, tapping each letter with his fingertip, intoning them in soft whispers, the words sounding strange and alien on his tongue.

He stopped.

Held the pyramid up, frowning, hefting it, thinking it certainly felt hollow now. Something shifted inside when he moved it.

An odd notion struck him. He raised the black pyramid to his ear, turned it upside down and heard it, the whisper of something sand-like.

Instantly, his rational mind scoffed at the muted dread the sound conjured. So it was a strange paperweight filled with sand, left for free by a pawnshop.

So what?

A strange paperweight with odd designs and incantations carved into it, his mind protested, *which jumped off desks and broke neighboring knick-knacks on its own.*

"Ridiculous," he scoffed, holding the pyramid up so he could see the strange words better. "Absolutely ridiculous."

As he stared at the strange words, rubbing them with his thumb, an acute sense of displacement fell over him. His office disappeared. His bookcases, framed divinity degrees, desk and his gigantic King James family Bible faded away, replaced by yellow stone walls depicting effigies of strange, unknown gods. In the far corner a great sarcophagus stood upright; its lid made of gleaming gold, fashioned into the arrogant visage of an Egyptian pharaoh long since laid to rest in layers of incensed wrappings.

All of this he only sensed peripherally as more

words appeared on the obsidian stone. He whispered them reverently, the words now flowing from him, as if they were his native tongue.

The pyramid quivered in his hand, as if it was squirming to life. Its tip peeled open. Inside lurked darkness. But as Norman tilted the pyramid for a better angle, a sandy whispering filled the darkness.

Something exploded upward into his eyes, covering his face. As a child, Norman once blundered into an underground hornet's nest in his backyard. The cloud of enraged insects which had briefly engulfed him had been like this, only this was worse because the grains were so much smaller, filling his throat, choking him, swarming up his nostrils into his sinus cavities to his brain, and all he could hear was the sand whispering and strange, alien voices screaming in the distance . . .

Screaming.

Alien voices, screaming, wailing, screeching.

Norman ran, clawing those buzzing black flies or gnats . . .

sand

ashes

. . . away from his face, his shoes crunching gritty sand; his earthen footsteps echoing down a long, dark corridor.

pyramid

inside the black pyramid

no, that's impossible

A voice chanted over and over, thundering in the air and the rock around him, and he could hear it, now, a *name* . . .

Nyarlathotep!

Norman heard a scrambling rustle behind him. Chasing him. Something was chasing him.

In blind terror he stumbled forward, legs shaking and nearly giving out as he felt the corridor's slight incline. Wherever he was; whatever this place was . . .

a dream, a nightmare
the pyramid, the black pyramid

. . . he was running slightly uphill toward a dim rectangle of light above, a room of some kind, perhaps somewhere he could hide.

The incline leveled out before turning a sharp left upward again. On the flat he indeed saw a dim rectangle, a doorway. Heart pounding and lungs aching, his mind trembling at the threshold of madness, he stumbled through the doorway and slid to a stop, gaping in bewildered horror.

Torches affixed to the walls guttered, flickering shadows across ancient paintings of Egyptian pharaohs and priestesses, like the ones he'd seen in textbooks as a child. Their faces sneered cruelly in a way he didn't remember, however, with an inhuman arrogance. In the center of the room lay a rectangular stone coffin, a sarcophagus, and a name kept thundering in his mind . . .

Nyarlathotep!

. . . as he stumbled toward the tomb, legs beyond his control. When he drew near he gasped, recognizing the stone effigy adorning the sarcophagus's lid. Wearing the garments and headdress of an ancient Egyptian priestess or queen, the face bore an unmistakable likeness to Mildred.

With a scraping groan, the sarcophagus's lid began to slide open.

Norman screamed and fled the chamber, running further up the inclined corridor. As he did, he glimpsed something lumbering up from below. A twisted figure lurching on two bent and crooked inhuman legs with a coiling serpent for a head. He stumbled on, the corner mercifully hiding the monstrosity as he scrambled toward yet another dim rectangle above. He wheezed, struggling to draw air into his tortured lungs; air which clogged his throat.

sand

ashes

The incline leveled again and the corridor once more angled sharply left and upward. On this level another dim rectangle beckoned. He didn't want to go through it, didn't want to see, wanting to keep running, but he heard something shambling up behind him, so he plunged through the doorway into another room whose walls depicted more scenes of ancient Egyptian pharaohs with cruel faces. In the middle of the room, waving snaky arms, wailing from mouths ringed with needle-point teeth, things shambled and swayed. Their naked, gray rubbery skin glistened in the torchlight. They bore only a passing resemblance to humanity but still he recognized them all.

The Food Pantry.

The loyal attendees of the Food Pantry. There was Willa May Zether, naked with gray leathery skin, sagging breasts, shuffling, hump-backed and stooped shouldered, lamprey-mouth wide and drooling. Behind it lumbered Cletus Smith, emaciated and gaunt, wide black eyes staring. Over there lurched Jed

Sykes, wide fish-like mouth moaning, tentacle arms lashing the air.

They were all converging on two forms lying prone and naked in the middle of the room. Humans. As the foul and unclean things slowly shuffled closer, Norman caught glimpses between their gray, sickly bodies to see the faces of their victims.

His blood turned to ice water.

His heart slammed against his rib cage, bladder throbbing painfully, demanding release. Mildred. Mildred, lying naked and unconscious, next to *him*.

The things screeched as one loathsome collective mind, their tentacles whipping the air, then with unnatural speed they descended upon the prone forms. Blood sprayed to the sounds of fleshy crunching.

Bile churning in his stomach, Norman staggered away from the unholy communion through the doorway. As he limped up yet another incline, he caught in passing a shadowy hulk lurching up from below. Moaning, he shuffled up toward yet another shining rectangle. The sounds of gristle crunching in sharp teeth throbbed in his ears as he plunged through the doorway into another room whose walls also depicted the past. On the far side, another doorway flickered with a much brighter, pulsing light. Next to it, another sarcophagus leaned upright against the wall, bearing *his* face. Hanging on the wall next to it was a human-sized, marble effigy of Christ on the cross.

With a creaking, rock-on-rock groan, the sarcophagus' lid trembled. Before Norman could spin and flee, he heard it, felt it lumbering up the passage and to the doorway, its heavy bulk scrambling across sandy rock toward him. He sprinted past the quivering sarcophagus and away from the huge lumbering thing through the shimmering rectangle into a room much grander than he'd yet seen. A floor of shining gold reflected the fires in scones mounted on walls. Murals depicted scenes of rites and practices so inhuman and abominable he gibbered, clenching and unclenching his hands in useless fists, teetering on the precipice of madness.

At the far end of this ornate room sat a golden throne inscribed with strange, alien symbols and characters, one of which he recognized dimly: Three hooks spiralling around a center. On each side sat not statues of sphinxes—as he'd seen in his textbooks as a child—but terrible statues of the thing lumbering behind him, an abominable two-legged horror with twining tentacles for arms and a serpentine head with no eyes but a gaping, fanged mouth.

In the center of the room shimmered a pool of water, which bubbled quietly. As Norman stared, the pool rippled outward from its center. Something rose from it. Not the serpent-headed horror depicted by the statues on either side of the golden throne, but a man. Or something that looked like a man. An Egyptian pharaoh wearing a high, glittering headdress and a curiously blank but cruel countenance, with a hard mouth, square jaw and deep, emotionless black eyes.

The pharaoh rose from the pool and stepped smoothly onto the floor. His blood-red robes were dry, the gold around the robe's neck glittering in the fire burning on the walls.

Norman's mind cracked. Heedless of the thing

behind him or the opening sarcophagus, he screamed and spun back out the door, away from this thing which looked like a man but wasn't.

The instant he left the throne room an angry hiss filled his ears. Nothing but a mass of reflexes and terror now, Norman spun and felt his last bits of sanity slip away as the marble Christ leaned away from His marble cross, craning His neck to hiss at him.

"Faithlesssssss. Faithlessssssss."

A great crack, the groan of stone pulling away from stone, and the marble Christ on His cross tore away from the wall and fell toward him. Norman flung up his hands, feeling a warm flush as his bladder finally lost its battle.

A strong, muscled hand shot out from beneath a blood-red robe and arrested the marble cross' fall. Norman peered through splayed fingers as the hand threw the cross to the far corner of the room. It shattered against the wall.

A great peace filled Norman.

Heedless of his wet crotch, he sank to his knees. Standing before him was something worth serving at last, a great and powerful force that could not be denied. An entity commanding absolute obedience.

The great pharaoh stretched out the hand which had saved him. In a paroxysm of ecstasy Norman grasped it, kneeling at the feet of something which could use him for A Great Service, indeed.

The pharaoh gazed at him, black eyes glittering as he intoned, "Follow me."

A moment of hesitation.

Deep inside, Norman knew he had no choice. He'd made his choice the instant he'd brought the black pyramid home. He nodded wordlessly, feeling something shift inside him as he opened himself in a way he never had, before.

The pharaoh opened his mouth, but instead of words, out flowed black sand . . .

ashes

. . . buzzing like the swarm of hornets he'd disturbed as a child. As the rippling mass flowed toward him and covered his face, filling his eyes, pouring down his throat, he didn't fight his new communion. He accepted it, eating of a new and terrible Body.

⁓⁓

Norman jerked with a sharp cry, dropping the black pyramid back to the floor, hands flying to his face to dig away the sand blinding him, filling his mouth, clogging his throat.

Only to find unblemished skin.

He glanced around and saw not an ancient, alien, gleaming throne room, but his church office.

He covered his face with his hands, closed his eyes and breathed deeply, letting an icy fear drain from him as his muscles relaxed. Must have dozed off while composing yet another message he didn't want to deliver and didn't believe in. And oddly enough the dream (which was already fading) of running lost through a maze of subterranean tunnels was frightfully appropriate. He'd gotten lost in his mission. He'd lost his purpose. But then, of course, there was the black pyramid.

The black pyramid.

He opened his eyes and gazed down upon the black

pyramid, lying on the carpet, next to the shards of ceramic Jesus on His cross. As he stared at the broken effigy of his faith, something shifted deep inside him.

He smiled.

Bent and grabbed the black pyramid with one hand, scooped up the remains of his faith with the other. He dropped the broken pieces into the wastebasket next to his desk, then gently and reverently sat the black pyramid on the edge of his desk. Right where it belonged.

At home.

"S'yknow how it is, Pastor," Jed Sykes cringed, whining in a high-pitched voice which normally made Norman grind his teeth but tonight didn't bother him at all. "My back's been actin up somethin fierce. I ain't been able to work at all, but cause itsa pre-existin condition workers comp won't cover it. I cain't get my insurance to gimme a referral to a chiropractor, so things is awful tight round home."

Norman smiled, hands folded on the desk, barely listening to a single word Jed Sykes said. He also ignored the man's thin face and unhealthy pallor, his bloodshot watery eyes and slobbery lips.

Instead, fantastic images wheeled through his brain. A majestic throne room with golden floors. Walls adorned with portraits of ancient men and women. A tall, regal man wearing a pharaoh's headdress and a crimson robe. A man with a cruel face. Norman, kneeling before him, reverently taking his strong hand.

"I been tryin real hard, Pastor, ta stay way from

that demon hooch, but it's powerful hurtin when ma belly's so empty."

At this the good Reverend Norman Akley gave poor Jed Sykes a wide, sincere smile. "No worries, Mr. Sykes. I have a feeling after tonight your belly will never be empty again."

Jed's eyes and face lit up with a beatific glow, one Norman knew well by now. "Oh, I know, Pastor! All I gots to do is ask fer the Spirit an He'll fill me up an I'll never feel that demon thirst no more!"

Norman stood, reverently took the black pyramid from his desk and handed it to a slightly confused Jed Sykes, offering another wide smile. "Indeed. You will be filled, I guarantee."

Fifteen minutes later, when eyes now deep and black (like Norman's) returned his gaze, the good Reverend Norman Akley knew Jed Sykes had indeed been filled, to the brim.

Unlike poor Mildred, who unfortunately hadn't been as accepting of the black pyramid's ministry.

No matter.

He wasn't the first prophet whose spouse couldn't find it in her heart to support him.

"Now," Norman said pleasantly, accepting the black pyramid back from Jed's suddenly steady, unwavering grip, "let's bring the others in and spread the Good News, shall we?"

9.

I WASN'T DYING after all. I heaved a big cough and blew little speckles of stuff—not insects, more like sand—all over me. Then I had a sneezing fit lasting about ten minutes or so before I finally cleared my throat with several hacking gasps.

I blinked dust and grit from my eyes. My mouth and tongue tasted gritty, but I was all right. Nearly passed out after that dark sandy stuff puffed in my face, but I was all right. I dropped the black pyramid to the floor damn quickly, though. No more rubbing it and reading those weird-ass words, for sure.

What was that stuff? I never found out. At the time I thought maybe it might've been some sort of hallucinogenic drug. Something that screws with people's minds, makes them hallucinate. The things I saw when I accidentally snorted it was worse than any nightmare I'd ever had.

I'm not sure how long I sat there, blinking and spitting. Felt like a long time. Weird images spun in my brain, the worst of them a snarling, hissing Jesus on a cross, some guy in Egyptian robes, and a lizard-snake-headed thing with no eyes and all teeth. Also, sidewalk sales, for some reason. Weird sidewalk sales, with body parts and heads on display. Or maybe used Barbie dolls? I dunno. Like I said: Thought I'd snorted some sort of drug.

Anyway, when I finally got myself together, another thought hit me. The back of the store. There had to be a way out somewhere back there, especially because the creepy shopkeeper had disappeared back there, right?

Here's the thing. I *knew* why I didn't want to go back there, why I'd subconsciously avoided it until then. When I first looked down that hallway, trying to figure out where the shopkeeper had gone, I hadn't liked it. It stretched out way longer than it should. It seemed endless. Some part of me was afraid if I started wandering around back there I'd get lost, kinda like the crazy lady on the iPhone was saying she was lost. The hallway out back had way too many rooms, too.

I'm not afraid to admit I was *not* a fan of going out back, but by then? I was desperate. So desperate, in fact, if I had my .38, the one I couldn't remember putting back under my bed in The Motor Lodge . . .

Well.

You get the idea.

When I finally got my wits about me, I managed to stumble upright and limp over to the counter. Steeling myself, I placed my hands on it, leaned over and peered down the long hallway with no end.

It *was* endless, or at least looked like it. Shelves ran on both sides for the first few feet, cluttered with all sorts of stuff. Old baseball gloves, football helmets, hockey sticks, books, old televisions, VCRs and DVD players. Some radios, too. Newer ones and old mammoth jobs with eight-track players. After that, the hall stretched away into darkness. Every few steps open doors led into rooms filled with who knew what. At the time, I had no intention of finding out, but I'd have to walk past them to get out, and that was working on my imagination.

There wasn't anything else left to try by then. So, legs shaking, I pushed open the swinging gate and stepped through to the back.

And *fell*.

Bounced and rolled, tumbling ass over tea-kettle so fast no coherent thoughts could form. I crashed onto a hard concrete floor, smashing my shoulder. I'm not gonna lie; I screamed, not only because it hurt, but because I was so pissed.

A door.

A *fucking* trapdoor. Why hadn't I checked when I'd stepped through? I mean, I guess no one expects an open fucking trapdoor under your feet, but you would've thought I'd gotten to expect about anything. I don't know. All I knew was I'd fallen down a flight of stairs to smash my shoulder into a concrete floor. I was hurt, pissed, and freaking out, big time. No, check that. I was *scared*. Out of my mind, losing it, for sure, maybe for real.

I lay there, curled in a fetal ball, holding my shoulder and swearing, kinda screaming the whole time, too. Finally, it weighed down on me how dark it was. Only dim light filtered down the stairs. If there was one thing I didn't want, it was to be lying in the darkness down in some storage cellar. As the throbbing pain in my shoulder eased, I rolled onto my knees and dug into my pocket for my lighter. I pulled it out, flicked it on and panned it around.

The walls were brick. Which was odd. Who would take the time to brick and mortar walls to a cellar? Also, the cellar wasn't nearly as large as I'd first thought. In fact, it was damn small. Too small to be much use, really.

I pointed my lighter to the far corner. I saw an altar or something like it made of plywood. An altar with shelves, and with things on it. Thick white candles, which had burnt out long ago. Dried up flowers. A garden hat. Toys. A football, basketball and baseball. Pictures, too, of boys, but I wasn't about to take the time to examine them closer.

Something scratched in the other corner, the one covered in darkness.

Common sense would say maybe a mouse. Still, when I heard it again—*scratch*—my heart leaped into my throat. Yeah I know it's a horrible cliché, but *that's what it felt like.*

Scratch.

Again.

In the dark corner to my left.

On rubbery legs, my knees buckling, I slowly stood. Backed up several tottering steps to the stairway leading up and away from the scratching sounds. I put one foot on the bottom step, turned to go up . . .

You know this part, of course.

I had to look, right?

Had to. Because it's what humans do. We look. Most *especially* when we shouldn't.

So I pointed the lighter into the far corner.

Opened my mouth wide.

And screamed silently, my mind falling to pieces, finally.

WHEN WE ALL MEET AT THE OFRENDA

T HE HORIZON ABOVE Hillside Cemetery was slowly bruising a crimson-purple, shading to the velvet darkness of an autumn Adirondack evening. Night birds sang. The crisp air nipped Whitey Smith's hands and face. Dry leaves rustled underfoot as he shuffled along the path leading toward the cemetery caretaker shed. His assistants, Judd and Dean, had raked leaves all week, but it hadn't mattered. Never usually did. When autumn came, leaves covered the ground. This was the way of things.

Flowers bloomed in spring. Crops grew during summer. Leaves fell in autumn, and things died during winter. Except Maria, who died a month ago of pancreatic cancer, which was the way of things.

People died.

He shuffled to a stop, grasped the knob on the shed's door, swallowing a grimace as arthritic pain arrowed glass slivers into his knuckles.

"Sonofabitch."

He turned the knob and tried to open the door but couldn't. It had rained yesterday, and the door had swelled as it always did afterward, catching in the doorframe.

He tugged harder.

The door popped open, but he was rewarded for his efforts with an aching pulse in his right shoulder. It had been hurting lately. Ever since he'd twisted it when burying the Jensen kid last spring, after he rolled his car on Bassler Road.

Whitey stood before the shed's open door, right hand still on the knob, left hand gently kneading the leathery meat of his right shoulder, which throbbed dully. Dr. Fitzgerald at Utica General said it was probably a torn rotator cuff. He'd recommended surgery. Or at least physical therapy. Whitey had waved off the recommendation, claiming he had neither the time nor the money for either, a self-fulfilling prophecy after Maria's diagnosis.

Whitey didn't enter the shed immediately. He stood there, eyes closed, rubbing his shoulder, savoring the heady scent of oil and gasoline from the lawnmower out back. It was one of his favorite smells because it reminded him of the night he first saw Maria.

He'd first seen Maria Alverez while standing outside the pit area at Five Mile Speedway, hands hooked on the chain-link fence separating him from the powerful cars tended to by mechanics wearing gray smudged overalls. Some of the cars were jacked up, tires being changed or their undersides inspected by men lying under them. Others had their hoods open, swallowing mechanics intently fixing either carburetors or changing spark plugs. A few cars roared as drivers tested their engines.

At age ten, the world beyond the fence appeared grand. Every Saturday night men conjured strange masculine magic from gasoline-fueled beasts. After spending his childhood watching the races with his father, Whitey Smith would race himself during the early years of his tenure at Hillside Cemetery. This, of course, earned his modified 1940 Ford coupe (number 72) the nickname *Grave Wagon*.

Those future days were distant dreams when he first saw Maria in the Five Mile pits. He'd only been ten, she an exotic twelve, handing her father tools as he worked under a chopped and stripped Chevy.

Whitey fell in love instantly. She hadn't been wearing anything remotely girlish, clad only in a smaller version of the gray overalls other mechanics wore, her hair pulled tight into a ponytail. Face composed and serious, she intently watched her father (Carlos Alverez, Whitey would later learn) work underneath the Chevy. Whitey fell in love with her focused expression, her narrowed eyes, pursed lips, (which he suddenly wanted to kiss), and the oil smudge—a beauty mark on her cheek.

He would chase her, worship and annoy her, woo her and then win her. He'd someday race for her, and would always cherish her.

Now he mourned her.

Whitey inhaled another breath of oil and gasoline, then reached in and flicked a light switch inside the shed's door. Dim orange light spilled from a single bulb hanging from the shed's ceiling, illuminating the

238

Spartan area, which had become his living space since he'd buried Maria here at Hillside.

Against the wall sat a simple cot, blankets tucked in. Next to it, a wooden crate served as a nightstand for a small lamp he'd bought at Handy's Pawn and Thrift. At the cot's end sat an old footlocker he'd bought at a clearance sale at Save-A-Bunch furniture long ago. Pushed into the far corner of the shed was a refrigerator, with his Coleman stove on top.

The tools of his trade hung neatly on the far wall. Two different sizes of shovel, several kinds of rakes, a weed whacker, a pick and a pitchfork. The small riding lawnmower, push mower and snow-blower (to keep the access roads clear during winter), rested in an adjoining small garage. In the center of the shed sat a kerosene heater.

Whitey grunted as he moved slowly toward his cot. The shed offered everything he needed, regardless what his eldest Carlos thought. Carlos kept saying he'd catch his death out in the cold. Claiming he understood Whitey's pain in one breath, accusing him of "playing Huck Finn" in the next. Ungrateful snot had grown too big for his britches, partying in New York City with his writer boyfriend. Said Whitey was foolish to believe all the old tales of Dia de los Muertos, that Maria wouldn't come back. Hell with him, anyway. When had Carlos . . .

(or was it Marcus?)

. . . valued his mother's traditions? All Hallow's Eve, Saint's Day, All Souls Day, Dia de los Muertos. Those quaint Mexican customs (of which his sons had acted increasingly ashamed) meant nothing to him, so how could Carlos (Marcus?) understand Whitey's need to be close to Maria tonight?

239

Whitey sat down on the cot, knees popping, his lower back aching. Didn't matter what they thought. He'd decided to spend October by Maria's side here at the cemetery, and he had. Only one more night left. Tonight, All Hallow's Eve. Dia de los Muertos. Day of the Dead. Technically it fell on November 2nd, but after they'd gotten married, Maria had insisted on celebrating it Halloween night. To her, it felt right to celebrate Dia de los Muertos the same night the whole town armed their porches with grinning Jack o' Lanterns while costumed youth patrolled the streets.

Some front yards on Halloween boasted haunted graveyards filled with foam headstones, skeletons and lurching zombies. Their front yard on Henry Street offered a monument to the Day of the Dead. Central to the display had always been the ofrenda, a wooden altar Whitey had built from sheets of plywood. On it, Maria always assembled an offering for their dead relatives and loved ones, to welcome their spirits on a night when the boundaries between worlds grew thin.

Sitting on his cot, Whitey recalled the days when Carlos and Marcus marveled at the ofrenda. For years it had lit their eager, drinking faces with soft electric light glowing from strings of orange and yellow bulbs and the flickering of ceremonial candles. During those innocent years, the boys thought they had the best Halloween exhibit in town. The finest touch? The Coqueta Catrina and Elegant Catrin (two opulently clothed foam skeletons), standing silent and grinning watch on either side of the ofrenda.

Their lawn did boast foam headstones also, but they were garlanded with bright orange and yellow marigolds. Before each, Maria filled plastic bowls full of candy apples, homemade pumpkin empanadas, pumpkin spice brownies, and of course, homemade Calaveras. Sugar candy skulls. She and Whitey—faces painted in Calaveras masks, dressed as the Coqueta Catrina and the Elegant Catrin—directed the children to these bowls.

Whitey sighed. As children, Carlos and Marcus had begged to sit before the ofrenda, long after the trick or treaters had gone. But it got "old" as they entered their teenage years. They'd gone so far as to accuse Maria— their *mother*—of not believing in Dia de los Muertos at all. She'd co-opted it, according to Marcus . . .

(or was it Carlos?)

. . . made it her "thing" to show how Mexican she was. Said she thought the stories nothing but superstition. So disrespectful, it made Whitey's hands shake with barely-restrained (but still futile) rage thinking about it. He sounded like his brother.

(but which one?)

Whitey bent and covered his face with shaking hands.

After being struck dumb by Maria's transcendent twelve-year-old beauty at Five Mile Speedway, Whitey didn't instantly pursue her. After all, she was twelve and in sixth grade. An unattainable prize for a lowly fourth grader.

However, as they progressed out of grammar school into junior high, a combination of happenstance and Whitey's own quiet determination kept them crossing paths. By high school they were friends. They walked home from school together. They sat together at lunch. During the summers they picked blueberries at Mr. Trung's, browsed garage sales, and once they braved the first floor of old Bassler House, the dilapidated Victorian farmhouse on the edge of town. They wandered through Raedeker Park Zoo, talking about nothing and everything. They watched the Wednesday night summer movies at Raedeker Park when it was a monster movie or a western, and they endlessly searched Handy's Pawn and Thrift for the trinkets only young people found fascinating.

The tipping point occurred Maria's senior year, when Whitey asked her to the annual Halloween movie at Raedeker Park. At the time, he hadn't understood her unusually excited acceptance of his invitation. Only later did it dawn upon him: For the first time he'd formally asked her to go somewhere with him.

When he knocked on her door and she opened it, he could only stare, speechless. Her usually light brown face was a startling white. Large black ovals circled her eyes, mimicking the gaping eye-holes of a skull, but they didn't make her eerie or frightening. She appeared mysterious. Otherworldly. Likewise, her nose was painted black—a skull's empty nose cavity— her lips were also white and sectioned by black lines into two rows of skeletal teeth.

On her forehead and cheeks, faint colored lines— yellow, blue and red—swirled in delicate patterns. Peering closer, he noticed the small blue circles bordering her eyes, as if a chain of sapphires circled each. As a finishing touch, a red flower blossomed on her chin.

She stared at him for a heartbeat. Whitey opened

his mouth and closed it, still speechless, because she was unearthly and ethereal. It flitted across his mind to ask if she was practicing for Halloween, but the painted mask invoked a seriousness which transcended a mere spook mask.

Finally he swallowed and managed, "Wow. You look amazing."

Maria smiled, transforming her face into a beautiful and disconcerting grinning skull. "Thanks!" She stepped out, shut the door behind her, and they left for Raedeker Park.

After a few steps, Whitey said, "It's awesome. Is it for Halloween?"

"Not exactly. We're doing a family heritage project in Mr. Groover's class, and I've been studying Mexican customs. Cause, you know," she jerked her head back toward her house, "Mom and Dad won't talk about Mexican stuff because they're trying so hard to be American. Which is fine. I've got no problem being American, except whenever Grandma Louisa tries to tell stories about Mexico, Mom and Dad hush her, as if she's going to spill all these embarrassing secrets, especially when she tries to tell us about Dia de los Muertos. So I decided to study it for my history project this year."

She offered Whitey a brilliant grin, which only made her more beautiful and ghastly. "My parents weren't happy. Got an 'ay dios mio' from Mom, which is impressive. But anyway, it's for a school project, and they know I hate school, so I guess they figured if it'll get me interested in schoolwork, they'd tolerate it."

They left Henry Street and crossed onto Main, heading to Raedeker Park. "Dios de los Muertos. Day of the Dead, right? Mrs. Millavich talked about it in Spanish last week, but . . . I, uh . . . "

Whitey shrugged. "I sorta wasn't paying attention."

Maria's painted-on skull smirked as she punched his shoulder. "Of course not. She was probably wearing one of her tight sweaters." Whitey said nothing and kept grinning, because of course, it was true.

"I'll skip the parts about the Catholic Church and All Soul's day. Day of the Dead is ancient. It recognizes death as a natural part of life. Not something to be feared. That's why the face-paint." She tapped her cheek. "This is a Calavera, representing the human skull not as something scary but something beautiful, because it's a part of life. They make little sugar candies in the shape of skulls. Can't buy them around here. Next year, I'm going to learn how to make them myself."

Samara Hill, which led to Raedeker Park, lay only a few blocks away, but suddenly Whitey wanted to walk slower, and make the time last. "What else is the Day of the Dead about?"

Maria talked excitedly, gesturing with her hands, warming to the subject. "Mostly, it's about honoring those who have gone before us. You decorate loved ones' headstones, offer their favorite foods in clay bowls, maybe sing their favorite songs or hymns. Nana always mentions it every year because Grandpa is buried out in the old Shelby Road Cemetery, and she gets upset we don't erect an ofrenda and celebrate for his spirit to return."

"What's an ofrenda?"

"An altar you place at a loved-one's grave. You put pictures of them on it, maybe some keepsakes they loved in real life, candles, or bowls of their favorite foods."

"Do you believe people's souls actually come back on the Day of the Dead?"

Maria shrugged, smiling wistfully. "I don't know. I know it's an important part of my culture, which my parents want to ignore. I'm not going to get all traditional with everything. I like America fine. But I want this one thing from my heritage, y'know? And I'm going to celebrate it from now on."

Blazing inspiration pumped Whitey's heart. "Can I celebrate it with you? Can boys have their faces painted, too?"

They'd reached the next-to-last intersection before Samara Hill. Maria turned and favored him with an earnest expression of affection which burned its way into his soul. "Of course boys can have their faces painted as a Calavera. And of course you can celebrate it with me."

She reached out and gently took his hand. Squeezed it, and held it. He smiled, and, because he didn't trust himself to speak (and maybe she likewise) they turned and crossed the street. Whitey realized he'd done something far greater than simply ask Maria Alvarez to the annual Halloween movie.

❧

A soft knock on the door pulled Whitey from his memories. His knees felt tired and sore (as always these days), so he didn't stand. Only glanced up and said, "Come in."

The door opened. Sheriff Chris Baker removed his campaign hat and stepped in. "Evening, Whitey." He gestured with his hat. "Your Elegant Catrin is wonderful this year. Wasn't sure you'd be celebrating, especially after . . . well. Happy to see you're carrying on."

Whitey smiled slightly. Sheriff Baker was young and relatively new, and he still had some things to learn. But he knew how to flatter his elders. "Thank you, Sheriff. I'm not so wonderful, honestly. A tired old man wearing white face paint and a dusty tuxedo bought forty years ago at Handy's Pawn and Thrift. Nothing more."

Sheriff Baker waved off Whitey's dismissal. "Humble as always, Whitey, but this town loves you as much as it loved Maria."

Whitey smiled fully now, blinking back an irritating wetness in his eyes. "You're too kind, Sheriff. Parents obviously taught you some manners."

"My mother didn't suffer fools, sure enough."

Whitey folded his hands in his lap, feeling mild impatience at being interrupted (something he'd felt more and more the past few years, because he was old, and tired, and interruptions wearied him, and he hated the whole feeling, which only made him feel older). "What brings you out here, Sheriff?"

Sheriff Baker shrugged. "Patrolling. Halloween and all. Wanted to stop by, make sure none of the kids were sneaking around here, getting into mischief."

Despite his irritation at the interruption, Whitey chuckled. "We haven't had any problems in the cemetery since before your time, Sheriff. Why don't you tell me the real reason you're here?"

Sheriff Baker's smile faltered. He actually appeared embarrassed. "Well. Understand, Whitey. No one's been talking behind your back. We all imagine how you're feeling right now, this being your first Day of the Dead without Maria. But a few folks have noticed you didn't put up your ofrenda or Day of the Dead decorations this year, and they're worried, I guess. Hoping you're all right."

Whitey forced a smile. "Death is a part of life, Sheriff. Maria taught me that."

He allowed his smile to slip a bit. He'd come to respect and like the new Sheriff, and believed he could trust him with some of the truth.

Some, of course.

Not all.

"But I wasn't quite up for it this year. I did answer the door for a few children, but I didn't have it in me for anything more." He offered the Sheriff a sad smile. "I'm sure you understand how much it weakens a man to lose his wife, regardless of the age."

Sheriff Baker nodded, distant pain glimmering in his own eyes. Whitey didn't enjoy taking advantage of the Sheriff's recent loss—the sheriff's wife had died shortly before they moved to Clifton Heights—but a growing impatience for the Sheriff's departure warred with his sense of propriety. The time was coming to welcome Maria's spirit from the Other Side. He wanted to be alone, and his desire outweighed his concerns for the Sheriff's own grief. "I know you understand what it means to lose your wife. I didn't have the gumption for the whole production this year."

Sheriff Baker nodded. He glanced around the shed, gesturing with his hat. "Got things nice and fixed up. You comfortable out here? Not too cold or anything?"

Whitey sighed and leaned back against the wall,

stifling a grimace at the small flare of pain in his lower back. "All right, Sheriff. Who sent you? Which of my boys called you, asked you to come out and check on me?"

Sheriff Baker frowned, confusion and also worry showing in his expression. "Your boys? Whitey, I don't understand. The boys . . . "

" . . . have been asking for you, Maria. They wanted to be here, but they can't come yet."

A weak, fluttering smile. Eyes sad and regretful, yet understanding. "You haven't told anyone, have you? About the boys? I don't think they'd understand."

"No, Maria. It's nobody's business. But they miss you. They miss their Momma."

Another sad smile, stretching tight skin over sharp cheekbones. "I know. But it is the way of things. We live then we die. So long as you build the ofrenda, light my candles on Dia de Los Muertos, if you prepare, I will come. I promise."

"I've made all the preparations. Like you always wanted."

Raw emotion closed his throat. He'd tried to be strong. God, he'd tried. He'd managed to put a good face on it; he'd managed to act brave, but he couldn't do it anymore. "Maria, please. Don't leave me."

A slow blink. Eyes dulling as their light receded, faint voice rasping, "I must. It is the way of things."

"But I can't. The boys. They keep nagging me. Night and day. They keep telling me what I can and can't do. I'm not a child. I don't want to move into an old folks' home or a nursing home, but the boys won't stop."

THINGS YOU NEED

On their first trip to Mexico, they saw the catacombs. They stayed in Mexico City on November 2nd because Maria wanted to see the Day of the Dead up close. They watched parades with hundreds of people dressed as the Coqueta Catrina and the Elegant Catrin, wearing exquisite

Calaveras face paintings. They ate sugar candy skulls bearing their names. They listened to men playing Guitarrones on the street corners. When night fell, they visited the graveyard on the outskirts of town and watched in awe and reverence as families lit candles on ofrendas at tombstones and sang songs to their beloved dead.

Maria was inspired. She asked Whitey to build an ofrenda in their front yard, for all of Clifton Heights to see on Halloween night. And it was on their trip, the next day, when Maria told Whitey—made him swear on his solemn word—how she wanted him to celebrate Dia de los Muertos with her, should she pass away first.

Whitey realized his slip soon as Sheriff Baker frowned. "The boys? I'm not sure I follow, Whitey."

Whitey offered him a weak smile, hoping he appeared as baffled as Sheriff Baker, who no doubt imagined he was. "Pay no mind to me, Sheriff. I'm an old, sad man rambling after losing the love of his life, is all."

Whitey could see he'd inflected the right tone, as the younger man's face relaxed. "I understand. After

Liz passed, I wandered in a daze for weeks. Didn't know which end was up."

He gestured around the cabin with his hat again. "Whitey. It's none of my business. But is everything okay? You managing all right at home? You mentioned the boys, and I . . . "

Another flickering, weak-old-man-can't-blame-me-I'm-losing-my-mind grin. "Apologies, Sheriff. I'm not myself right yet. Still haven't gotten my wits about me."

Sheriff Baker nodded, sympathy glimmering in his eyes. "I understand. Certainly do." He replaced his campaign hat on his head and moved to leave, but paused before stepping out the door. "Listen, Whitey. If you ever need anything, don't hesitate to call."

"Thank you," Whitey said sincerely, lying with his next words, "I will."

Sheriff Baker nodded, tipped his hat, said "Happy Halloween, Whitey. Feliz dia muerte," and stepped out into the night.

Whitey eased himself down the ladder, rung by rung, into the cellar he'd dug under the shed when he'd rebuilt it shortly after accepting the head caretaker's position. Back then he'd only the barest idea as to why he'd dug the cellar. The old shed he'd rebuilt because it had been a ramshackle affair. He'd wanted something sturdier, so he'd erected a finely built shed which doubled as a surprisingly comfortable sleepover when he occasionally drank too much at The Stumble Inn. Maria had nothing against drinking and had never persecuted him for having a few too many, but he'd never felt comfortable coming home drunk, worried one of the boys would see him stumbling to bed.

Oddly enough, he hadn't any booze the entire time he'd slept here since Maria passed.

He stepped off the last rung and onto the cellar's concrete floor. He put his hands on his hips and gazed around, appraising his handiwork, thinking how pleased Maria would be when she saw it because, after all, it was what she'd asked for. The day after Dia de los Muertos, in Mexico City.

"Ay dios mio," Maria whispered as she descended the rickety wooden ladder, following Whitey and their guide into the subterranean depths of the catacombs outside Mexico City. "I've read about it and seen pictures, but I've never . . . "

Their tour guide, a plain-faced man named Juan, glanced at her in mild surprise. "You are Mexican, si?"

Maria smiled apologetically at him. "Si. But I was raised American. My parents became citizens before I was born. But all my life, I've felt something in here," she thumped her heart with a closed fist. "A wish to know who I was. To know my culture. I've studied and read for years, but this," she gestured at the shadowed depths of the catacombs, lit by flickering orange bulbs hanging by wires from the ceiling, "this, and the celebrations, Dia de los Muertos. Seeing this is a dream come true, since I was a teenager."

Juan nodded once with a small smile, as if he'd seen it before, and didn't find it strange. "Well then, senorita." He waved ahead. "Welcome to the catacombs."

As they followed Juan down the narrow corridor dug out of red hardpan and rock, Whitey marveled at how dry the air was, but also how cool. It didn't smell foul or rotten, as he'd feared it would. The only scent tickling his nostrils was of dust, an ancient spice he couldn't place, and the musk of old books.

They passed the corpses leaned upright against the wall. Whitey was amazed at their condition. Their desiccated skin had pulled tight without rot. No maggots, rats or any of the more sensational signs of decay. Something about the dry, cool air, perhaps. Or something done special to the bodies themselves, like with Egyptian mummies.

Or, perhaps it was their good luck they hadn't descended into the catacombs *after* a recently interred body. In either case, the experience—especially for Maria—of walking down the softly lit dirt corridor, past rows of the dead, wasn't ghoulish, or ghastly, or stomach-churning in the least. It was intriguing, mysterious, enthralling, and peaceful. The corpses' faces appeared composed and relaxed. Their hands folded on their midsections (Whitey had never been sure how the arms had stayed put; perhaps they'd been wired into place), their empty eyes gazing nowhere.

"Oh yes," Maria murmured, hands clasped together in eerie pantomime of the corpses leaning against the wall, her eyes shining. "Yes, Whitey. Like this someday. Promise me, all of us together."

"Of course," Whitey murmured, thinking nothing of it, thinking it was only inspiration from the moment, nothing more.

"Promise me, Whitey. Please."

And he did.

THINGS YOU NEED

Whitey stomped his boots on the cellar's cement floor. Thankfully, he'd poured several feet of sand and gravel before laying the concrete. Amazingly, after all these years, the floor was still relatively smooth, with few cracks and no heaving.

He placed a hand on the brick wall he'd mortared himself. It felt cool and dry, mostly, as did the air. Not quite as arid as the Mexican catacombs, but it was the best he could manage in the Adirondacks, and would have to suffice.

Flickering light drew his gaze to the cellar's far wall. He faced the ofrenda he'd so lovingly constructed for Maria years ago, when she'd first decided to celebrate the Day of the Dead on Halloween night. He'd had to disassemble it, bring its parts here to reassemble. It hadn't been easy. His hands shook these days, and his shoulder and back hurt. Of course, he'd had since Maria's diagnosis to complete it. He'd sensed from the beginning hers was a losing battle.

For a moment, gazing upon the ofrenda, sharp grief twisted his insides. Thick white candles had been lit on all the ofrenda's shelves, firing the bouquets of red, orange, and yellow marigolds with an unearthly glow. Framed pictures of Maria from when he'd started dating her to pictures from before her illness lined the top shelf. Next to them, sugar candy skulls he'd made himself, with her name written on their white crystalline foreheads. Also, some of her favorite bits of jewelry. The floppy gardening hat she always wore when tending the flowers lining the front walk. Sheets of wax paper and the thick black sticks of wax she used for her tombstone rubbings, a hobby she'd begun ten years ago.

The ofrenda's second shelf burned with candles and was lined with marigolds also, but featured pictures of both Marcus and Carlos. Next to the pictures, toys from their youth. A football, basketball, soccer ball, and a baseball. Marcus' old Nikon camera, from before he'd discovered writing. A hammer, saw, and a clutch of nails, because Carlos had fallen in love with Whitey's hobby of carpentry and had pursued it as a career. Both of them, good boys. Strong boys. Devoted boys, as unique as day and night.

Before the car accident which had stolen Marcus, five years before. Before the unexpected heart attack claiming Carlos a year later. Suddenly, he and Maria had been rendered childless, having survived their children, which no parent should ever have to suffer.

But it was all right, now.

They were together again at last. Whitey had been worried, initially, how the boys would fare. This, after all, wasn't the cool and dry catacombs of Mexico. The cement floor and brick walls had helped, and it never got hot here, even in the summers, but there had been spring thaws to deal with. He'd a mess to clean— simply from seeping fluids and general decay—the first several springs. Also, Marcus had suffered a maggot infestation which had been unpleasant. Since then, however, they'd weathered the years well.

He hadn't been able to stand them against the wall, however, as was done in the catacombs. The embalming process had made them too rigid. He'd managed to prop them, seated, backs against the ofrenda, hands folded in their laps, sightless eyes gazing at him, somewhat accusingly, which did bother him, when he was honest with himself. For what could they accuse him of? What had he done wrong? He was only honoring Maria's wishes, after all. Bringing them together as one family, forever.

He turned and grasped the rope hanging from the rectangle opening above, attached to a stick propping open the door he'd installed into the floor when he'd dug out the cellar. With a quick tug, he pulled the stick into the cellar. The door swung shut with a thump and the click of the special latch and lock he'd recently installed. A lock which could only be opened from the outside, which he'd also fused shut with an acetylene torch. He'd fastened a throw rug onto the hatch, concealing it from passing eyes. Perhaps, when he turned up missing, someone would eventually discover them down here. Perhaps for them, it would be like Maria descending into the catacombs so long ago.

Regardless, Whitey made his way in the flickering candle light—which cast shadows on his family's faces, and in those shadows he saw them gazing at him—to Maria's side. He lowered himself to the dry concrete floor, gathered her stiffness into his arms, and waited for the Day of the Dead.

Uncountable hours later, candles long since extinguished, a heavy presence—an intangible weight—filled the small catacomb. Whitey smelled Maria's perfume. Her rich chestnut hair, before it had fallen out. The warm baked-flour odor of fresh empanadas. Whitey sat up and stared into the darkness, heart pounding with joy as he whispered, "Maria? Is that you? Maria? It's me. I'm here, darling."

Her head—light from decay—shifted against his neck.

Whitey cried out, fear squeezing his heart (because her dry touch was so cold) as he pushed weakly off the wall to his feet, tottering away into the darkness, stiff joints screaming. Hands out, searching the blackness, he felt brick, turned and flattened against the far wall. He frantically dug into his pocket for his lighter . . .

And heard it.

Scratching.

Dragging. Something, several somethings . . .

Carlos

Marcus

if I believe in it, it will happen

wasn't supposed to be like this

. . . shifting and crawling toward him.

Whitey's hand closed around the lighter in his pocket. He squeezed it, feeling the cool metal housing a cleansing flame.

No.

Fear drained away.

He tottered several steps toward the dragging, clicking, sliding. His legs trembled, and he fell to his knees. Opened his arms.

Waiting.

Maria reached him first. And she didn't smell bad at all (not like her perfume or hair or freshly baked empanadas, but not bad, either) as she nestled her withered mouth at the base of his neck. Sighing, he craned his head back and, gently holding the back of her head, pressed her to him, so her teeth could get a better grip on his on jugular.

And with his other, he welcomed his sons as they came together, at last.

As he'd believed they would.

IO.

I COWERED AGAINST the stairway, shaking. The hand clutching my lighter with a white-knuckled grip jittered, throwing its faint orange light over their withered faces. Lips peeled back from white, jutting teeth. Blind eye sockets stared, stopped up by crusty dead matter. Wispy cobweb hair—what remained—clung to skulls sheathed in tight, leathery flesh. Mouths gaped wide in silent screams.

I can't tell you how many there were, exactly—three or four—nor can I say how they were positioned, because I couldn't hold my hand still. It kept jerking up and down, the light flitting across their faces, filling up their blind eyes. Maybe two of them were embracing, one's head buried in the other's neck. Lovers? Husband and wife?

I've told myself maybe those weren't real corpses at all. Could be they were old, cast-off Halloween decorations. Very *genuine* Halloween decorations. Made of foam, or something, and dressed in old rags. I've told myself this, and on some days, I actually believe it.

Other days?

I ask myself who would build such a small cellar

under a store, and take the time to brick and mortar the walls? I wonder about the lingering scent of oil and gasoline, the kind of smells usually associated with lawn mowers.

Anyway, I'm not sure how long I cowered on those steps. Mesmerized, transfixed, seeing *things* through those corpses' (or decorations) eyes, I lay there silent and still.

And then I started blubbering.

Hell, yes. Blubbering and bawling, right there on the steps, but not for the reasons you might think. Sure, I was scared out of my mind. Lost my wits completely, broken as broken could be.

But it wasn't the corpses themselves. No, I was broken because even dead folks had each other. They had what I'd never had growing up. Hell, they had it *still*, in their moldy afterlife, more so than me. *Family*. People they belonged to. Someone to hold them.

Family.

While I'd never had anyone, *didn't* have anyone, and knew I never would.

Sobbing, I flicked my lighter off. Those corpses (or maybe decorations), fell into merciful darkness. They deserved their privacy with each other. I left them, at first crawling backwards up the steps, sobbing more quietly. About halfway up, I rolled over onto my hands and knees and crawled up a few more steps. Then I lurched to my feet for the last two, staggering back up behind the sales counter. My thighs were weak and quivering, threatening to spill me to the floor.

I glanced down and saw what I'd missed: The cellar's trapdoor had been left open, held by a hook and eye screwed into the counter. The open door had been flat against the counter, out of the way. If I'd glanced down first, I would've seen the dark open rectangle in the floor, but as it was, I'd only looked along the endless hallway (which I had *no* desire to explore), not down at the floor.

I didn't bother wondering how the shopkeeper had walked around the trapdoor without falling, or if he'd opened it special for me before he'd disappeared. Not thinking anything, I unhooked the door and flipped it down. I sat on my ass, put my head in my hands and sobbed incoherently. My shoulders were shaking, chest heaving. God, I was wailing. Wailing at the top of my lungs.

Of course I was. No one to call my own. No place I belonged. Nothing to do in this world but sell fucking magazine subscriptions, and I wasn't even doing *that*, only conning others into selling them for me. All alone, for as long as I could remember.

Considering everything that had happened, I suppose what came next was inevitable.

I grabbed my shirt and wiped my face. Glanced up and saw them, arranged in orderly piles on shelves under the sales counter.

Hand guns.

Pistols.

Old revolvers and a few shotguns. I didn't know what kind of pawn shop sells used guns. Didn't know if it was legal, or if they had to do background checks or anything, or if they needed a license to sell them. But I was getting the idea by then, you understand, that no license existed for what Handy's sold, and there they were. Hand guns, pistols, revolvers, shot guns and some rifles, all stacked neatly. And of course, sitting nearest to the counter's edge, newer and more polished than the rest, practically *gleaming* bright silver: A .38 exactly like the one I'd left back in a box under my bed at The Motor Lodge.

See, the one thing which kept niggling away at my brain but I'd kept repressing was not remembering what I'd done with the .38. Did I put it away? Bring it along? Use it? I certainly remembered sitting on the bed, holding it, sorta caressing it with the pad of my index finger, but I didn't remember putting it away. All I remembered was driving around Clifton Heights and eventually pulling up in front of Handy's, where they sold "things you need."

I didn't remember putting it away.

And where the hell was my rental?

Did I even drive to begin with? It was a blur.

I reached out and grabbed the pistol. Same one? Was it the pistol I didn't remember putting away?

Did it matter?

No.

My hand suddenly steady, I flicked the .38, and the cartridge cylinder popped open. Was it loaded?

Sure it was. Four barrels, anyway. The other two only had empty casings. What happened to them?

It didn't matter.

I did the only thing I could've done right then. I stood up, not wanting to go out on my ass. Slapped the cartridge cylinder back into place and spun the cylinder, its rhythmic clicking filling my world. When it came to a stop, I cocked the hammer back and stuck the muzzle in my mouth, gazing into an old mirror propped up on a shelf near the sales counter, seeing the truth of everything in my eyes as my finger tensed on the trigger.

Almost Home
"How much longer?"
"Not long, I don't think."
"*How* long?"

❦

Mary blinked at the rain-slicked windshield while her mind struggled against the wipers' droning metronome. She was so tired. Tired of driving, tired of not knowing when it would end.

I chose this. Shouldn't complain.

She touched the .38 under her belt. The cold metal chilled her fingertips. Shivering, she pulled her hand away. Bile churned in her gut, made her mouth taste sour, because she couldn't blame anyone but herself for this. She'd known what Barry had been like—God help her, she'd known—and it wasn't as if people hadn't warned her. But she hadn't listened, because she'd thought she could change him. Make him better.

And now, here they were.

"Shit."

"Johnny. Watch your mouth." She glanced over her shoulder into the backseat. "What's wrong?"

The old Gameboy she'd bought for him at a thrift store in Clifton Heights warbled. Arcs of light from the tiny screen played across Johnny's forehead, accentuating the angles of his nose and cheeks, flaring in the hollows under his eyes.

"Only two lives left. Thing's fuckin' hard."

She faced forward and squinted at the rain-blurred road. "Don't swear, honey. It's crude."

"Dad swore."

She swallowed all the sharp words she wanted to

spew about *him*. "Well, I don't want you to. It's low. You're gonna do better. Okay?"

Tiny stars blossomed over Johnny's cheeks while his thumbs raced. "Whatever."

"No. You can change, Johnny. If you want to."

"Sure."

It wasn't much of an answer, but they were both tired, and Johnny was too absorbed in the Gameboy for her to push the issue much further. Still, she persisted. She was his mother, after all.

Fine time to pick that responsibility up. Where was she when the bruises on his arms had started showing? When he started complaining of back aches? Where was she when Johnny got his first black eye "falling down outside?"

She sucked in a deep breath, swallowing her self-recrimination. "You can always change, Johnny. Always."

"Okay. When's the next stop? My ass . . . my *butt* hurts."

She bit her lip. They hadn't seen anything for miles, and the highway stretched out before them into the dark: A black strip broken only by pale yellow lines. Wet darkness swirled around them as it rained. Only a few pinprick stars glimmered through night's velvet curtain, along with snatches of bone-white moon.

They'd gotten lost. Probably took a wrong turn after Clifton Heights. The next stop could be minutes or hours away, and she had no way of knowing. She could try the map, but all those lines and interstate numbers only confused her.

She glanced at the gas gauge. The needle trembled inside the yellow of *Caution*, above the red of *Empty*. Her stomach cramped.

"I dunno, kiddo. Hopefully we'll find something, soon."

Vinyl-seating squeaked and electronic trumpets blared. "Whatever. Just want to get up and walk around a little."

She didn't answer, swallowing bitter fear. Her stomach chewed on doubt and empty promises. Here was the truth: Things were no better now than they were before. Barry's behavior had been erratic, impossible to predict, and life with him had been a violent roller coaster ride, but they'd had a home, at least. A place to call their own. A roof over their heads. Food, shelter, warmth.

Now?

She gazed in the rear-view mirror. Its cracked glass reflected her worn face, her skin pulled tight at the corners of her mouth. Old bruises shadowed her eyes. Johnny looked much better than she did. Thankfully, young skin healed faster.

She frowned.

That's not my face.

Her mirror eyes laughed. The gun pressed against her belly. She dreamed of pulling its trigger soon and making all her regrets and nightmares disappear for good.

No.

Not yet.

Mary drove to the tune of the Gameboy's warbles.

Johnny had shut the Gameboy off and fallen asleep in the back. The silence made her eyelids flutter as she drove. She'd tried listening to the radio to stay awake, but all it seemed to play were angry evangelists and shouting politicians. She'd turned it off, and the silence had swallowed them whole.

Her arms trembled. Fatigue burned her stomach.

Something caught her gaze. Up ahead, on the right side of the road, a building shimmered through the raindrops. A rest stop and welcome center, built of night-washed brick, its parking lot empty. Understandable, given the late hour.

Still, something about the place bothered her. She frowned, glancing over her shoulder at Johnny. Curled up on the backseat, he seemed babyish. Hard to imagine him swearing. Stringy brown bangs sprawled across his forehead and eyes. She risked reaching back and brushing them away. As her fingertips grazed his smooth skin, a chill coiled around her spine.

She glanced forward, flicked on the turn signal, slowed, and pulled off the highway and into the rest stop's parking lot. Dim halogen lights spilled piss-yellow splashes over the building and onto the ground. Nearby sat a small, neglected park sporting a few leafless trees. Shadowed shapes of picnic tables and grills huddled among them.

She parked at the building's entrance, where a sign read: *Welcome to Webb County*. She stared at the gas gauge and saw the needle hovering over red.

Fear chilled her stomach. She had no money left for gas; had spent her last few dollars on Johnny's Gameboy. She'd almost said no, but something made her give in. She wasn't sure what. Maybe it had been her desperate need to see Johnny smile, showing the grin all boys his age should wear. She hadn't seen him smile in such a long time, not since before Barry had been laid off from the lumber mill.

Or maybe it had been the kindly shopkeeper at that thrift store. A tall, regal man with white hair and deep green eyes, smiling so gently at Johnny, offering to knock five dollars off the price.

Now, staring at the fuel gauge, she felt guilty for buying the Gameboy. A few dollars wouldn't have made much difference, but still the guilt—along with a million other sharp regrets—jabbed into her heart. Something crumbled deep inside her.

She bowed her head, wiped her eyes with the back of her hand, then reached under her shirt and pulled out the gun. Her skin reveled and recoiled as she touched it. Here was power. Here was weakness, too.

Here, also was truth.

She cradled the gun in her lap and thought, hard. For a long time.

"Wake up. We're here."

"Did we stop?"

"For a while, yes."

"Are we there yet?"

"Not yet. Just taking a rest. We've got a little more to go. Only a little more."

A sharp report shook the car. She woke and shivered, suddenly cold from the night air Johnny had let in. She rubbed her eyes and glanced into the backseat. He'd already buckled himself up and was once again playing his Gameboy.

Somehow she found the strength to smile. "All set?"

A bare nod. "Yep. Kinda hungry, but there weren't any snack machines here. Maybe at the next one."

She glanced away as she backed the car out. She hadn't told Johnny she'd spent their last few dollars on the Gameboy. Maybe enough quarters still rattled around in her purse to buy a bag of chips or cookies, so she could avoid the issue a little longer. Besides, maybe at the next stop she'd see someone she could borrow a few bucks from . . .

Beg.

Beg a few bucks. Why lie to herself?

As she drove on, the night swirled around them. It had stopped raining, and was now only misting. She looked at the gas gauge. It had dropped deeper into the red band, but it hadn't hit bottom yet. Maybe, if she reached the next stop, she'd find help. Maybe.

The gun rubbed against her waist, mocking the thought, reminding her of its presence; always reminding.

⌒⌒

"We're close, aren't we?"

"I think so. Maybe. Hard to tell."

"I hope so. I'm so tired."

"I know, and I'm sorry. But it'll be better, soon."

"Promise?"

A nod and a smile. "Promise."

⌒⌒

She blinked and sat up. Raindrops tapped the windshield, roof, and hood. The car felt warm and close, stifling. Her head swimming with fatigue, Mary tried to brush off sleep, tried to focus.

They'd found another rest stop. Johnny had left . . .

to buy snacks? Use the bathroom again? Had he found change in her purse after all?

She squinted at the building through the rain, lips unconsciously forming the words on its welcome sign. Then she yawned. She hadn't dozed nearly as long as she could've.

Something had woken her. Raindrops?

It kept raining. It would stop for a while, and then, inevitably, it would start raining again. So, the raindrops had woken her up.

Settling back into the driver's seat, she frowned at the thought. No. That wasn't quite right. Things felt wrong. Disjointed. Like a CD skipping in the middle of a song, getting hung up on the same phrase over and over. Worse, the sensation felt familiar, but she wasn't sure why.

Her gut twisted into knots. Of course it felt familiar. It was her life. It had always been like this, right? Ruined CD, ruined song . . . ruined life.

A sudden need to move consumed her. She reached under her seat, pulled her purse into her lap, and started rummaging through it. At first she found nothing but old lipstick tubes, crushed tampons, and a few brittle sticks of gum.

No money. Either she'd given it to Johnny and he'd gone inside to buy something, or he'd needed the bathroom again.

Strange.

She couldn't remember.

Her searching fingers found a folded, brochure. She dug it out and opened it. A 'Welcome To' brochure, the kind found at rest stops everywhere.

A tiny pinprick of alarm blossomed in her heart.

She tried to swallow but her throat clenched, tight and dry. Under a rising tide of panic, cold realization bloomed. She couldn't remember what state or county this was. How far had they come since their last stop?

She flattened the brochure on her thigh.

It read "Welcome to Webb County."

Her heart skipped a beat. She looked at the sign outside the car again.

Welcome to Webb County.

Back to the brochure. It was worn. Soiled. Colors faded, as if it had languished in her purse forever. Her desperate eyes read the sign once more, hoping for something different.

"What the hell?"

Something was wrong. She and Johnny needed to get back on the road until she sorted this out. Had she made another wrong turn? Gone south when she'd wanted to go north? Accidentally doubled-back the way they'd come?

She grabbed the door handle, but then stopped. Something nagged her. Opening the door felt wrong, out of place. How long had she been driving? Her stomach quivered.

She didn't know.

Stupid. You're tired. Need sleep.

That's all.

She shut off the ignition so she wouldn't waste gas. Breathing deeply, spots clouding her vision, she exited the car.

❧

"Johnny?"

She stepped inside the rest stop, turned right into

an empty lobby. Grit crunched underfoot. The place hadn't been swept in ages. Pale fluorescent lights flickered above, throwing ghosts on the walls and floors. Something dripped back in the shadowed recesses. The information center in the far corner was in a shambles, brochures scattered on the floor. The air tasted stale, as if she was the first person to breathe it in years.

Her hand strayed to the gun, but she clenched her fist. "Johnny? You're creepin' me out, chief. C'mon."

Something shifted. She turned and faced two doors—bathrooms. Light glimmered around the door on her left, pulling her toward it. Each step dragged, her own breath roaring in her ears, heart pounding.

Something waited behind that door.

"Johnny?"

Another step.

Her hand trembled near the gun.

"That you?"

Rustling and sliding, behind the door. She bit her tongue, tasting copper saltiness. Sweat chilled her forehead, and a rotten scent crept into her nostrils.

She reached beneath her ragged sweatshirt for the gun. Sweaty fingers closed around the grip, index finger curled on the trigger. She breathed frosty-white plumes; the air suddenly much colder than it had been moments before, as if someone had abruptly turned the thermostat down.

She pulled the gun from her waistband. Her nerveless fingers fumbled with the pistol, nearly dropping it as she *felt* more than heard something sliding behind the door. She licked sour, cracked lips.

Headlights splashed through the glass front doors,

living in your small apartment, existing hand-to-mouth, writing ad copy for all those small radio stations?"

It came to me quickly, immediately, with crystal-clear clarity. "Sitting in Mass Media's office," I said, "interviewing for my job."

"And do you remember all the traveling?"

To my amazement, I did. Every school I'd visited over the past twenty years. Every gig. Every little bar, every tired bar whore, teachers, principals, student council vice-presidents, I remembered them all.

I nodded slowly. "Why? Why not anything before?"

The shopkeeper didn't answer that, either. Only gazed at me with those kind green eyes, his expression soft, gentle, and sad. The answer came to me, as if I'd known it all along. "She killed me, didn't she? She *did* shoot me in the head. But somehow I'm still here. On the road. Always on the road."

I glanced down at the Gameboy in my hand. My voice cracked, throat tight and dry. "How is that possible?"

The shopkeeper shrugged. "Sometimes things slip through the cracks. They get lost and go wandering." He gestured at the store's cluttered shelves. "Like items on a pawn store shelf. Lost and forgotten. That's why this store and others like it exist. To collect the lost things which have slipped through the cracks, and to give them new homes, if possible. To give them new purpose."

"Have I been dead? Dead this whole time? But still sort of alive?"

"Maybe not alive. *Existing* is a better word. As for being dead, haven't you always wanted to return to that state? Since your first week on the job? How long ago did you buy that," he gestured at the .38 sitting in my lap, "really?"

I glanced down at the .38, seeing it anew. "I've always had it, I think. It's always been there. Hasn't it? Because it was Mom's."

A slow nod. "Yes. She passed it and death on to you. She shot and killed you but you traveled on regardless. Always on the road. And the gun's always been there with you, and you've always wanted to go to it. Embrace it. Become one with it."

"Did she find peace?" I stared at the gun and the Gameboy. "Did she find rest?"

"That's not for me to say, unfortunately. In the end, we only know our own stories."

"What about me, then? Will I find rest?"

The man sighed. "You want it, I know. But as I said when you first came in, we all know what we *want*. So few of us know what we *need*."

I looked up at him, tears swimming in my eyes. His face wavered out of focus. "What do I need? Please. What do I need?"

He held out his hand, saying nothing.

I took it.

12.

S O THERE'S NOT much more to tell. You're probably expecting some big reveal, right? A twist? Maybe I signed a contract with the shopkeeper and traded my soul for my continued life, or existence, as the guy called it?

Well, I hate to disappoint. No such thing happened. The guy shook my hand, took the gun from me, stood up, walked past me, down the long hall with no end (and believe me, in the time since I've explored it, and there is *no* end) and he disappeared, never to be seen again.

I never did get his name.

I sat on the floor for a long time. Finally, obeying an urge I didn't understand, I got up. Brushed myself off, ran my hands through my hair, and got ready to open Handy's Pawn and Thrift for the day.

I've been here ever since.

This town isn't so strange, now. The people here in Clifton Heights are mostly good folks. Sheriff Baker is a good man, and I feel bad about him missing his wife. Gavin Patchett—the English teacher who took me out to dinner a lifetime ago—is a surprising aficionado of pawn shops. A hell of a writer it turns out, too. Shame what happened to him, why he had to leave town last year, but that's how it goes. I know better than most, as I've just told you.

Kevin Ellison, the owner of Arcane Delights, is always stopping by, searching for used books. Father Ward, the Headmaster at All Saints High is a sound fellow, for a priest and all. He comes in often to chat.

Of course, none of them recognize me as the "magazine salesman." And for good reason. When Sheriff Baker first came in, hunting for fishing lures one day, I was a little surprised he didn't seem to know me. I took a quick glance into the mirror sitting on the shelf nearest the sales counter while he was searching. Honestly, I really *wasn't* surprised to see the face of the mysterious shopkeeper staring back.

Am I me still? Did the shopkeeper switch places with me, somehow? Or does the face simply come with the job? A job I accepted when I shook his hand. Who had the shopkeeper been before *he* came here?

I still haven't met the shop's owner, Mr. Handy. I will someday, I'm sure. We're all gonna meet Him in the end, I believe. It'll be on *His* schedule, however. Not ours.

What do I think He's like?

I don't know, honestly. Lots of wonderful things in His store. Some not-so-wonderful, horrible things too, I'm afraid, as you can tell from my story. But what can I say? We need ugliness to know what beauty is, and the light shines brightest when surrounded by darkness. As someone once said: *That's the way of things.*

Believe it or not, I've never again seen anything strange when handling items in this store. Not since that night. I suppose it's because I found what I needed, and I don't need to see anything more. In here, people only see what they need. Some folks need small things, others, big things. I don't control what they see, or who sees things. I only manage the store. As for the folks I saw when I first came here? Don't know about them, either. Like the shopkeeper before me said: In the end, we only know our own stories.

And the trapdoor behind the counter? That one I fell through? Gone. I've checked several times, thinking maybe the door fit so snugly the edges were hard to see. Far as I can tell, there is no trapdoor anymore, with no sign one ever existed.

But I'm fine not knowing the answers to all these questions. I've enjoyed working here. I enjoy the folks who visit—locals and tourists alike—and not only have I sold many interesting things (things I didn't even know we had) I've helped lots of people find what they need, too.

It wasn't always pretty, though. Sometimes, what folks needed was the last thing they wanted. But every customer—especially the chosen ones—always come away with the things they need.

Which brings me to the point of all this. Sorry for the long-winded sales pitch. Still got some of my salesman mojo, I guess. Of course, you *did* ask me how I got here, and all. But now that we've gotten everything out of the way—take a look around. No rush. We stay open late, as you can guess from my tale. Take all the time you need. And don't be shy. Ask any questions you want. More importantly, though . . .

Tell me, friend.

What do you *need*?

Hi readers,

It makes our day to know you reached the end of our book. Thank you so much. This is why we do what we do every single day.

Whether you found the book good or great, we'd love to hear what you thought. Please take a moment to leave a review on Amazon, Goodreads, or anywhere else readers visit. Reviews go a long way to helping a book sell, and will help us to continue publishing quality books. You can also share a photo of yourself holding this book with the hashtag #IGotMyCLPBook!

Thank you again for taking the time to journey with Crystal Lake Publishing.

We are also on . . .

Website:
www.crystallakepub.com

Be sure to sign up for our newsletter and receive two free eBooks: http://eepurl.com/xfuKP

Books:
http://www.crystallakepub.com/book-table/

Twitter:
https://twitter.com/crystallakepub

Facebook:
https://www.facebook.com/Crystallakepublishing/

Instagram:
https://www.instagram.com/crystal_lake_publishin
g/

Patreon:
https://www.patreon.com/CLP

Or check out other Crystal Lake Publishing books for more Tales from the Darkest Depths. You can also subscribe to Crystal Lake Classics where you'll receive fortnightly info on all our books, starting all the way back at the beginning, with personal notes on every release. Or follow us on Patreon for behind the scenes access.

With unmatched success since 2012, Crystal Lake Publishing has quickly become one of the world's leading indie publishers of Mystery, Thriller, and Suspense books with a Dark Fiction edge.

Crystal Lake Publishing puts integrity, honor, and respect at the forefront of our operations.

We strive for each book and outreach program that's launched to not only entertain and touch or comment on issues that affect our readers, but also to strengthen and support the Dark Fiction field and its authors.

Not only do we publish authors who are legends in the field and as hardworking as us, but we look for men and women who care about their readers and fellow human beings. We only publish the very best Dark Fiction, and look forward to launching many new careers.

We strive to know each and every one of our

readers while building personal relationships with our authors, reviewers, bloggers, podcasters, bookstores, and libraries.

Crystal Lake Publishing is and will always be a beacon of what passion and dedication, combined with overwhelming teamwork and respect, can accomplish: unique fiction you can't find anywhere else.

We do not just publish books, we present you worlds within your world, doors within your mind from talented authors who sacrifice so much for a moment of your time.

This is what we believe in. What we stand for. This will be our legacy.

Welcome to Crystal Lake Publishing.

THANK YOU FOR PURCHASING THIS BOOK

CPSIA information can be obtained
at www.ICGtesting.com
Printed in the USA
FSHW01n0620290918
52435FS